NOTHING

Linda Naseem

ISBN: 0692499164
ISBN 13: 9780692499160
Library of Congress Control Number: 2015914185
Linda Naseem, Colorado Springs, CO

For everyone whose life has been touched by meth

I see him climbing out of the dumpster.

I'm rolling through the alley behind my apartment, coming home from an early morning visit to the doughnut shop on the next block, and out he pops: a gaunt shadow with rowdy silver-streaked blond hair. An unlined face scowls through an auburn beard mottled with crumbs and gray patches. Garbage splotches his clothes, and a worm---really?---hangs lifeless from the corner of his mouth. His laceless running shoes yank him down from the height of the dumpster. They reach the ground before he does.

"You can't have my diamonds!" he yells at me, crouching to put his feet back in his shoes, raccoon eyes never leaving my face.

"Are you hungry?" I offer the bag of doughnuts.

"Give me a stick."

"Sorry. I don't smoke."

"Fuck you." He limps quickly away, his body a skeleton inside his worn jeans and ragged black and orange San Francisco Giants jacket, a plastic bottle of orange juice slipping from his pocket to splatter open on the asphalt, a rain of yellow buttons trailing the bottle.

I wheel up the ramp to my door and let myself in.

W ho the fuck does he think he is? I don't need no kind of food from a fucking wheelchair creep. I don't need nothing from nobody I'm my own CEO. I ate last night a taste of this and a taste of that all night long cuddled up in my sweet little dumpster bed the Dumpster Hotel and Buffet. All you can eat for free. Only serving special people fuckers like me. Wormy old ham sandwich and I found some carrots and apples that were only a little bit rotten and some juice that wasn't even open and stuffed them in my pockets so I got something to eat when I come down and I'm hungry and none of those fuckers'll give me another hit. And all those diamonds I swallowed and those gold buttons I hid in my pocket. I bet he's the one I heard breathing standing right outside the dumpster so he could snatch them from me when I climbed out. "But I pulled out all your wires and smashed your TV on the ground so you couldn't spy on me. Fucker." And now I gotta shit them out before I can take them to the pawn shop. Fuck him! I'm going to take them all down there at the same time the gold and the diamonds there ain't no point in going down there twice it's only going to take a day or two I'm going to go lay on the lawn by the library and take my shirt off and get a tan I get brown real quick. Maybe I'm going to see her going out for lunch my Annie my sexy Annie. I ain't going to let her see me she's going to call the cops. I don't want to see her. Life's good now I don't need her. Fuck her! I'm going to go find the guys and maybe they'll front me a hit I gotta stay as high as I can so I don't gotta deal with this fucking world that won't give me nothing. I'll tell them about the diamonds and I bet they're going to give me a hit on good faith. When I sell them I'm going to pay them back. I ain't going to tell them about my gold buttons if word gets out about my gold buttons all those fuckers that want money from me are going to come running I bet they're twenty-four carat gold can't let my Annie see me I gotta forget about her she cheated on me the fucking whore same as every other bitch on the planet. Cheated on me. So I stole some of her crap and made her cry. Fuck! I screw up everything. Fuck the library I gotta go find Cam he's going to give me a hit he's a good kid. He always shares his shit. I gotta shut up these crazy thoughts shut up this motherfucking brain gotta figure out a way to make it stop she warned me. I didn't believe her with her praying all the time like she was holding God's hand and walking side by side with Him. She loved Him more than she loved me. God's a lie! I ain't going to ask Him for nothing no more He's a lie. He always gives me what I want and then I screw it up fuck it off lose it and if He was real He'd let me keep it all no matter what I done man I gotta stop thinking so much. When's it going to end? It hurts like knives stabbing me in my heart. My Annie. So fucking sexy.

My first husband was a scientist with doctorates in biochemistry and pharmacology. Invented drugs for infertility, erectile dysfunction, breast enhancement. One wall in our house was papered with his awards. He was chair of the biochemistry department at UC Berkeley. His cold gray eyes petrified his students but they melted me, at least in the beginning, into a lump of malleable flesh.

He had walked into the university library one day when I was doing post-graduate work, lifted my chin with one hand and with the other gently ran his index finger along the plunging neckline of my red sweater. Chills skated down my back and those gray eyes shot arrows through me. They pinned my will to the back of my mind where it fluttered like a slack cobweb and every wish of my own expired. The focus of my life became the search for ways to please him, and what pleased him most was sex.

When my parents were killed in a car accident he held me close throughout that long night, wiped away my tears, promised he would take care of me forever. We were married two weeks later in a private ceremony in the university chapel. Instead of a white gown he had me wear a tight gray two-piece suit ("You can't wear white. We've been having sex for a year.") with a push-up bra that turned my breasts into creamy pillows mushrooming out of the suit's low neckline. "I'm a forty-D. I don't need to advertise." "From now on these belong to me, and I'll tell you what to do with them. Today you're going to put them out there so everyone can see what I own."

I clung to his arm at his many award ceremonies, a haughty half-smile on my red-stained lips as I turned my eyes away from the women escorted by lesser men. This highly intelligent famous man had chosen me to be his consort. It was an acknowledgment of my own intelligence and talents, proof that I had something to offer the world. I was as close to being his equal as a woman could be. I wore the slinky bosom-divulging silk gowns he brought home for me, my flawless face hidden under layers of makeup, waist-length red hair piled on my head, a million dollars' worth of diamonds twinkling from my hair, earlobes and neck, and peppering the revering crowd with glittering lights.

I'm not sure when it sank in that he saw me only as an alluring possession. Someone he could show off to let everyone know that yes, he was brilliant but he also appreciated beauty. Silent beauty. Someone who kept her mouth shut and did what she was told. Someone who did not win awards or excel in her work or was even noticed by other people. Someone who, in the eyes of his world, didn't exist except as an exquisite shadow at his side.

I think it was during the third year of our marriage. We—no, not we: I. I had been trying to get pregnant. I knew a baby would make me happy. It would chortle with delight when it saw me, not ignore me or sneer at me. It would hang on every word I said, its sparkling eyes following me with adoration. It would hug my friends and play with their children. A baby would bring giggles and nursery rhymes and lullabies to an increasingly bleak household. But I didn't get pregnant. The doctors told me it would never happen. A tipped uterus. "What about surgery?" I asked. Maybe.

He said no surgery. No baby. "You don't want to stretch that little waist of yours. You wouldn't fit into those tight dresses anymore. And having a brat sucking on those hooters would make them sag." "Is that what you think is important to me?" I asked. "It's important to me. I married you because you're hot. What the hell would you do with a baby? Probably lose it or forget to feed it. And what about all that cooking you like to do? You wouldn't have time for it. We'd have to eat take-out. It isn't healthy. My cholesterol would go up. I could have a stroke. Is that what you want?" "I'm not your employee," I answered. He didn't speak to me for a week, but that didn't stop the sex: a refusal would have brought a more-than-playful slap to my cheek.

We didn't keep a television in the house because he knew it would fill my head with Hollywood frivolities. On the evenings that he wasn't out with his scientist cronies he would sit in his little office off the living room, pounding away on his computer keyboard, his cherished companion a glass of Kentucky bourbon, an open bottle standing pertly next to the glass. I balanced on a bar stool in the kitchen in the hot pants and halter tops he made me wear, pouring over cookbooks with a glass of wine in my hand, seeing myself sneak out the kitchen door and slide into my car and drive across the Bay Bridge and down the coast. I worked at the West Portal branch of the San Francisco Public Library back then, and had seen a little pink stucco house on Taraval Street with a For Sale sign in front of it. When my dream-clotted eyes saw my car finally swing around, they saw it park in front of that little house. They saw me scamper up the pansy-bordered walk, climb the stairs, turn the key in the lock and slip inside. They saw a television and soft cozy clothes that let me breathe. And they saw a little dog joyfully bouncing up and down when I opened the door.

The final straw came a couple years later when he was being honored for creating some kind of sex-enhancing drug that had allegedly improved the lives of millions. The Chancellor and the Governor were at the ceremony. Someone represented the White House. He'd started on the bourbon when he got home from work at noon, and by the time we arrived at the auditorium he was openly intoxicated. The dress he'd bought for me was sea green, skin-tight, and the V-shaped neckline fell below my navel. A thousand tiny diamonds made a belt that held the thing together. "I'm a Christian," I screeched. "I can't be seen in a dress like this." "Christian? You? You haven't set foot in a church since the day we were married. And what good Christian woman spends her evenings making out with a bottle of wine? Get dressed. No one is going to look at you. They're all going to be looking at me. I'm the star here. Put on this dress or I'll drag you there naked."

He accepted his award, his right hand whipping the air as if he were hailing a cab and his left hand balancing a full glass of bourbon that emptied during the ten minutes he tottered on the dais. The words of his acceptance speech sloshed around in the glass, spilled on the floor. Then people were pulling me out of my chair and pressing me forward. He was introducing me. "You all know that behind my behind iz a v-vo-lup-chew-us obe-di-obedi-obeying woman." Polite laughter from the audience. My stomach was a bag of acid. I stood next to him, blinded by spotlights, a smile sliding off my quivering lips. "You s-see what a goddam beautiful beauty she iz," he said. He pushed me to the edge of the dais. "You like the dress? Stunning, izn't it?" A few claps and whistles. "She didn't think it waz good enough for her." A final noisy sip from his glass. "T-twirl, my dear, my doe, my love, my honey, my bee, my b-better half," he ordered. I turned slowly. "Look at those honkers! Damn! If those things could sh-shoot we'd win the war." "That's enough," I said. "I'm going to sit down." I walked away from him. "You'll s-sit down when I damn well tell you to s-sit down," he yelled, grabbing the back of my dress. "I want everyone to s-see my beautiful wife, my life, my death." He yanked the shoulders of my gown down to my waist, baring my breasts in front of five hundred open-mouthed people, the Chancellor, the Governor, and the White House. I heard one loud collective gasp. "Look how f-firm, like they're c-carved out of marble," he said, cupping one breast with an ice-cold hand. I slapped him as hard as I could and his hand dropped, a surprised look on his face. "I jus' wanted them to s-see how b-beautiful you are," he said. I ran. "You're a g-goddess," he called after me. I jumped into a taxi that took me to San Francisco. I bought the house on Taraval Street and never went back to him. For months he left apologies on my answering machine at work. I let my lawyer return the calls.

I went back to church. Begged God for forgiveness because I knew it was my pride that had led me into that situation. Ignored the wine on the grocery store shelves. Joined the Mary-Martha Ladies Auxiliary and knit caps for newborns in hospital nurseries and mittens for homeless children in shelters. After a couple years of whispering prayers through stiff lips I felt clean again. I gingerly started dating. Men from my church. I always let them go before we got as far as the first kiss.

Then I met Cleo. So sweet and funny. Didn't have much money or a prestigious job or a college education: what a relief! Absolutely no arrogance. Took off his baseball cap when he spoke to me, twisted it in his hands. He didn't lay a finger on me until I asked him to. Nothing more than a peck on the cheek for weeks, until I invited him home and showed him where I wanted him to touch me.

I met him in church.

He said he believed, and I believed him.

I fell for him the second he turned those intense blue eyes on me. It wouldn't have mattered if he believed or not. In that short second I was his.

I was thirty-five years old. Too old to be so foolish. After my first marriage I should have known better.

I'm forty-two now, an old woman. Childless and husbandless. I have no brothers or sisters, no cousins, no aunts or uncles. No grandparents. I have no future; he left me as flat as a piece of paper completely scribbled over with bad memories, no room left for dreams.

I thought he was the one. You know, from the fairy tales. The one who sweeps you off your feet and carries you off on his white steed into the sunset and life is perfect forever. Your true love.

I know he loved me. He enshrined me in his beautiful heart, bowed down to me and worshipped me, enthroned me on a gilded pedestal, genuflected before my bare flesh every morning and made love to me every evening, but in time his heart shriveled to the size of a pebble and then it fractured into a few pieces of gravel that he lost somewhere in the alleys south of Market Street.

I knew his worshipping me would not bring us happiness, but after the disdain of my first marriage I was overjoyed to be appreciated and I let it go to my head. I opened my heart wide with the exhilaration of it. I slaved blissfully over the stove, cleaned and polished and cleaned some more, laughed the same way he laughed, head thrown back and mouth wide and baying. I head-banged with him to the heavy metal music he loved, wearing one of his tee shirts and nothing else because that was what he liked. I filled his closet with expensive flannels, leather jackets, steel-toed boots and the black jeans he adored. I let him touch me any time and any way he wanted. But I am not God and I am not perfect and I should not be worshipped. I became intolerable to him. My dedication to my work, my love of sassy skirts and low-cut lacy blouses, my education; he saw them as signs pointing to another man, someone I loved more than him, someone more educated, more refined, smarter. The gilded pedestal cracked. Jealousy drove a wedge into the crack and insecurity hammered on the wedge until the pedestal shattered and we lay rough-edged and broken on the carpet.

He didn't truly believe, and without belief, without faith, life can be unbearable.

And me: I believe. But so many times every day I ask myself why.

Look where it got me. I trusted and I was betrayed. I tried to be obedient to the laws of the church and God allowed someone who didn't care about those laws to bruise my heart with steel-toed kicks, crimp it with fear, pervert it with drugs. He allowed him to try to obliterate me, the only person in his life who had loved him and stood by him.

I can't talk to men anymore. My veins clot when they smile at me. I am terrified that they, too, will plunge through the thin ice of their fears into their own murky depths. They, too, will drag me under as they grab onto me, hoping I can save them.

I wish things could be different. It's been more than a year since I've seen him. Most nights I sit on the couch staring at the television until the alarm goes off, but those times when I lie in bed my body cramps with self-pity and I sob until morning.

Then I remember the tantrums, the fights, how many times I raced out of the house half-dressed to escape his anger, how many times I didn't escape.

If I were to see him I would run the other way as fast as I could and hope he hadn't seen me and come chasing after me. That is my nightmare. I've dreamt it many times. He is dead, dead and buried. I am standing at his grave weeping. Suddenly he rises up out of the ground and lurches after me. I throw stones and dirt and twigs but they don't stop him. I smash him in the face with a shovel and his head falls off and bounces on the cemetery grass and still he shambles, faster and faster, after me. I yell for help but no one answers. As his decomposing fingers stretch out to seize me I shriek myself awake, my hands flailing and my sprinting feet shackled by the sheets.

When someone you love degenerates into empty body parts and soulless pieces, and you watch each tiny fragment disintegrate, you disintegrate, too. You disappear atom by atom until, by the time your loved one has become nothing more than a pinch of dust, all that's left of you is a lifeless shell.

I haven't cooked since I last saw him. I eat micro-waved food, junk food, fast food. I stopped knitting when he complained that I should be paying attention to him instead of playing with yarn. I stay up and watch late night talk shows. I watch soaps on my days off. I hate soaps and talk shows but they keep me from thinking and they get me through the aching hours. I used to wear leather boots and prissy three-inch heels and he accused me of trying to find a boyfriend, so I switched to Reeboks. The same black pair every day, everywhere. I wore lace and ribbons, flouncy skirts, ruffled blouses baring the faintest inkling of bosom and dangling earrings that sprayed dots of light every time I moved. He screamed, his hands wrenching my hair and his face an inch from mine, that I was trying to look sexy for the people who came to the library. He popped in on me at work to see what I was doing, convinced I was sleeping with the library patrons. He picked fights with them and was repeatedly escorted out by security and finally banned. I took to wearing long dark shapeless skirts and men's shirts two sizes too big, buttoned to my neck, cuffs swallowing my hands. Plain gold posts in my ears, barely visible. And those Reeboks.

I don't want anyone to notice me; they will see how far from God I have fallen. They will know that he gave me drugs and I didn't stop him, that I fought with him as if I were an uneducated piece of trash. They will see my shame.

When I look in the mirror my face is blurry. I'm not sure it's mine. My pain and my guilt and my fear have altered my features. My nose isn't straight anymore. My skin is blotchy; it used to be snow-white and perfect. My eyes are no longer green; they are gray, the color of an ocean hiding under winter clouds.

How long do you mourn someone who dies? They say life goes on. There are rituals, ceremonies, wakes. You say goodbye to a body in a coffin, and eventually the space in your life that belonged to that person shrinks. It becomes a single thread in the tapestry that tells your story. But what about someone who is still alive? Someone who was kind and caring and, as you watched with your horrified mouth gaping, mutated one cell at a time into a monster. Someone who shuffles zombie-like down the street with no joy, no hope, no love, no chance for rebirth. There is no final goodbye, no funeral, no acknowledgment of a life lived and now ended. How do you get over that? How do you move on?

Aflash of silver rivets his eye.

Running shoes. Tucked into the shadowy alcove at the top of a flight of steps. Silver stripe spotlighted by a random ray of sun.

Sockless feet in the shoes and, above them, skinny legs in washed-out jeans. The face floating higher up in the shadow is talking to the empty space on its left.

"Cam!" Cleo calls from the sidewalk. "Give me a hit."

Cam's voice doesn't stop. "...And you really gotta start taking care of yourself, bro. You stink. When was the last time you took a bath? Don't give me none of your excuses, anyone can go to the Y and take a shower."

"Cam!" He tosses a pebble at the silver stripe. His feet are throbbing and those fifteen steps are as daunting as Mount Everest.

"Can't you see we're conversing here?" Cam's muddy eyes scrape across the edges of his no-man's land to glare at Cleo with the impudence only a fifteen-year-old dares to have. "You always think the world's gotta stop for you, Cleo. Well, I got other friends, too, and right now Jim here's all fucked up. Besides, I ain't got

13

no shit on me. Maybe later." He turns back to the empty space. "Man, Jim, I'm really sorry. That bro is hella rude."

"How about a stick? Give me a stick Cam."

"I stopped smoking. I really did stop smoking, Jim. I stopped for you because you told me your mom died of lung cancer when she was only twenty-five, and you said you didn't wanna lose me, too."

"You're a fucking cuckoo bird!" Cleo yells. "Who needs you!" He totters away, every step forcing sizzling lava from his feet to his knees. "Man even a cuckoo bird don't wantto help me out no more. How come everyone hates me?"

He forces his feet to keep hitting the sidewalk until he is out of Cam's line of vision, and then he collapses. Takes off the shoes. "Fuck. These don't even look like feet." The tops of his toes and the backs of his heels are decorated with pus-filled cabochons surrounded by scarlet leaves, their crimson vines spiraling up his legs. His fingers massage the inflamed skin and screaming fireworks shoot through the vines. "No pain. Feel no pain." His teeth cramp and sideburns of sweat sprout on his face. "I'll take care of them later. Right now I gotta go and get me a hit. Gotta stop the fucking pain."

The sidewalk is a bed of burning coals. "What are you looking at?" he taunts a young woman at the bus stop, his bare feet hopping. "You want a piece of this?" He unbuttons his fly. She skitters across the street, horns beeping, brakes squealing. "Then stop looking," he roars at her retreating back. "You ain't my kind anyway. You ain't got no tits."

Fucking bitch. All of them want a piece of me and then they all leave. Look at my mom she didn't need to go and die did she? And my first girl when I was fourteen. Sat there in the next desk with her sly blue eyes peeking at me and her skirt sliding up her leg until her lacy pink underwear stuck its tongue out at me and said "Come on Cleo meet me in the woods after school." We were just past the volleyball court and she was all over me and her lacy underpants were on the ground and her skirt was up around her neck and she was screaming. I was so good even the first time. And that evening the cops came to my foster parents' house and handcuffed me and threw me in juvey and lost the key. The fucking bitch told them I raped her. And all those bitches in their fancy guard uniforms whispering behind their fingers about me and smirking when they paraded me through the halls. But the men winked at me like they were saying "Yeah man good job." I had to stay in solitary most of the time and no one'd let me out no matter how much I banged on the door and screamed. Wouldn't give me no clothes to wear not even a blanket. Every time those bitches saw me they slapped me and stuck their ugly wrinkled faces right up in mine and sneered "Rapist!" and spit on me. And my stepmom years before then. She made my dad fuck me and stood there laughing so hard she almost pissed her pants. And my Annie fucking every bozo in town behind my back. I hate them all.

A large cardboard packing box squats in the alley behind the Den of Doom, a heavy metal gay bar. Fingers of white smoke beckon from slits in the sides of the box.

"Chris!" He raps on the cardboard. "Chris!"

"Get outta here, man!" a muffled voice answers. "I ain't got nothing you want."

"Anything man, I'll take anything. Give me some of your crack I'll take it."

"Aw man, you ruining my high, man. You know you don't smoke no crack. Now get your pitiful self away from here before I hop outta this box and fix you so's you can't never smoke nothing no more."

"Okay. Sorry Chris. Sorry. Give me a stick."

"I said get the fuck outta here!" Chris yells. The cardboard shudders. Cleo limps backwards, wary in case Chris jumps out with the machete he keeps inside the box. Jumps out and swings

15

it at Cleo's head. You don't mess with Chris. Someone tried once and his bloody body parts were found scattered around the city, a shoed foot in Golden Gate Park, an ear at Pier 39.

Cleo rounds the corner and falls. His feet refuse to carry him farther.

T his sucks man. How come they all gotta be so mean? I just
want a stick and a hit that don't cost nothing a twenty. I got
diamonds and gold and I'm going to pay them someday. My feet
are killing me. Wish my Annie was here. She'd take care of them.
Met her in church. I used to go to churches looking for God. I
used to believe in Him. I didn't lie to her about that some old
man sitting up in the clouds sure why not? I went to every kind of
church Catholic Methodist Buddhist. I went to a synagogue. Every
time I said I believed good things happened to me. First time I
saw her I knew. Her red hair was rolled up in a bun on top of her
head and all lit up by the sun and glowing like a fire a red halo like
she was some kind of angel. Green eyes and tits big as cantaloupes.
I couldn't believe she wanted me. I just got out of aprogram and
stopped using that shit. None of this fur on my face. Had a little
job. I swept the sidewalk in front of a couple stores for pocket money. Told her I was a manager in one of them. See what love does
it brings you down. Man my feet are fucking killing me. I looked
so good back then all the bitches wanted a piece of me. Now it's
only my feet want me and they want to hurt me. Where's my knife?
I had a pocket knife where'd it go? I gotta slice them open and

drain them which fucking friend of mine stole my knife? When I find out I'm going to take that knife and slice a piece off him he don't want to lose. Oh yeah I traded it for a hit I remember. I'd kill someone for a stick right now kill them. And when I was done smoking that stick I'd kill someone for a hit. A teeny little one just enough to kill my feet and my heart it keeps on beating no matter what I do and every beat's a switchblade slashing through it. There ain't nothing in my chest but chunks of bleeding heart. I'm sorry for what I done to her. I broke her heart didn't mean to. Too bad she couldn't see what I really am. Nothing. I ain't nothing. Not worth loving. Fuck I gotta get a hit. I'm just one big pity party today I think I gotta fever.

"Aw, now, Cleo, why are you lying on the sidewalk? You can't be sleeping. You never sleep. You look hot and I don't mean hot, I mean hot." He drapes an icy hand across Cleo's clammy forehead. "You've got a fever, sweetie."

Cleo's eyelids flicker open. "Hey Pete. I don't feel too good."

"You look awful, man, worse than usual if that's possible, and take a look at those feet. Damn! What did you do to them? You need to get to a doctor. And they stink, too."

"You gotta hit man? I just want a little hit and then I'm going to go over to the clinic. I promise. Just enough to make them stop hurting so I can stand up on them. I'm going to pay you later. I ate a bunch of diamonds."

"You know you aren't going to pay me and I don't want any diamonds that come out of your ass, sweetie. But here, I'll give you some shit, I don't want the word to get out that Pete Ducharnay is a stingy bastard. Might scare off my honey, that gorgeous young hunk I'm looking for with the muscles rippling on his biceps and a six-pack bulging through his tight little tee shirt. Nobody likes a meanie." He drops a tiny plastic baggy blinking with fine white crystals into Cleo's damp palm.

"You gotta point?"

"Now you're pushing it. Take care of yourself, Cleo."

"Wait. Give me your coffee."

"Jeez! Try to do you a favor and you milk it for all it's worth. Here, take it. Happy now? I have to run, I've got a big date tonight. You know. See ya."

Yeah right. A date serving booze. It's called a job you fucking bozo you stupid old man. Every hair on your head's gray and your face's full of lines running every which way looks like a road map. Ain't no young hunk's going to look twice at you.

He trickles the crystals into an eddy of coffee.

It ain't a point but sometimes you gotta be creative.

One gulp and the coffee's down. He leans against the wall, eyes shut.

The sun veers behind a cloud and a soothing gray blanket drops over him. He waits.

His head pulls his neck up, up, up, stretching it until he's as tall as a giraffe. He can see over the roofs of the parked cars and nibble on the highest branches of the withered trees that guard the sidewalk.

A cool sip of fresh air whirls up and down his elongated neck. His biceps bulge against his jacket sleeves, his thighs balloon inside his jeans and strain the seams until the stitches pop one by one and his legs break free. His feet heal and he can walk. No pain.

I'm just like Jesus He healed the sick with shit way back then. It's been around a long fucking time.

He smiles. What's he going to do now?

M an here's that same fucking dumpster. But this ain't the same place where it was las night it's been following me or maybe it's been sending out radio signals that made me come here they turned me into a robot. That wheelchair creep out there I bet he put a chip in my brain when I was sleeping in the dumpster the fucker. He's sending signals to me through that chip and forcing me to come here no creep in a wheelchair's going to do nothing to me I'd knock his teeth down his throat before he even got those wheels turning. Maybe he buried something good in here for me cuz he was so fucking mean to me yesterday maybe some more diamonds man life's so fucking good! I got steamy sunshine dribbling like fucking paint all down my back and there's a million dumpsters and garbage cans in the city just standing around waiting for me to dig through them I could find anything. A cat a fucking rattlesnake man I'd sic it on all those fucking assholes who won't give me nothing. Candy bars now that'd be cool I'd go down to the pier and munch on them all afternoon use them to score a sexy bitch and have my way with her they all want a piece of me anyway don't even gotta give them candy all I gotta do is flash my sexy come-and-get-me-baby smile at them and then fuck!

I gotta smack them off me. Need a cop to save my ass. Look at my muscles! I'm ripped man! Look at my face! I ought to be a movie star every fucking bitch in this city wants a piece of me.

I watch him from the window, that same skinny blond dude marching back and forth in front of the dumpster. He's lost his limp and his laceless shoes, and his bare feet have been slapping the asphalt all afternoon. I know he's talking because I can see his mouth moving. He's fried. Or mental. Those are the only possible explanations.

I should be working. My computer is warmed up and ready for me to slave over it. My online business. I buy and sell Mexican and Central American crafts. When you're in a wheelchair it's easier to sit at home and work. That's one good thing about the computer age. I have customers from all over the world without stepping outside my door. It's actually pretty cool.

But I can't tear myself away from the window and that wasted specter eroding a trench down there in the alley. His head sags as if he were carrying the weight of the world on his back and his lips flap.

When dusk blankets everything but the light bulbs over the alley doors I go back to my computer. Is he going to keep this up all night? Will he still be there in the morning, forcing those tattered feet to run a marathon in front of the dumpster?

Around midnight I go to bed. I'm out as soon as my head hits the pillow, but visions of him twirling, skipping, hopping get tangled in my sleep. He sails up to heaven, sprouts wings, sings. Plays a harp. I gasp myself awake. Why am I dreaming he's an angel? He is rude, filthy, aggressive and probably violent.

As soon as dawn whispers into my bedroom I roll back to the kitchen window. He's still there but now his feet, powerful as the hind legs of an irate mule, are kicking dents in the dumpster. I can hear his screams through my closed window.

I have to stop him. Someone will call the cops. Or someone will jump him and I doubt he could fight them off. After pacing all night he has to be ready to keel over, even if he is kicking the shit out of the dumpster.

Fucking stupid dumpster! Didn't give me nothing no diamonds no gold buttons no candy bars not even a bottle of moldy juice. And I got so fucking dirty digging through it look at my hands black sons of satan and they're my fucking hands I had the world in these hands yesterday and now I don't got nothing not even a fucking crumb! And now the fucking thing's talking to me telling me about my Annie. "If you wait here she's going to prance by at midnight," it says to me. "Oh you're fucked," I answer. "You don't know my Annie." "I swear I do," it says. "By the god of the dumpsters she's a whore and she's out here every night at midnight looking for a john with his pockets full of money. Been doing this for years long before she met you. You thought you were fooling her telling her you had to go to work or you had to help a friend and letting her sit there all by herself in her pretty pink house while you were out getting high and fucking other bitches but she was on to you and she was out there doing it too. Shooting up shit and everything." "You're a liar! I never fucked no one but my Annie." "You left her alone every night to go out and fuck other bitches." A big belly laugh explodes out of the dumpster. "Anyone who'd share their shit with you dumb-ass." "Liar! I'm going to kill you! You hear that noise like a machine gun shooting everything in the alley? That's my bare feet kicking in your fucking sides. Kicking holes in them my feet are hard as rocks and sharp as machetes and I'm going to kick huge gigantic holes in you and all your fucking garbage is going to spurt out of you like blood garbage blood all over the ground and you're going to look like the jolly green giant's sieve when you're all smashed up and dead in the dump all full of holes from Superman's steel-toed boots! I never fucked no one but my Annie! Even though she was out there fucking everyone else in the whole city." Man who's there? That wheelchair creep again.

"Get out of here leave me alone!" Fucker.

"Hey, dude," I call him.

He ignores me and continues to scream at the dumpster.

"Dude," I call him again. "Take it easy. Someone's going to call the cops on you."

"Can't you see I'm fucking busy here? I gotta kick the life out of this fucking dumpster. It lies man lies like hell. I don't got time to talk to a fucking wheelchair creep."

"I'm just letting you know. You don't want to spend the night in jail, do you?"

"Yeah and what else is new? They love me in jail and what the fuck do you care anyway? I'll show you who's boss you fucker." He viciously kicks the dumpster again. "Did you come down here to get a piece of me man?"

"Me? No, dude, I'm not that way. I just don't want you to get in trouble."

His foot freezes for a second in mid-air, then it settles to the pavement and he glares at me, swirling gray clouds smudging his bright blue eyes.

"You been fucking my Annie."

"What?"

"You been fucking my wife. That's how come you're out here acting like you care. You want to see who you're up against. See the profile?" He faces the dumpster. "Like a fucking Greek statue." He turns back to me, widens his eyes. "See the eyes? Bluer than a summer day. And the hair you don't got thick hair like this." Blackened fingers comb through the mass of blond and silver curls on his head. "No fucker does. See? You lose. I'm so much better than you it ain't funny I look better I got more money and I can walk. Yeah you heard me. I said it." Another kick to the dumpster. "You been fucking my Annie." He raises his fists and steps towards me.

"Hey, dude, look at me." He's crazy. Why on earth did I come out here? "I'm in a wheelchair. I broke my back in a car accident ten years ago and I haven't been laid since. I can't do it. Nothing works from my waist down. Look at me, dude."

He looks. His hands fall to his sides. "I never punched a guy in a wheelchair and I ain't going to do it now." He sways a little. "What's your name?

"Tim."

"I'm real fucking tired Tim." His eyelids drift downward. "Real...tired..." His chin hits his chest.

Damn. "Look, dude, come up to my apartment and sleep it off."

A soft snore.

I wheel forward and tap his arm. "Wake up."

"Huh?"

"Come up to my apartment and sleep."

"I'm a thief man. That's what everybody says. You don't want to let me in your place."

"Is that true?"

"Fuck no."

"Then come up with me."

His eyes close.

"Hey!" I nudge him. "Push me."

"Okay fuck it. Which way?"

"This way."

He clutches the back of the wheelchair and pushes. "Where's the handles on this fucker?"

"It's streamlined. Goes faster."

His head sinks to my shoulder. He stumbles.

"What's your name?" I ask.

"George."

"George?"

"How come you want to know?"

"You know my name."

His head slides off my shoulder and pushes against the back of the chair. His feet drag on the asphalt. "Cleo." Almost too soft to hear.

"Leo?"

"CLEO. Dumb-ass. Are you fucking deaf too? My name's Cleo!"

"Okay. Cleo." What the hell am I getting myself into?

H e sleeps for two days straight. It doesn't seem like he's sleeping: he jabbers nonstop. Gibberish, profanity. He sings, sits up and whinnies. Lies back down and meows. Cackles, crows and screeches. Gets up and pisses in the corner and stumbles back to the couch, doesn't answer when I yell at him. His hands punch an invisible punching bag and his feet kick a continuous can-can.

I am mesmerized. What a miserable life this man must have. He can't even rest when he's asleep. It's as if he is losing the battle with his demons and they're taking over his soul, tossing it around like a football, running it down the field and doing a victory dance as they bounce it into the end zone.

His kicking feet are puffy and covered with oozing abscesses that shoot red streaks up inside the frayed hem of his jeans. They have that death smell, the smell mortuary flowers try to hide. I can't get close enough to touch them but in between kicks I douse them with peroxide. He doesn't respond, doesn't seem to feel the peroxide fire eating at his wounds. Those legs move and his mouth blathers as a volcano froths up, covers his feet, drips onto the pad I put down to protect the couch. I do this several times during those two days. Not once does he react.

Toward the end of the second day he is still. He lies on his back and snores. His feet are quiet, the swelling has gone down a little, the red streaks have faded to dusty rose.

He snores all night.

In the morning I peek into the living room on my way to the kitchen.

He is sitting on the couch, hunched over his knees.

"Hi," I say.

He looks up. "How come I'm here?"

"You were asleep on your feet. I brought you in to let you catch a few winks."

"How long you been holding me here?" Chipped grime-caked fingernails dig into his arm, scratching, squeezing, gouging. He picks something off his bleeding skin and holds it up to his eyes. "This look like a bug?" He shows it to me. "You got bugs in your couch man? What kind of place you running here?"

"No, dude, no bugs. None at all. You've been here two days, to answer your question."

"Two days! Did I shit?"

"Nope."

"You're a fucking liar!"

"Why would I lie about that? You did piss in the corner, thanks a lot."

"You sure I didn't shit?"

"Unless you did it in your shorts, and I think I would've smelled that. Why is it such a big deal?"

"None of your business. I gotta go."

"Aren't you hungry? I'll fry you some eggs. You could take a shower, too. I've got some clothes you can have. You're about my height."

"How come you're being nice to me? You don't know me."

"I have a brother who's spent most of his life down on his luck. I always hoped someone would help him if he needed it."

"Where is he?"

"Prison."

"Okay go and fry your eggs and give me a towel. I'm going to make you happy. But I don't need your help."

While he showers I crack two eggs into a frying pan, spread toast with raspberry jam, section a grapefruit, pour a cup of coffee.

He walks out of the bathroom, a scarecrow in my old jeans and sweatshirt, stuffing wisped away by the wind. My shoes have turned his sore-footed gait into a hobble.

"How do you take your coffee?"

"Black. Fuck. My feet are killing me."

"You need to see a doctor. They're infected."

He empties the coffee cup in one swallow without sitting down at the kitchen table, snatches the toast off the plate and crams it in his mouth.

"Gotta go. Gotta be at work in a few minutes."

"You work?"

"Yeah I'm the president of the Bank of America. The one down on Market and Third."

"Is that what you wear to work?"

"You gave me these clothes. Something the matter with them? They got bugs? That's how come you gave them to me?"

"No, they're clean, dude. But a bank president? Where's your suit and tie?"

"Shows what you know. I'm the president. I can wear any fucking kind of clothes I want."

He picks up his reeking Giants jacket and slams the door as he leaves. Through the window I see him limping away at half the speed of light.

President of the Bank of America. And I'm Miss Universe.

I go to grab the wet towel he dropped on the bathroom floor and the bedroom door flutters as I pass. I push it open.

Everything has been rifled. The dresser drawers dangle, clothes hanging out of them. The closet shelves spill their guts through their gaping doors. The lid stands up on the tooled Spanish leather box where I keep my mother's jewelry, a red flag signaling me. I navigate through the mess on the floor, panic crushing my throat with iron fingers. The box is empty. Mama's onyx rosary and the gold crucifix and chain that her grandmother gave her. Gone.

"Damn!" I say it out loud and it pierces the wall like a spear and sticks there. I only let him out of my sight to take a shower. When did he take them?

He's my brother all over again, the same kind of miserable lying stealing addict as Teddy. I should've known.

"May I buy you a cup of coffee?"

I look up from my desk. A tall slender man with a trim gray moustache, thick gray hair curling over his collar, and eyes that are the deep brown of pools hidden beneath a layer of autumn leaves stands in front of me.

He is smiling.

"Do I know you?"

"You helped me find a picture last fall. From Sturgis. A photo of me in a magazine with my Harley. Remember?"

I blink. I have no memory of him. A slow sizzle starts at the place where my brain ends and the unforgiving bone walls of my skull begin.

"I told you I ride up there every year. You said it sounded like fun."

"Oh, Sturgis. I do remember. But I don't have time for coffee, thank you." I can't do this. Please go away.

"It doesn't have to be now. We can get coffee any time."

"I'm sorry, I just don't know when I would be able to do that." The sizzle in my brain chops my breath into hiccupping gasps. I want to say I have a husband but I can't bring myself to tell him a lie, and my naked left ring finger is as obvious as a traffic light.

"I'm not a bad guy. My name is Joseph Wall. Actually Joseph George Wall, Jr. Everyone calls me Joe. I'm a substance abuse counselor at a drug treatment center not far from here. I have a good income and I'm clean, see?" He holds his arms straight out from his sides, palms up. "And shiny. I polish my shoes." He points to them but I don't look. "Leather. No gym shoes. I have my own house in Haight-Ashbury, a motorcycle, a Camaro...But that's not what interests you, is it?"

I turn my eyes toward the picture windows, hoping the sunlight cascading through them will blind me and I won't be able to see him.

"I wanted to let you know how much I appreciated your help. I figured you'd turn me down, so I stopped at the store and bought a bunch of different drinks. I don't know what you like. Take your pick." Curiosity pulls my eyes back to him. I watch his long fingers re-move a cold bottled cappuccino, a mango Snapple, an Arizona lemon ice tea, a diet Coke, and a Seven-Up from a plastic grocery bag.

"I...I'm not thirsty, Mr. Wall." The words stick to my tongue and I have to scrape it against my teeth to get them to slink out of my mouth. "Thanks anyway." Sweat sloshes in my armpits, drib-bles down between my breasts. I squeeze my trembling hands with my knees and frantically look at my computer screen. Is he never going to leave?

He stoops down to my eye level and I peek at him. His brown eyes hold mine for interminable seconds.

"The tops are all sealed," he says quietly. "Check them."

"How did you know?" I whisper. He guessed my secret. A gust of cold air chills my suddenly exposed soul.

"I said I was a substance abuse counselor. I'm also an addict, but I've been clean for more than twenty-five years. I know what addicts do. I know all the different ways they hurt the people who try to love them."

A sigh rocks me from deep inside the eon-thick walls of brick and thorn I'd built around my heart to protect it from Cleo.

"I suppose I could take the cappuccino."

I don't drink it. I slip the bottle in my handbag and take it home. I set it on the dining room table and plunk heavily down on a chair and stare at it, not seeing the bottle at all. Seeing Cleo.

Cleo was six feet tall, with curly Viking hair that could only be tamed by shaving it off, and a large-boned wide face, twinkling Paul Newman-blue eyes, and lips that were twin pencil lines perpetually curled in mirth. He loved to laugh; he even laughed in his sleep.

He swept me off my feet with roses. Every day he brought them to me at the library, red roses, violet roses, maroon, white, scarlet, orange and yellow, pink and cream, every color imaginable. I knew he hadn't bought them. He'd taken some from Golden Gate Park, stolen some from people's yards. I didn't ask, didn't care. I was in love.

We slow-danced on the beach at sunset and he sang "Annie's Song" in my ear, twirled me around until our legs buckled and we lay in the sand crowing like roosters. Our mouths filled with salt-water as we kissed. Wet sand plastered our hair and clothes. We chased each other and he bayed, head thrown back and hands and feet pawing. "I'm the Wolfman baby and you ain't going to get away from me." He snorted and snuffled and licked my face, his tongue leaving a clammy trail from my jaw to my forehead. I squealed like a toddler.

He chased the dog, the Chihuahua I'd gotten after I moved into my house. The big man and the tiny dog were inseparable, the dog bobbling in and out of every room at his heels. Poquito would bounce in the middle of the living room and bark at him. One bark meant he needed to go out. Two barks meant food. Three barks meant "Chase me," and off they'd dash, the towering man running after the shrunken dog. Then they'd switch and the dog would run after the man. They'd do this for hours at a time, Cleo taunting "You can't catch me you little mutt. Your legs are too short," and Poquito yipping and yapping. I'd be on the couch knitting a sweater for Cleo, feet tucked under me so I wouldn't trip them. Every now and then a chuckle would break through my skeins of yarn and from a quiet place inside me a prayer of thanksgiving would work its way up to God. Life was good.

One Friday evening we ate dinner as usual. He made coffee afterwards and we drank it in front of the television the way we did every Friday. For some reason we didn't sleep that night: we talked. About our day, our plans, our jobs, the dog. We made love and got back up and talked some more. Decided to go for a drive at one in the morning. Drove forty miles to San Jose, then up the other side of the bay to Oakland and back across the Bay Bridge to San Francisco. We were still chatting but now his angelic smile had twisted into a taut braid, and the conversation carried long-buried barbs, wrongs never forgiven, parents unable to love, teachers who bruised with rulers. Black clouds crowded the car and smeared a greasy film across the windshield. He started talking about me, hinting at sins he thought I'd committed, making accusations but unwilling to pin my name on them.

"Some of you fucking bitches hook up with a boyfriend when your husbands are at work."

"Some do," I agreed, wondering why he'd said that.

"Some bitches act like they're going to go to work in the morning but they're really going to go to their boyfriend's house."

"I suppose."

"You suppose? You don't know? You do too know. Fucker. You just don't want to admit it."

"Admit what?"

"Admit it. Bet you didn't think I was going to figure it out did you. You're always acting like you're so fucking holy always telling me about God and how I gotta tell the truth and look at you you're a fucking liar." He was screaming now and banging his fist on the dashboard.

"Cleo! I love you. I would never…"

"Shut the fuck up! I can't take no more of you. Stop the fucking car."

The inky San Francisco streets were deserted. I pulled over to the curb.

"Not here you fucking bitch. You think I'm going to walk halfway across the city? Drive me to Ninth Street."

He told me which way to go, pitching words at me as if I were a batter trying to hit his fastballs at home plate. My fingers had iced over. They dropped off the steering wheel several times, too frozen to hold onto it. My feet were cold, too, the feet of a snowman, but my body was feverish and dry and my armpits reeked. A snake had found its way in between my chapped lips, swallowed my tongue and was flickering in and out in its place. My words slithered out with a lisp I'd never heard before. "What's going on?" my brain asked.

"You fucking whore." He spit in my face and bolted out of the car in the unlit alley he'd directed me to. "I'm going to file for divorce." He left the door open and sauntered away shouting "She's a fucking whore!" to the deaf night. I had to get out of the car and wobble around to his side to close the door. In that brief minute he'd already been gobbled up by shadows. It was as if he'd never existed.

"Hey, baby," a deep voice rasped next to me in the dark. "I want you if he don't."

I shrieked and ran back to the driver's side. Hopped in, gunned the engine and zoomed down the street without looking to see who the voice belonged to.

When I got home all I could do was pace. Living room, dining room, kitchen, bedroom, bathroom, living room. My trembling legs could barely hold me up but I was too anxious to sit down and too stunned to cry. I turned on the television to have some voices in the room other than the "What's going on?" that was pounding my brain to pieces.

I called in sick for my Saturday shift and kept pacing. Peed every few minutes. Couldn't bring myself to eat a thing. Questions highlighted the whole day: why did he leave me? What did I do to make him so angry? I paced. The sun went down and came up and I finally collapsed on the couch and fell asleep.

Three days later he called. "You okay?"

"Okay? How could I be okay?"

"I miss you."

"You mean you don't want a divorce?"

"I never wanted a divorce. I don't know why I said that. I love you so much."

He begged me to let him come home. After we made love I fell asleep with his arms wrapped around me, my head sandwiched against his chest. His embrace was tight and I felt secure again.

I awoke at four in the morning. His side of the bed was cold. I found him on the couch in the living room, smoking.

"Is something wrong?"

"Can't get to sleep. I'm just going to finish smoking this stick and then I'm going to crawl back in bed and rub my hands all over your sexy body."

"You have to get up soon and go to work."

"Man I forgot about that. They ain't real nice at that job. Always talking about me when they think I can't hear them. I'm going to get me another job. Don't go and get that worried look on your pretty face I ain't going to quit until I get a real good one. A lot of money and no people bothering me. Come on over here and sit with me baby." I snuggled up next to him and smelled the sleep scent of his tee shirt and inhaled the wisps of cigarette smoke straying from his lips. He swaddled me in his arms. "Thank you for letting me come back," he murmured to my hair. "I'm going to stay here with you forever. You know that don't you Annie? You know I'm going to be here with you forever."

"I know."

He didn't go to work that morning. He called in sick and had me call in sick, too. We made love all day. I wept at the intensity of his tenderness and every time we were done I wanted more. By evening we lay splattered across the bed, too exhausted to care that the sheets were crumpled on the floor and the damp pillows had lost their cases.

My thoughts floated in hazy circles as I drifted off to sleep. Is it the pull of the moon? He's so sensitive. Maybe it's the moon.

T he phone jangles.

"Obregon Imports," I say, pinning the phone to my shoulder with my jaw, my fingers battering the computer keyboard as I order Guatemalan clay pots. "How may I help you?"

A deep voice hums on the other end.

"This is he...What?" My fingers hang in the air for a couple seconds and then fall to my lap. "How did it happen?"

More deep rumblings.

"What do I have to do?...Okay." I drop the phone.

Somewhere in my chest there used to be lungs. They could suck in air and release it without any effort on my part. Those lungs have moved out; I can't catch my breath. "Oh Jesus." Teddy is gone. Shanked through the heart by another inmate.

I rest my forehead on the cool computer screen. "I failed you, Mama." I'd promised her I would help him, and I hadn't. I'd turned my back on him after the crash. It was his fault. I blamed him for my wheelchair, my paralysis, my life of confinement, my loneliness. "I always meant to go see him. You know that, Mama. I wasn't going to stay away forever."

I remember her in her hospital bed, her tiny cancer-yellow hands clutching mine. "Forgive your brother," she pleaded. "He needs you. You're all he has now. Forgive him and be his friend."

"I will, Mama. Don't worry. I'll help him get himself together. I promise."

She'd died a few days later. Teddy was in prison, serving five years for assaulting a cop. They brought him to the funeral, discreetly handcuffed to two officers in twin black suits with black ties and glaring white shirts. His sneer told the world "I'm in prison, so what? I can get out any time I want." There was no sadness, no sign of pain at the loss of our mother. I sat by myself next to the front pew and studied the blood red dust specks drifting past the stained glass windows. I couldn't look at him.

He'd had that same sneer on his face after the accident. He'd come by with a new car.

"Tim, you gotta see this baby. Awesome car. Rides like a Ferrari. I got it legal, too. I know you don't believe me but I did. Bought it from a friend."

I didn't want to go with him. It was ten o'clock on a Saturday morning and I had a case of beer to work through. That was how I spent my Saturdays back then. Sundays, too. And I would grab a cold one as soon as I walked in the door after work. I'd have to set the open can down to take off my jacket.

"Rosa's coming over." The girl from down the block. We used to go to bars on Saturday nights, drink our whirling thoughts to extinction, dance until closing time and then make wild love in my bed until dawn. Over the years she gradually drank less and I drank more. Eventually all she did was cook dinner for me on Saturday nights, sit next to me on the couch and watch me chug beer until I was comatose. She'd go home after I passed out. Maybe she kept coming around because she thought we would get married someday. I haven't seen her since the accident.

"C'mon, Tim. Don't be such a pussy. Rosa won't be here 'til evening."

"All right."

"Wait. Gotta use your bathroom."

He was in there a long time. I guzzled two beers before he reappeared, his pupils flaring, words zipping out of his mouth in a frantic tap-dance.

Okay, so what? So he got high. To each his own.

A year later when I finally returned to my apartment I found the syringe in the bathroom sink, a couple drops of blood permanently staining the counter and a tiny empty baggy floating in the toilet.

"Look at this!" He kissed the hood of a canary yellow '69 Mustang with double chrome tailpipes. Glass packs. The car roared like a jet plane when he accelerated. We blasted away from the curb, horns honking and drivers yelling out their windows as he cut them off.

He headed south on Highway 101. Through bloodshot eyes I watched the speedometer climb to eighty, ninety, a hundred.

"Slow down, Teddy," I yelled, and downed the beer I'd brought with me.

He cackled.

Any thoughts I'd been thinking were whisked away by the sight of electric poles rushing by too fast to be counted. The only thing in my head was a ricocheting mantra: "Oh God, please don't let us get busted." I was drunk and he was high. I was a social worker in the county jail and I didn't want to be an inmate there.

I gripped the edge of my seat. There were no seat belts.

"Look at those fools!" he shouted, both hands waving at the people who were staring with noses squashed against their car windows as we passed them.

The driver next to him slammed on the brakes as we veered into his lane. Teddy hooted. Started singing at the top of his voice. "Born to be wild." Closed his eyes.

"Teddy!" The red tail lights of a white Ford van were ten feet in front of us.

"Huh?" Eyes still closed.

My own scream filled my ears along with the shriek of tires, of metal French-kissing metal, and the clink of shattering glass as I shot through the windshield. I hit unyielding pavement and crumbled. I couldn't move. I heard sirens and saw red lights flashing and wondered where Teddy was and then I saw him lounging against a police car, talking to a cop, a maroon trickle wending its way down one side of his face. I heard him say "He gave it to me, Officer. I'm sorry. I was trying to stay clean and my own brother gave it to me." He sneered as he looked at me spread across the freeway in a sloshing ocean of my own blood. I watched my life disappear as that taunting sneer sucked it up. His sneer was to become a scar, a permanent fixture he would wear like a badge. Only a plastic surgeon would be able to remove it.

As what was left of me was being loaded onto a gurney, his face appeared in front of me. It drifted closer and he whispered in my ear "You know why I'm still walking around? Angels saved me. I saw them. When I flew out of the car they caught me and lay me down on the ground, so soft it was like laying down on my own bed. Angels. I don't know why they didn't help you."

The word "forgiveness" vanished from my vocabulary in that instant. It was replaced by a hundred different words for anger. My favorite one was rage.

Ten years later that rage still bubbles under my skin, pierces me like cactus needles at night when my hands hoist my dead legs onto my bed. My dreams are maroon jello garnished with Teddy's sneer as it chews me up and spits out my dead parts, the parts that will never walk, never make love. The parts that need suppositories, that need catheters every six hours. The pale feet bloated and motionless in high top leather running shoes.

I'd told myself many times that there was nothing I could do for him. "Mama, I can't help him," I'd said when my pledge prodded my heart and I saw my dying mother smiling at me, the love for her two boys shining through her eyes. That love was the road she followed into eternity, sure-footed and head held high. It was the halo of her angel self, her achievement in this life. Her essence.

Why don't I have that love? I can't blame it on the accident. Teddy hurt Mama, too. He came home high and beat her. Put her in the hospital more than once. Stole from her, jewelry, money, credit cards, checks. Precious mementos of her dead husband, our dad. Still her love wrapped around him without flinching.

I sigh. "Okay, Mama. Time to make good on my promise." I can't help my brother. He's with Mama now, she can deal with him. But maybe I should try to help Cleo. Will that get me off the hook with her?

"I'm sure not getting in a car with him if he's driving," I say to myself, teeth clenched. "And I'm not going to let him use me. I'm going to get Mama's things back. That's what I'm going to do."

A couple weeks later it happened again.

We were cuddling after dinner, steaming fingers unbuttoning buttons, slipping inside waist bands. Our throbbing clothes had not yet left our bodies when I glanced at the clock and the hands were pointing to eleven. There was a knot of anxiety in my stomach. My fingers and toes were chunks of ice. We had sex in the living room, the bedroom, the bathroom and on the hall floor. He was ferocious, not the tender lover my body ached for. I had rug burns on my back and vermillion teeth marks, some of them groaning out beads of blood, from my jaw to my ankles.

"Who is he?" He was still inside me, ramming me into the wall so hard that I was crushing my hands against it to keep my neck from snapping.

"Who?" I was choking on the sweat storming off his body.

"Don't act like you don't know who I'm talking about." He slapped me.

"Cleo! Don't!"

"I smell the fucker on you. You think I'm too stupid to figure it out? I know the way you smell and you smell different."

"Maybe it's my new soap." Trying to keep the wave of fear that was lapping at my frozen feet from dragging me out to sea.

"I'm out of here." He jumped off me and jammed his legs into his jeans. "Fucking whore. Everybody told me 'Don't marry her she's a whore.' Did I listen? Man I'm one stupid piece of shit. I had to go and marry her and now you see what I got a goddam fucking piece of shit whore. Where's my shoes?"

Please, God, make him hurry. I lay scattered across the hall floor, a dismembered manikin. I slid my eyelids shut so I wouldn't have to see him. Held my breath so it wouldn't pull his attention back to me. My slapped cheek tingled. Blood clanged through my temples and my barreling heart was digging a tunnel out of my chest. Nausea skulked up the back of my throat. If he didn't leave soon I was going to vomit on the carpet.

The door finally slammed behind him and I heard the car speed away. My eyes opened cautiously. Deep gusts of air flooded my lungs. I kneeled for a few minutes while the whirl in my head slowed to an occasional teeter and the shiny white spots of volcanic ash falling in front of my eyes settled into a mound on the floor.

My hands crept up the wall, dragging me to my feet. I lurched to the bathroom and heaved. Crawled to the bedroom, climbed into a nightgown and fell into bed.

What if he came back?

I knew he wouldn't. I didn't understand what was happening but I knew he'd be gone for days.

I lay there with lightning arcing through my brain. Was he psychotic? But I was affected, too. Something in the food? I'd made the dinner myself both times. And he made the coffee. Maybe we should switch to decaf.

This became the race we ran, always on the same hoof-marked track with the same garish sights at the sides of the same stretches. We passed Friday dinner, we passed the frigid hands and feet and the churning stomach, we passed the accusations, the threats and slaps, the malignant sex, and we passed him walking out. A couple days of respite with palm trees and beach chairs appeared at the side of the track. And then he came home and we passed Friday dinner again.

I knew I should leave him but the idea immobilized me: he was the reason I got out of bed every morning. Who would put excitement in my life if he wasn't there? Who would I preen for, cook for, flutter around? Who would tease me and caress me? I could barely stand to be away from him for the eight hours I had to be at work. By lunchtime my heart would be struggling to break free and run to him, and my body would be shivering in anticipation of his fingers, my clothes unbuttoning themselves, ready to fall off the second I was in his arms. What would every dreary day be if I didn't have him?

I would become a desiccated skeleton, the sheets pulled primly to my chin, my rib cage deserted, my veins barren.

I had to figure out what was going on. Maybe it was something we could fix.

I tried discussing it with him but he insisted he didn't know either, and he assured me it wouldn't happen again. "Sometimes I'm funny that way," he said.

"But what about me? I'm not funny that way."

"No baby you ain't funny. You're awesome. You're the awesomest thing I ever got in my whole life. I ain't going to make it in this world if I lose you. You're the only friend I got."

One Friday evening the nausea began earlier than usual. We were still in the euphoric stage of the nightmare when it hit. I threw up repeatedly until my stomach was a deflated balloon, wrinkled and empty. Dry heaves took over. Chills shook me. My teeth chattered. Thunder blasted in my ears and my eyes looked out at a world of strobe lights.

"Take me to the Emergency Room."

"How come?"

"I think I'm having a stroke," I sobbed. I was only thirty-nine. "Take me there now. Or I'll call 9-1-1." I stumbled toward the phone. My legs vanished and my face hit the floor.

"Okay baby."

The vomiting had scraped my insides clean and there was not a drop or a crumb left inme but there it came again. I covered my mouth with my hand while I retched.

"I'm sorry you're feeling so bad Annie." He carried me to the car.

The nurse checked my blood pressure. 185 over 150. My pulse was 180.

"Let's get you into a bed right away," he said.

He started an IV. Injected some kind of medicine into the tubing. Drew blood, had me pee in a cup.

A while later the doctor came in. "Could you step out for a moment, sir," he said to Cleo. "I need to speak to her in private."

"What is it, Doctor? Am I dying?"

"Are you trying to?"

"What do you mean?"

"You have toxic levels of methamphetamine in your blood."

"I do?"

"You sound surprised."

"Doctor, I'm a Christian. I go to church every Sunday. I pray every day. I don't drink, let alone use drugs."

"Why do you think your blood's full of meth?"

"I don't know."

"Who is that man with you?"

"My husband. You don't think..." Oh no. He used to use speed. He'd told me that. But not in a long time. And he was never going to use it again. That was one of the promises he'd made when I agreed to marry him.

"If you think he did this to you I can have him arrested. In your condition it would be considered attempted murder."

"No, no arrests. I need to think. I'm sure it wasn't him. I have to figure this out."

The coffee. It wasn't the caffeine. He was mixing speed in the coffee.

Why would he do that? I knew he didn't want to kill me. He loved me. So why?

I confronted him when we got home.

"No baby I ain't going to pull no crap like that. I know you don't want none of that shit."

"How did it get in my body? It isn't billowing in with the fog. I didn't breathe it in somewhere."

His forehead corrugated while he thought. "I bet I know. Sonofabitch. The coffee. I asked the guy at the coffee shop to grind it. He slipped something in it. Fuck! I'm going to go and knock his teeth down his throat in the morning! Let me throw it out right now." He chucked the bag of coffee in the garbage.

"What about all those times when you went crazy and walked on out me? You weren't high then?"

"No baby no. I promised you remember? I always keep all my promises. That's one of the few things I do right." His eyes rolled upward and inspected the ceiling. He inhaled all the air in the kitchen, let it out slow enough for me to remember the starfish. Buckets of starfish he had brought home from a day clambering on seaweed-dripping rocks made visible by an ebbing tide. He parked them outside the back door and forgot about them.

The water covering them evaporated, and when they were rubber corpses bobbing on stinking green slime I returned their bodies to the sea.

He turned his eyes on me. "Okay. Here's the truth. I'm bipolar. I was going to tell you before we got married but I loved you so much I was scared you wouldn't marry me if you knew. The docs made me take dope but it made me feel like I was sleepwalking so I don't take it no more. And it made my thoughts crawl by as slow as a snail one fucking word at a time and I didn't know how to deal with that."

I stared at him, face blank as a cave entrance.

"You don't believe me?"

"I don't know."

"I ain't being bad now right?"

"No."

"If I was an addict Annie you know there ain't no way I'm going to give you some of that shit and not take most of it myself. You know that's what addicts do don't you? And man if I used some of it now I'd be in the hospital too. I'd be bat-assed crazy. That's how come I stopped. Don't want to be 5150'd."

"Then why do I get sick when you're being bad?"

"Cuz you and me baby we're one. You feel all the same things I feel. That's what happens when two people really love each other. We got one heart we beat together."

"If you love me that much, why do you hit me?"

"I never hit you baby. I love you. How come you're saying crap like that? It stabs me like a knife just to think about hitting you. I ain't never going to do that. My sexy Annie."

Did I imagine it? Was it because of the drugs he was giving me? Was he really giving me drugs? Maybe the lab results were wrong.

I bought drug tests. Ignored the smirk on the cashier's face. But the next weekend nothing happened. We ran errands, fingertips touching, lips teasing. Friday night we ate dinner and watched TV. Saturday evening we sat on the beach while the hot orange sun sank with a sizzle into the slate-blue sea, melted marshmallows over a fire and smeared them into each other's mouths, cuddled naked and ecstatic under a blanket until our energy was spent and the ocean-chilled air forced us back into our clothes and sent us home. We slept normally. I went to work Monday and felt fine.

Maybe he is telling the truth. All we have to do is find the right medicine for him. The anxiety that had taken root in my heart and sent up shoots blossoming with ugly black buds withered into a tiny dead twig, a smile peeking out from behind it. The stack of duties at work pushed his need for a psychiatrist to the back of my mind, and he was so charming for the rest of the week that I told myself I was over-reacting. My hot German blood.

Then it happened again. This time he snatched the three-foot-wide mirror off the bathroom wall. "Two-way mirror did you think you were going to fool me?" He smashed it on the floor and stomped on the shards with his bare feet, leaving glass slivers submerged in bloody puddles. "See what did I fucking tell you?" He punched holes in the naked wall. "Take that you motherfucker! Think you're going to spy on me?" I backed silently away, feet an inch above the carpet and lungs on hold. I had almost reached the front door when his hand wrenched my shoulder back.

"Where do you think you're going? You got all those fucking FBI spying on me now huh. Not no more. They're dead I killed them all. Now what am I going to do with you you fucking bitch. You working for the FBI? Think you're going to turn me in? You ain't gotta thing on me bitch." He knotted his fingers in my hair and dragged me headfirst to the kitchen, grabbed a steak knife out of the drawer, jerked my head back and caressed the vulnerable skin under my chin with the tip of the blade.

"You promised you wouldn't hurt me," I squeaked, lips ripping as the words sliced through them.

"I did? And you believed me?"

"Yes. I believed you."

"Okay then I'm going to fuck you so hard you ain't going to forget it. Take your clothes off."

My fingers, shapeless as water, couldn't undo the buttons on my blouse. He used the knife to rip it open, tore off my bra, shoved me to the floor and tried to slit my jeans but cut me instead. He yanked them off and shredded my panties, already blood-stained from his efforts with the knife.

He glared at me for a minute.

"Know what?" he said. "You ain't even my wife. She's sexy. You're ugly and wrinkled as an old hag. Looks like your fucking face is a bunch of footprints carved out of stone. Bitch who the fuck are you? And what did you do with my wife? You're fat. Those fucking tits are as big as pigs and your belly's spilling out all over the floor and that butt like the back end of an elephant. What did you do with her? Tell me or I'm going to kill you. What do you think I got this knife in my hands for?"

"I'm Annie," I sobbed but he wasn't listening. He had gone somewhere. Not even his angry self was present in that room. The person he had turned into raved for six hours, hurling obscenities, accusations, threats of dismemberment and death at me. I lay naked on the icy linoleum, forcing my body into rigor mortis to control my shivers, feeling my bladder expand to the size of a water balloon. Poquito always hid under the bed when Cleo was in a bad mood, and I heard him whimpering but he wouldn't come out. I shut my eyes and prayed. Cracked them open from time to time and peeked out between bolts of lightning to see what he was doing. He stood rooted to the kitchen floor, voice changing pitches at a dizzying rate, now deep and gravelly, now satanic and hissing, now a squealing witch's cackle. Sometimes the English became a babble in strange syllables and he'd throw back his head and bay until he was breathless. Then he'd switch back to English. "Fucking whore. Bitch. I saw you down there on Ninth Street. I followed you all the way up to the room where you fuck your johns. Shut up Cam. You're such a fucking cuckoo bird you can't even tell who's real and who ain't. I told you she's fucking everybody in San Francisco. And every piece of shit in the city jeers at me when they see me out on the street. Every one of them thinks I'm stupid cuz I'm letting her get away with it. Cuz I love her. She's my fucking life."

After six hours of madness he left. I ran to the bathroom and peed in the cup. Waited for the results. Positive for speed.

The next Friday it was positive. And the Friday after. And the Friday after that. Positive. Positive. Positive.

I met with Pastor Brown. A man my age with kids in grade school and a kind sedate wife. We had said our marriage vows in front of him.

"You have to leave him, Annie." Very gently.

"Leave him?" I couldn't do that. He was my soul. My heart. The oxygen that kept me alive. The glue that held together the dust I was made of.

"I know it's difficult. But for the sake of both of you, you have to let him go. You aren't doing him any good if you let him harm you."

"There has to be a way to help him."

"Does he want help?"

"Of course he does. I don't know. Maybe. What do I do? What do other people do? I can't be the only person in the world in this situation."

"You can't help someone who doesn't want to be helped."

"I have to try."

"Then keep yourself safe, Annie. Don't drink anything he gives you. And come over if you need a place to stay. We'll be happy to put you up."

I thanked him. I could do that: not drink the coffee he laced with speed. It sounded easy enough. I knew the real Cleo was still alive inside that howling madman.

It worked for one week, although he was not happy and he refused to drink the coffee, too. "I paid a lot of money for this crap it's a special blend. You know today's the anniversary of the day we met. In your fucking church remember? But if you don't want to celebrate I'm just going to dump the coffee no point in drinking it all myself."

The next Friday I didn't drink anything he gave me, but after dinner my heart took off on its night-long race. The gabbing began that would take us to the other side of the universe and back. And the seductive closeness that I knew would become an abusive explosion, blowing us through opposing walls, severing limbs and dribbling blood on the carpet.

Oh God, why are You doing this to me? My heart plunged down a spiral staircase into a dank black basement. This time he must have sneaked it into my food. There was no escape other than to leave him. But I couldn't do it. Did I have to die before he understood?

I don't want to die, God. Please make him stop.

I take the cappuccino Joe Wall gave me and toss it unopened into the garbage.

W onder when those diamonds are going to come out. Bet that pisshead Tim or Tom or Tinfoot or whatever the fuck his name is lied and stole them probably sitting with a cup under my ass while I shit them out. And all my gold buttons are gone. I put them in my pocket. He took them so I took his crap that's fair ain't it? Don't need a judge and jury to figure that one out. Look at this cross solid gold. Jesus hanging on it and He's solid gold too. Gotta trade this for some shit bet it's worth at least ten hits. Man what the fuck's the matter with me? My feet are killing me. My gut's trying to kill me too feels like someone's slicing me open with a chainsaw. Oh man I'm going to puke.

H e floats in a curdled pond of his own vomit. "Oh God yes I believe in You. I swear I do. I know I said it before and I didn't mean it but now I swear I mean it. Help me God. Please help me. I'll be good I promise." Skin stretched drum-taut across a belly the size of a small watermelon, pain screeching through it with every choking heave. Retching and nothing coming out except shrill animal sounds, bleats, whinnies, moos.

"Hey, Cleo Deo, what's wrong song with you shoe?" Light blue eyes against a backdrop of short spiked neon-green hair peer into his face, breath like a cherry sucker so sweet he can taste it. Scabs and open sores from digging bugs out of her face and long skinny arms. Sylvie.

This is the bitch who took my Annie away prancing around stark naked with all her bones sticking out and all my Annie's johns telling her they saw me with her. Getting high with me and that's what everyone does when they get high is fuck. So she left me. If you blew me up with C4 I'd keep right on fucking someone but only my Annie not that fucking Sylvie. She's just a bunch of bones no tits no ass. She's crazy and ugly as an old dog turd laying out on the street. She told my Annie we fucked all the time and she came over to our house when she was pregnant like she was saying the bastard was mine. She told my Annie I didn't love her no more and I was going to marry her.

Words slip out of his mouth in filmy shreds. "Get the fuck away from me."

"Oooh, is that puke duke you're lying sighing in? Ugh bug. Who wants to fuck suck you? Not me see. Yuck chuck. But those shoes dues are hella cool school. I'm going to borrow sorrow them, met a dude crude who's going to give me some shit split and fuck pluck me if I trade parade him something." She wrenches the shoes off his feet and a train of fire jolts up his legs from the red-ringed abscesses and collides with his gut.

He screams.

She romps down the street, tearing off her shirt and brandishing it at the passing cars, her flat rib-striped chest burnished to glowing copper by a sun that forces her clothes off and ravishes her long body as often as it can.

"Thank you God," he breathes after she's gone. "You're still up there looking out for me."

The stench of rot and excrement sidles from his belly up to his nose. He retches again.

I comb through all the pawnshops on Mission Street. No one has Mama's things and no one remembers a guy fitting Cleo's description.

"I'll bet he's traded them for drugs," I mutter.

I sit in a coffee shop, inhaling a mocha and wolfing down a couple brownies. Where should I look for him? Where do all the addicts hang out? The Tenderloin. That's mostly crackheads. Crack doesn't last all night, doesn't keep someone kicking a dumpster for hours shoeless and with feet spurting pus. Crack takes you up quick and drops you right back down with a thud. It has to be speed, and that would be the Castro. Or Ninth Street.

Ninth Street: furniture shops, expensive antiques. The freeway exits onto Ninth and you take it straight to Market Street, crossing Harrison, Folsom, Howard, and Mission Streets. On one corner of Howard and Ninth is a busy gas station with a car wash and a fast-food restaurant, and directly opposite lurks Asia, the cross-dressing night club. Alleys silent as graveyards open up off Ninth, sepulchers where the dead still breathe (usually), crammed behind dumpsters or in them, sleeping on stoops, hugging the shadows the houses throw at them. The dead who are trying to escape the morning sun before it bleaches the jewel tones of their fantasy worlds, degrades their joyful dancing night images back into the tenacious cobwebs that crowd their lives when the drugs wear off and they come back to life.

I roll slowly down the sidewalk. I don't like this part of town. The scent of skunk whispers in the clouds of pot smoke seeping from open windows, barely masking the reek of decay pervading the street. High-pitched cackles dance above me. Strange people skulk by, ski masks or baseball caps hiding their faces. Or they trail tuxedo tails, flowing skirts, shawls, motley ribbons, their lips forming symmetrical orange or red or purple smiles, their eyes inert.

"Cleo!" I see him curled up on the sidewalk a block away.

I wheel up to him.

"Cleo! Why did you steal..." I stop. He's drowning in a frothing puddle of what looks like melted chocolate ice cream. His stomach is bloated to the size of a basketball, his face is gray, only the whites of his eyes are visible between his half-open lids. "Cleo! Talk to me!"

A groan falls out of his mouth. "My belly man." Voice a faded breath of air.

"I'm calling an ambulance. Dude, what happened to you?"

"Those eggs you gave me."

"You didn't eat them, remember?" I pull my cell phone out of my pocket. "Operator? I'm on Ninth just south of Harrison. Got a man here too sick to move. We need an ambulance quick."

Cleo heaves. Nothing comes out but the same stink that permeates Ninth Street.

"They'll be here soon, dude. Hang on."

"Y"ou get my diamonds out Doc?" Cleo is sitting in a hospital bed, his belly bound with white bandages. IV fluid drips into one arm and a plastic tube makes a bridge from his nose to a bottle on the wall.

"Diamonds?" The doctor in his tired white lab coat and faded green scrubs looks at him over splotched half-glasses.

"The diamonds I ate."

"You ate diamonds?"

"Yeah I didn't want no one to get them. I found them in a dumpster. If you took them I'm going to call the cops. They're mine."

The doctor's mouth clenches. His nostrils flare.

"You ate them," he repeats.

"Come on Doc don't play your fucking games with me I want them back."

"Your intestine was completely blocked with gravel. If you'd gotten to the hospital half an hour later you'd be dead. As it is we had to excise a large portion of your bowel because your so-called diamonds, your gravel, killed it. If you people would stop distorting your vision with your mind-bending substances I would be out of a job. Unemployed. Everyone who comes through the ER comes because they did something idiotic while they were high." The volume on his voice goes up a couple notches. "I didn't spend eight years in college and three more years as an intern and a resident, going sleepless for days and too exhausted to spell my own name and alienating my wife and having her leave me, just so I could sew addicts back together. If it were up to me I'd let you all die. That's what you want. But the laws of this country require me to keep you alive, no matter what."

"You're full of crap Doc. I seen you out there on the street as high as the rest of us. And I bet you go to your fine house at the end of every fucking day and guzzle a bottle of whiskey and smoke a couple joints right there in front of your TV. Bet you even do a line every now and then. Maybe shove a little cocaine up your fucking nose. Yeah? I knew it. So don't act like you're better than me cuz you ain't. What did you do with my diamonds? You took them didn't you? Gravel!"

The doctor stomps out of the room. He returns in a few minutes with a bulging green surgical drape, stained dark brown and reeking. He sets it on Cleo's lap. "Take a look. I saved it to remind myself how disgusting you addicts are. And you call yourselves human."

Cleo tears open the drape and finds a stinking mass of gravel mixed with sour black blood clots, green slime and stiff worms. He blinks as one of them opens its mouth and laughs at him. He sifts through the mass with both hands. No diamonds. Only gravel swaddled in the same curdled stench that had bloated his gut and flumed through his nose and mouth when he lay puking on the street.

"You stole them!" He heaves a handful of the putrefied mess at the doctor. It misses him and lands instead on the foot of the bed.

The doctor laughs as he leaves. "What an idiot."

"I ain't no idiot!" Cleo shouts. "You stole my fucking diamonds!"

H e sits outside the Den of Doom's alley door. The sight of
Chris' cardboard box with little puffs of smoke wisping out
the slits comforts him. He rests against the wall, points his eyes
toward the box and lets them drift out of focus.

His belly squeezes big purple splotches of agony all the way
to his teeth. A deep breath a minute ago ripped him apart. The
pain crunched him hard enough to make him carefully measure
further air intakes and outflows.

He fled the hospital after the confrontation with the doctor.
His insides burst into flames whenever he thinks about that lying
thieving piece of shit, and he wants to plan his revenge but the
pain in his gut is the only thing he can focus on right now. He's
just trying to make it through the next five minutes. The nurses
pumped him full of morphine and it's wearing off. His nose drips.
Chills rattle across his shoulders and down his arms. His eyelids
stick together.

"Hey, Cleo Deo!"

He waves her away with a flick of his hand. Keeps his eyes shut.

She doesn't leave. "They said you were sick thick. That's what I
thought caught when I saw you puking fluking up your guts nuts."

Her face right in his. She pulls apart his eyelids and stares into his eyes. "I'm sorry, Cleo Deo. Look, I have your shoes clues." She holds them up. "Took them away okay when he was sleeping peeping. Told you I'd bring fling them back sack, didn't I pie?"

He doesn't answer.

"Cleo Deo, what's wrong strong?"

"I ran away from the hospital. Maybe I should have stayed. I gotta get a pain shot."

"Hey play." Kneeling in front of him, holding his hands. "I have some shit split, you want to get high sigh with me tree?"

"I gotta line." He holds out his arm and shows her the IV catheter.

"Cool fool! Let's do moo it!"

She rummages in her backpack, brings out a half-empty bottle of water, a tiny baggy of white crystals, a syringe. Carefully swirls water into the baggy and watches the crystals dissolve. Fills the syringe.

"Me first thirst."

He moves slowly, his breath held prisoner by pain, his eyes seeing only her outstretched arm. He finds her vein, pulls back on the plunger until he sees a scarlet puff, then pushes in half the meth. The rest goes into his IV catheter.

His breath grunts out. "You're a good girl Sylvie. Now you head on down the street and I'm just going to rest here for a while."

"Don't you want to fuck duck me like you always do blue? You put this ring sing on my finger dinger, remember September?" Her left hand flutters before his pain-narrowed eyes. "Don't you love dove me anymore tore?"

What he wants is to sit iceberg-still and let the meth kill the pain. He doesn't want to hear her stupid rhymes or have her spin him around with her games. Luckily he is too sick to listen to her. Otherwise he'd get caught up in her soap opera world for sure, she always manages to pull him in. He doesn't mean for it to happen but before he can catch on to what she's doing, she's tossing a ball at the wall and when he looks closer he sees that he is the ball.

"Tomorrow Sylvie. I'm going to fuck you tomorrow. Be right here with some more shit tomorrow morning okay?"

"Sure, Cleo Deo, hubby chubby. Tomorrow sorrow."

She bolts over to Chris' box. Rips off her clothes on the way and they flap to the sidewalk, a yellow silk blouse with the price tag dangling from the sleeve, her jeans, a pink satin thong she stole from Macy's.

"Chris Piss! Chris Piss!"

"Goddam, Sylvie. What you want?"

"Fuck chuck me, Chris Piss! I'm so high sky."

"Aw, shit! I ain't fucked no one in years, Sylvie. I ain't never fucked you and I ain't gonna start doing it now. Ain't gonna catch none of your damn diseases. Now get outta here and let me be."

Through the slits between his eyelids Cleo watches her hippety-hop down the alley, her bald bones flinging dancing shadows behind her. On the corner she runs into a guy they both know and the two of them gambol up the steps to the nearest house and disappear into the alcove that curtains the front door.

He leans back against the wall. The purple pain oozes out of his body and drips onto the pavement, leaving his belly swathed in a sepia bruise.

A brilliant yellow sun floats over the rooftops. It opens an orange-lipped mouth packed with fire-coated rows of crocodile teeth and swallows the sepia bruise in one flaming gulp. The pain is gone. The space inside his skull grows big enough to contain the whole universe. Planets, constellations, asteroids and comets dawdle in their orbits, waving at him as they float by. "Hey Cleo! Wha'dup man?" There is Orion guarding the heavens and the Big Dipper pouring out a glittering cascade of diamonds. Saturn swishes its shimmering rings as it sashays by, trailed by a screaming baby Pluto, diapered and crying "Mama! Wait for me!" "Pluto!" Cleo says sternly in a thunderous God-voice. "Stop that fucking yowling." Pluto stops.

Cleo smiles. He knows everything is going to be all right. This is God's view of things. He controls it all, he is in charge. He is God.

W here is he?
He said "Tomorrow" and that's today. Here I am with the shit he wanted. Den of Doom back door, same place as yesterday.

He's still mad at me. Says I broke up his marriage. Of course I did. An addict can't be married to someone who doesn't use. That won't work at all.

He thinks I'm a moron but I know a lot more than he does. Everyone thinks I'm a moron because I make rhymes. To fool them. If they think I'm short on gray matter I can get them to give me anything I want.

See, I've always known what I am. I'm a whore. Plain and simple. I'm not pretending to be anything else. The dudes have always wanted me. Right from the beginning, even my dad and my brothers. The boys at school. The teachers. When I was in kindergarten everybody knew what I was. I can't help it. This is how I'm made. For me to deny them would be to deny my purpose in life. There's something about my body. They all want it. It's sleek and long as a supermodel's and my legs reach almost to my chin and my skin glows like a new penny because I take my clothes off and dance around in the sun every chance I get. No tan lines.

Someday when Cleo is a rich CEO we'll have our own tanning bed, but for now I let the sun do the job.

They give me anything I ask for. All the dope I can stand, and money, clothes, food. Although when I'm high I don't eat, and I tend to lose the clothes. I go into some dude's room with new leather boots, a fake fur jacket and jeans I lifted from Macy's. We shoot up a little shit and the dude fucks me until my brains are jouncing out of my ears and when I leave I'm barefoot and wearing his shirt and nothing else because I don't remember what I had on when I got there and I don't care. Half the time I don't even wear the shirt.

The one thing I really want I can't seem to get. Cleo. Deep down inside he's hella nice. He needs to take care of someone. It makes him feel important. He doesn't need a wife who is independent and can manage on her own. He needs someone weak, someone who can't make it without his help, someone to protect. Someone like I pretend to be. That's what I want. My own dude who will come running when I call him, bring me coffee in the morning and cook dinner in the evening and pay the rent on a nice big flat. I want children, too, a bunch of them.

And Cleo wants kids. That redhead can't have any.

So I had a baby for him. And then he said it wasn't his and he left me.

I'd already had four and my mother was raising them but only because I didn't have a place to keep them.

Cleo is the one. I know in his heart he loves me. He doesn't mind if I fuck other dudes. He waits outside the door to make sure they don't rip me off or beat me up, and when they're done he takes me to wherever we're staying and I give him whatever money they've paid me and we score some shit on the way and shoot each other up when we get there. I know I will hear that big heart of his beating like a snare drum when he fucks me. All night long.

That's a real marriage. Two addicts sharing shit, sharing space, sharing dreams. Kids all over the flat, a little head popping up from behind the couch. Another one on top of a chubby tummy, pudgy pink hands flushing toys down the toilet. A little doggy-baby with paws on his jammy-feet crawling on the floor. Cleo and I popping needles into each other's arms, sitting on the couch and laughing at all the funny little kids.

That's what I want.

We want.

"Good morning!"

It's Joe Wall again, looming over my desk with a big grin scalloping the edges of his face. He's wearing a black Harley Davidson tee shirt and black corduroy trousers.

I stare at the "Guadalajara" cup I use as a pen holder and pray that he'll go away.

"You didn't drink it, did you?" he asks.

His ability to see through me is unnerving. It's also annoying. "No. Is there something I can help you with? If not, I have work to do."

"There's a Narcotics Anonymous meeting not far from here at five. Come with me."

"Why?"

"You have to move on, Miss...." His eyes read the name plate on my desk. "Wickham. You have to move on and you can't do that until you understand."

"I don't see that it's your problem."

"It is. It's very much my problem. I go to this meeting every week. I told you I'm an addict. This is my medicine. I need it the same way a diabetic needs insulin."

"Even after twenty-five years?"

"Yes. I will always be an addict. There is no cure. So I go every week. Plus my job. I see the ravages of drugs every working day and that helps, too, because it reminds me that I'm only one hit away from being in the same position as my clients. And I don't ever want to be in that position again."

"Well, Mr. Wall, I'm not an addict."

"Call me Joe."

"Joe. I'm not an addict."

"Thank God! So humor me and come along."

"What if he's there?"

"Are you afraid of him?"

My eyes look past him. Somewhere out there Cleo lurks, waiting for me. He never came to the house or the library after we split up. The fear that he will has set up housekeeping in the pit of my stomach, agitating acid up my throat on bad days, and on good days simmering quietly as I placate it with crumbs of my sanity.

He swore he would kill me if he ever caught me with another man. He would knock my teeth down my throat, that's what he'd promised that last day after the sex had been so rough he'd pushed me off the bed. "I smell the fucker on you," he'd shouted when he was unable to come after an unbearable night of trying while I had lain as still as a log, afraid to tell him to stop, fighting nausea and the thought that this might be the time the speed he'd given me would cause permanent brain damage. "That's how come I can't do it you fucking bitch!" Sweat sobbed off his body and the sheets were a sodden mass dripping off the sides of the bed. I lay crumpled on the floor where I had fallen and he kicked my head with such force that a jolt of electricity shot down my right arm. I tried to crawl past him but he slammed me into the dresser and then his fist was a jackhammer pounding me in the face.

"You're hurting me, Cleo! Stop!" I clung to the dresser. Flickering pinpoint lights twirled in the damp air between us and my pulse thudded in my temples. Nausea steeped my tongue in bile.

"I'm going to kill you! You think about that when you were fucking your boyfriend? And then I'm going to go and hunt that motherfucker down and skin him like a deer from his ears all the way down to his ankles." He was nose-to-nose with me, his sweat stinging my eyes, his hot angry breath scalding my cheeks. I saw his arm draw back for another punch and without thinking I grabbed a book off the dresser and smashed it in his face.

In the brief shocked second before he responded with an outraged howl I ran for the phone in the living room. I managed to dial 9-1-1 before he reached me. He ripped the phone out of the socket, grabbed me by my hair and rammed my head against the wall. I dug my nails into his hands until he let go. Blood gushed over my face as my fists battered his chest. He laughed. "I'm the man of steel bitch. I can't even feel those fucking tiny hands of yours." An atom bomb went off inside me. "I hate you!" I screamed. "I hate you! I hate you! I hate you!"

"You called the cops didn't you! You called the fucking cops on me and I'm your husband. I thought you loved me. Why did you call them? You fucking a cop? Is a cop your new boyfriend?" He knocked me to the floor and stood there for a second. He sneered. "You think you're going to hurt me? Bitch! You ain't going to do nothing to me." His taunts continued as he dashed to the bedroom. He came back buttoning his jeans. "Fucking whore! You bet I'm going to kill you. You can't stop me and the cops can't stop me. You wait! I'm going to be spying on you from the bushes outside the fucking library. I'm going to be riding on the roof of your fucking car when you drive home. I'm going to be as black as a shadow and hide in the darkest alleys and glue my eyes to your twitching butt when it prances right past me. I'm going to sit in the back of your goddam hypocrite kiss-my-fucking-ass-God church. You better be looking over your shoulder every fucking place you go cuz I'm going to be waiting to get you you fucking bitch."

He sped barefoot out the door, chest glistening and hair dripping.

Poquito bounded out of his hiding place and licked my face. "Oh baby puppy," I sobbed into his neck.

There was a knock at the door. "Police!"

"Just a second." My naked skin was still a pile on the floor. Where was my robe?

I found it, tied it, and opened the door.

"We had an incomplete 9-1-1 call from this number." Two policemen, one tall as a skyscraper, one broad as a sand dune, blue caps blinking on their heads and pistols ready for battle in their hands, peered into the room. "Who did this to you?"

"My husband." Words flopped out of my mouth in little pieces. "He pulled out the phone. He said he was going to kill me."

"And he cut your face?"

"He banged my head on the wall."

"Is he still here?"

"No, he left after I called you."

"May we look around?"

I let them in. They saw the rat's nest of sopping sheets in the bedroom, smelled the overpowering stench of sex and sweat. Their faces wrinkled and I could guess what they were thinking: "Are these people or animals?" Perfumes and lotions had flown off the dresser when he'd thrown me against it and were scattered across the room, broken bottles gasping their last bits of scent into the already saturated air.

They looked around the rest of the house.

"What's his name?"

I told them. Skyscraper punched it into his cell phone.

"He's got a long rap sheet. Domestic violence, drugs, weapons, petty theft, breaking and entering. What's a nice lady like you doing with a scumbag like that?"

I didn't answer. I couldn't remember why I was with him.

"I have to take a picture of that cut, Ma'am, and then we have to get you to the hospital. You might need stitches."

"All right." My head throbbed.

"Open your mouth."

I did.

"You've got a big bruise inside your cheek. Let me get a picture of that, too."

My muscles had disintegrated into grains of sand blowing across the Sahara. I needed to sit down. Were they never going to be done? I wanted to lock the door and, hidden from the eyes of the world, let my misery break me in two like the Titanic so I could lie dead and unfeeling on the ocean floor.

He explained the procedures to me, the temporary restraining order, the need to go to court in three days to make it permanent.

They brought up an ice pack from their car. I held it to my forehead.

"Do you want an ambulance?"

"I'd rather not go to the hospital. It isn't bleeding anymore."

"You have your own doctor you can go to?"

I nodded.

"We're filing this as a felony assault and there will be a warrant put out for him. When you go to your doctor have him write a report and fax a copy to us. Here's our number."

Skyscraper handed me his card. "If he shows up here keep your door locked and call us right away."

"I will."

"Maybe you should change the lock, too."

Oh. Did he have a key? Of course he did.

As soon as they were gone I showered off the fetid stink that had seeped through his pores and smeared itself on me. I looked at my forehead in the mirror and saw a small gash on a lump the size of a quail egg. I didn't think it needed stitches. A bruise pretending to be an ink blotch was pinned to my cheek.

My neck ached and my right arm tingled all the way to my fingertips.

I brewed a cup of tea and sat on the couch sipping it. The cup rattled on its saucer; I couldn't stop my hands from shaking.

I was surprised: there were no tears. Then I remembered fighting with him like a jungle animal and a water main in my heart broke and flooded the room. I had hit another human being with intent to injure. Not once but many times. I had yelled like a dog-eared scrap of street life. Is that what I'd become? Instead of him rising to my level, I had fallen to his. I might as well be a five-dollar prostitute, brawling over food and garbage-stained clothes and gossiping about who slept with whom, with no concerns other than where I'd get my next meal and my next hit and where I'd find my next customer.

The awful awareness of how much I'd changed turned my tears into a fruitless memory. I sat with rigid limbs and a heart that had gone to sleep. I didn't know if I still loved him, but I couldn't bear to live on his level.

Poquito climbed into my lap. My hand stroked him. "No more," I told him.

When my heart awoke, whenever that might be, I knew I would feel it shattering. I couldn't let myself think of that. I had to pull myself together and find the place where life held joy and not fights, fear, hatred, anger.

When my tea cup was empty I called a locksmith. I would do this one step at a time. Locks first.

The San Francisco Club. A place dedicated to the treatment of alcoholics and drug addicts. Narcotics Anonymous and Alcoholics Anonymous meetings are held here several times a day, seven days a week. It nestles in an alley behind the Opera House, a couple blocks from the library.

I sit at the back of the room, Joe Wall beside me. A fine tremor holds my hands captive and my mouth is lined with sandpaper. I'd considered sitting up front, close to the door, so I could escape if Cleo walked in. I decided to sit in the back where I can hide and where people can come between us if the need arises.

"Did he go to meetings?" Joe asks.

"He said he did." He knew the Twelve Steps by heart, told me stories he'd heard at the meetings. Told me about the many times before he met me when he'd gone only to eat the cookies, and afterwards had shot so much speed that his blood boiled. He'd be high and hunger-free for a week and then he'd go to the next meeting to eat more cookies. After we were married he went once every couple of weeks but he never invited me to go with him. Not to the one on Monday that was sometimes held on Wednesday, or the one on Friday that, without forewarning, became a weekend retreat and he wasn't allowed to let me know because outside contact wasn't permitted.

The speaker today is an elegant ageless woman in a well-tailored gray tweed suit. Her subtly made-up face could be on the cover of Vanity Fair. I get caught up in her story and forget about Cleo. He hasn't shown up, after all.

"What do you think?" Joe asks after the meeting.

My misted eyes turn his features into water-color trickles.

"She sold her children for drugs." The tears spill over. All my life I've longed for a baby of my own, to hold, to comfort, to teach, to watch walk its own rocky road through life, to offer a supporting hand when it was needed. "How could she do that? Her own babies!"

"You really don't understand, do you? Let's go talk."

"I don't understand," I admit. We are sitting in the Opera House Restaurant, sharing a slice of chocolate cake the size of a dinner plate. "A baby is the most precious thing in the world. The only thing worth fighting for."

"Ah, now that's a completely different discussion," he says.

"You don't agree?"

"It doesn't matter if I do or don't agree. There are a lot of people whose lives don't conform to that standard. Have you ever been in love?"

"Of course."

"So in love that you inhaled the scent of his skin everywhere you went? So that you saw him in every shadow, every cloud, every passing face? So that every dream you had was about him? And you would swim oceans and crawl across deserts to be with him, would shun your friends, disobey your parents and lie to your boss if he asked you to?"

"That's..." I squeeze my eyes shut to hold back tears. I have to gulp in a couple deep breaths before I'm able to answer. "That's how I felt about Cleo."

"Then you understand. That's how an addict feels about his drug of choice."

"Then he didn't love me."

"How could he not love you? You are sweet, intelligent, gorgeous. Of course he loved you. But not as much as he loved his meth."

"How does anyone ever stop?" Now the tears fall.

He dries them with his napkin. "Have you stopped loving him?"

"Part of me has. But part of me still thinks he can change. He can be good again. The person he becomes when he's high isn't him."

"Addicts think they can use again just once and it won't matter. They've been clean for a while and life is good and one little hit won't do any harm. But it does. It starts the whole terrible mess all over and they go right back to square one, their years of sobriety gone, their hopes chopped off at the knees, their lives back in the gutter."

"What made you stop?"

"My son."

"You have a son? You're married?"

"I was never married. We were together five years. She was an addict, too, so we were oblivious to each other's bad behavior. We stole from each other and everyone we knew. We lied so much that we no longer knew what was true and what wasn't. We fought until we didn't have the strength to stay standing. She pushed me down a flight of stairs once. Broke my back. I was in the hospital for months. I shoved her out the door of a moving car. Gave her a concussion. On and on, it was an endless nightmare and we didn't care."

"And your son?"

He takes out his wallet, shows me a picture of a young man in a dark blue graduation cap and gown. "David. He's in his last year of medical school at UC San Francisco. My son is going to be a doctor."

I wait.

"She took him from the hospital two hours after he was born. Shot up in her dealer's flat and they were raided by the cops. Everyone there was arrested and the baby was taken. I was in jail for possession. When I got out my friends told me he'd been born. He'd been placed in foster care, and I wasn't allowed to see him."

"I can't imagine not being able to see your own child."

"It tore me up. I went to court to get custody. I was living on the street, had no job and no job skills. I was dirty. My clothes were rags I'd found in a trash can. I shot up before I faced the judge. I yelled at him. He told me no way. Said I had to get into a program and only if I finished it would he permit supervised visits. And if I came to those visits high he would have the baby adopted and I would never see him again."

"So you went into a program."

"I did. And I took child care classes and learned CPR. My program hired me as a peer counselor and got me to enroll in college."

"How old was he when you first got to see him?"

"Eight months. He was already crawling. I'd missed eight months of his life and I kicked myself about it every day. But I made up my mind that I wasn't going to miss any more. The first time I saw him he crawled over to me, grabbed my leg, pulled himself up and stood there smiling. He snatched my heart right out of my chest and he's been carrying it around ever since. I owe him my life."

"And his mother?"

"I haven't seen her since David was born. I heard she died a few years later, beaten to death by someone she shot up with. I never checked it out. Couldn't go there. I had to protect what I have and not get involved in that scene again."

"Why couldn't Cleo stop? Wasn't my love enough? I'd counted on him to grow old with me. Most nights I stay awake replaying our marriage over and over in my mind. I speak to him. Try to reason with him. I feel like he used me."

"I'm sure he wanted to grow old with you, too. But you have to remember that he's an addict and until he met you he probably thought he was happy. You gave him a choice. It doesn't sound as if he could decide which world he wanted. He kept coming back to you, didn't he?"

"I kept letting him come back."

I go to the hospital the next evening. No Cleo. The first day after his surgery and he's disappeared.

How am I going to get Mama's things back?

I hear a child crying. I'm waiting at the bus stop on my way home. I took one bus to Sixteenth Street and now I'm waiting to transfer to the next one and this kid is crying. I spin around to see what's wrong.

A young boy, maybe five, maybe six years old, is running toward us. "¡Mamá!" he screams. "¡Mamá!"

"Hey!" I call. "What's wrong?"

"¡Mamá! ¿Dónde estás?" His shriek is the shrill of a before-dawn alarm clock, and it echoes in the ears of a sleeping monster and wakes it up.

"¡Espera! Wait!" But he stumbles on and the crowds on the street swallow him. I hear his screams long after he's lost to sight.

"I hope he finds her," I mumble. Should I have gone after him? Tried to help? I could've asked him where he lives and at least taken him there and his mother would have shown up sooner or later. I don't want to see a missing child report on the news this evening.

I should've gone after him.

Wails cut through my sleep and jar me into consciousness. The pitch black room is blank. I rummage behind my eyelids for my half-finished dream but the monster, snoring contentedly until that screaming little boy woke him up, grunts and rubs its eyes. I sit straight up in bed. I remember.

After the accident I'd let rage expunge the memory, but now it crowds my dark bedroom, as fresh as the day it happened.

Teddy. Five years old. We had gone to the Cinco de Mayo parade. Half a million partiers on the sidewalks. "You hold his hand tight now," Mama instructed me. I was eight. "Hold tight and don't let go. Papa and I are going to get us something to eat. Stay right here."

"Yes, Mama."

Teddy tugged my hand. "Look at that big clown! Let's go over there and see him."

"We can't. Mama said to stay here."

"But he's so tall. I want to go see him."

"He's on stilts, Teddy. He's not really that tall."

"I still want to see him. Come on, Timmy, he's right there. Mama can see us over there."

"Okay." I allowed Teddy to lead me, never letting go of his soft hand with the jagged fingernails, black from digging in our back yard even though Mama had already cleaned and clipped them once today. I gripped it as hard as I could.

The crowd surged in on us. Everyone was so much taller than I was and I was taller than Teddy. He didn't seem to notice. He pulled me closer and closer to the clown. I felt a flap of fear in my stomach.

"Hi, Mr. Clown!" Teddy's little duck voice yelled up at him. The white-painted face with the scarlet bulb nose looked down at him, red lips stretched cheek-to-cheek in a happy smile.

The mob pushed forward, jostling the stilts.

"Hey!" the clown yelled. "Get back!" The stilts shuddered and he tumbled into the sea of people. Everyone roared. Teddy's hand disappeared. I didn't think I'd let go but now the hand that had been holding onto him as if he were my own heart was holding onto nothing.

When the wave of people receded and a space appeared where the clown could climb back up on his stilts, there was no Teddy.

"Ai!" Mama sobbed. "Ai, Madre de Dios, my baby, find my baby."

"We told you not to let go!" Papa shouted at me. I cringed.

"I didn't, Papa," I whimpered.

"Yes, you did, Timoteo. Yes, you did. Or your brother would still be here."

"Scolding him won't help," Mama said. "It's my fault. How could I think you could watch him in this crowd?" She drew me close, kissed the top of my head. Her arms were trembling.

"You baby him!" Papa scowled. "He will never succeed at anything because you baby him. He will never be a man. A man has to be strong. None of this whining and making excuses."

"He's only a small boy, Jorge. Understand. It was my fault."

"Bah!"

We searched for hours, Mama and Papa and me. We called his name over and over even though the clamor of the crowd kept our voices stuck between our lips. Described him to the police. Squeezed our eyes between people laughing and dancing and hugging. Peeked around people in costumes, people in rags, people who looked ordinary and people who were scary. We searched behind their backs, above their heads, under their baseball caps. We stopped at every vendor, asking if a little boy with brown eyes and buzz-cut black hair and a green and white striped tee shirt had come to them, maybe asked them for a drink or an ice cream. Nobody had seen him.

Mama crumpled onto a step. The parade was over, the throngs of people had been gone for hours. The only things on the street were the creeping forepaws of night and ten thousand weeping bits of confetti. "I can't look anymore," she said, tears muting the contours of her face. "My baby. He's only five years old," she wailed, "my baby is only five years old."

"Stop that!" Papa bellowed.

She didn't stop. I covered my ears to block out her wails. I mashed my eyes shut but I could still see her: a lump of flesh in a limp dress and stockings zigzagged with runs, exhausted shoes flopping off her feet, her mouth open so wide you could see all the fillings in her teeth and the gap at the back where one tooth was missing. For years I saw her that way in my dreams and heard the wild wounded animal howl that brought up entrails as it poured out of her.

That moment went on and on as if time had frozen. Papa angry and Mama wailing and me wishing I had never been born and had never had a little brother named Teddy. I wanted to bolt down the street and dive off the edge of the world so I wouldn't have to see her like that. Wouldn't feel the terror that gripped me by the shoulders, making my sunny world of Mama's kisses and Papa's gruff growls and Teddy's giggles disintegrate as I was forced to watch. I didn't know what was going to take its place, but I knew the world I'd been living in was gone. My family would never be the same.

And it was my fault.

The police phoned the next day.

Mama had gone to church the evening before, lit a candle and prayed. "Hail, Mary, full of grace." Over and over. Papa and I slunk out after fifteen minutes. She stayed until the priest walked her home. Then she went to her room with its little shrine, the pictures of her dead parents flanked by rows of holy candles, the porcelain Mary standing with folded hands, serene face, and hair discreetly concealed by a long blue scarf. She lit more candles and knelt there all night fingering her onyx rosary. She prayed until her voice was a whisper stuck in a paste-dry mouth and her reservoir of tears was empty, white lines running from her eyes to her chin the only proof that tears had been shed.

She slowly rose from her knees, an old woman although she had been young the day before. She dragged herself to the phone.

"Yes?" Voice gray, hesitant.

"What? Are you sure?" Life sprinted back into her voice and her stooped shoulders straightened. "They found him!" she shouted to Papa and me. "Can we come now? Okay, thank you, thank you, thank you, thank you, we'll be right there."

She hugged Papa. "You see? God does answer prayers!" She ran out of the house without her shoes or sweater. We dashed after her. Papa grabbed her shoes but in his excitement he got two that didn't match. We chased her all the way to the hospital.

A policewoman held him. She was crooning a lullaby, his arms wrapped around her neck. He seemed so tiny in his miniature hospital gown.

"My baby!" Mama screamed. He began blubbering. The policewoman put him in her arms. "Where were you? Where did you go? Oh my baby." She turned to the doctor who had entered the curtained cubicle and was silently watching us. "Is he all right?" He looked at me and then he motioned my parents outside with him. Why did he look at me that way?

Yesterday's terror had evaporated when Mama ran out the door to get Teddy, but now it billowed around me, a fog slithering in from the ocean, cold, wet, obliterating everything in the room except the policewoman in her dark blue uniform. Maybe she was here to haul me off to prison. I was the one who had let go. I was the one who had lost him.

They returned. Mama kissed Teddy over and over, her tears staining his cheeks. Papa threw his arms around the two of them. I'd never seen so much anger in his face. His skin was purple and his eyes bulged. His lips curved into a tight half-circle with the corners twisting down to touch his chin. He hugged them, silent while Mama wept and Teddy bawled.

I backed out of the cubicle.

They didn't notice.

T hey never told me what had happened. I heard them whispering in their bed late at night, muffled sobs fizzing in
Mama's voice. I heard Tia Bela and Tio Rigo discussing it when
they thought I wasn't listening. Our neighbor Señora Ramírez
consoled Mama across the back fence and brought the priest to
pray for Teddy. Mama, clotted tears on her face, served tea and
cookies to neighbors who took over our living room and tried to
comfort her. I heard them say a word I didn't know. Sodomize. I
heard them say blood. Naked. Teddy walking on the street naked,
howling, bleeding, lost.

He must have been very cold, I thought. Maybe that's why he
screams at night. He's cold.

I brought more blankets and tried to add them to the pile already smothering him but he fought me off in his sleep, writhing
and grunting, arms flailing and strong enough to give a good hard
slap to my face.

After one try I stayed in my bed with the covers pulled up to
my eyes, peering at him through the shadows cast by the Mickey
Mouse night light. I knew he hated me. I had let go of him. I had
let him get hurt and bleed.

Mama would run in when she heard him screaming. Tears again, so many tears these days. Mama cried all the time.

"It's all right, my baby," she'd shush him, rocking him until he was quiet, with Papa glaring darkly from the doorway. "It's all right. Mama's here. I won't let anyone else hurt you. Ever, my sweet angel, not ever." Then she'd tell me to go back to sleep.

Because I was the one who had let him get hurt.

I held his hand and it turned into blood and flowed down my arm and became a sloshing puddle on the sidewalk. The crowd walked back and forth through the puddle, hiding the street, the grass, the sky behind a web of burgundy footprints. Then the people vanished and only his green and white striped shirt and his tan shorts remained. No Teddy. The clown on stilts crowed, his mouth so enormous he could choke me down whole, his teeth as big as elephant tusks. "I didn't mean to let go," I screeched at the clown before he got close enough to impale me. I woke up. Papa stood there, yelling at me. "Stop that damn noise! Don't we have enough screaming and crying going on in this house?"

I burrowed under my blankets. It was dark as tar under there but inside my head a million people were pointing at me. Cackling, squealing, shaking their fists in my face. I couldn't make them go away.

Papa started drinking more. Every night after dinner he got out a bottle of Vodka, made himself comfortable in front of the television and sipped at it until he fell asleep. I thought it might help me sleep, too. Maybe it would make all those people go away. Maybe it would deafen my ears to Teddy's screams and blind my eyes to Mama's tears. It seemed to work for Papa. So one evening when he was asleep and Mama was upstairs praying, I tasted what was in his bottle. Nasty, it tasted so nasty. But it spread warmth all through me and chased away the guilt that had taken over my life. It made all those people disappear---pouf! That night I fell asleep smiling.

"Liar! Liar! Liar!" My screams wake me up. His side of the bed is a toothy leer in the dark room. I lie still for a few seconds, wondering where he is, stomach cramping and panic ulcerating my veins. Then I remember. We are divorced. He's gone and I will never let him back in my life.

I dreamt he was speaking to me on the phone. "Car broke down baby and I ain't going to make it home tonight. Car - broke - down. I'm over here at my boss's house he's going to let me stay here tonight and help me with the car in the morning. He's going to help me me me." In the background I heard a woman's voice say "Hurry up, Cleo Deo. It's ready steady. Come on, hurry up pup."

"Shut up bitch," he yelled to the voice. "Bitch bitch bitch."

"Cleo?" His name ricocheted between my ears. Cleo Cleo Cleo.

"I'm going to call you tomorrow. I love you love you love you." I heard the dial tone. I could still hear it after I'd hung up.

"Liar!" I scream, completely awake.

Most weeks he was gone at least three nights, sometimes four. He rarely called to let me know he wouldn't be home. He'd turn up after x number of days, always with a flimsy excuse: a sick friend with no phone and he'd lost his cell phone (the one I was paying for), the friend he was riding with got a flat tire and had no spare, he was doing side jobs for his boss and he was positive he'd called and told me.

Once, as I walked in after work, he greeted me with "Gotta go baby. My boss called. Some sonofabitch called in sick for the evening shift." His new black jeans and white Western pearl-buttoned shirt didn't look like the clothes a stock boy wore to work. He asked me to save dinner and wait up for him. I made a casserole and a salad and sat in front of the television, too anxious to eat. At eleven o'clock I went to bed. I woke up every half hour hoping to find him lying beside me. Each time emptiness howled like a wolf from between the sheets. When the alarm went off I was worn out. I forced myself to put my feet on the floor; I'd already called in sick twice that week.

I phoned his job. He should've been there. He started at seven.

"He doesn't work here anymore, Ma'am."

"What do you mean? Why not?"

"We haven't seen him since last week. No call no show. Makes for immediate sayonara. I'm sorry, Ma'am. He was a hard worker and we all liked him."

A fist punched me in the stomach and every breath scraped my throat like a razor blade.

I collapsed on a chair, my face in my hands. Where is he?

Maybe he'd been in an accident. Or maybe he was in jail. That happened a lot, according to him. He could never explain why he'd been arrested; it was always someone else's fault. Most of the time he got out in two or three days, although there were a couple instances when he was locked up for several weeks, and one year he was in jail over Christmas. He wanted me to visit but I wasn't about to go down there and publicly acknowledge that my husband was a criminal. I refused to sit in the lobby and breathe the same sour air as those gossipy wives whose lives had neat little bulletin boards where they posted jail visiting hours next to their children's finger paintings.

I phoned the hospitals. I phoned the jail. I dropped my knees to the carpet, folded my hands and prayed. "Dear God, please help me and please help my husband. Keep him safe, dear God, dear Jesus. Help me make it through today and let everything be just a big misunderstanding. Oh God, please hear my prayer. Amen. Please."

He returned that evening. The Western shirt had been replaced with a Grateful Dead tee. "He probably thought you were talking about someone else. I was there today. I got paid. Here." He held out twenty-five dollars.

"That's a week's pay?"

"They take out tax you know. And social security and health insurance."

"You don't have health insurance. That's from my job."

"You calling me a liar?"

"Yes, I am."

"I ain't going to lie to you Annie. Let me call my boss. He'll tell you I still work for him." He dialed the number. "Hey! Charlie my man did you talk to my Annie this morning? She says you told her I don't work there no more. How come you told her that? You got me in all kinds of crap here man…Okay I'll tell her. See you tomorrow." He hung up. "He says he thought you were someone else."

I stared at him.

"Why are you looking at me like that? I told you what he said."

"Why didn't you let me speak to him?"

"I guess I should have huh. I'm sorry Annie. I swear I gotta job. Let's go out and eat. I got all this money and I want someone to cook for you tonight instead of you doing all the work."

We ate at Burger King. He noisily gobbled down his Whopper, gleefully shouting at people as they came through the door. "Hey

Tom!..Hey Sammy. I know him from work... Marie! Where you been girl?" None of them acknowledged him. A rising tide of flesh-eating crabs nipping at my stomach made it impossible for me to swallow my food. What was he doing?

But we went home and he went to bed and slept all night. He got up in the morning at five o'clock like he was supposed to and left for his job on time. The crabs stopped nipping. I went to work and looked the library patrons in the eye.

He wanted a baby and that redheaded bitch couldn't have one. I knew if I did she'd be out of the picture.

I stopped using condoms but I didn't get pregnant. Actually I never did use them with him. I knew from the first time I saw him that I was going to love him with all my heart and soul and body, and I wanted every part of him he'd give me, so I never used them. I left them lying around their house for her to see, hoping she'd get mad and leave and then we could live there and I could be his wife. It was a small house, neat and clean and warm. I wouldn't have to be out in the rain and the fog. I could snuggle up in that big bed where he slept with her at night and slept with me while she was at work. I'd pull that fluffy pink and purple comforter up over my head and lie there all safe and cozy and listen to the rain pitter-patter on the window.

But she didn't leave and she didn't kick him out, either. She was crazy. Maybe she really loved him.

T eddy's nightmares didn't stop. Everyone said they'd get better with time but they didn't. Night after night his shrieks ripped through the house. I'd jump out of bed and smack him, partly to wake him up, partly because I was mad at him for being such a cry-baby, mostly because I was mad at myself for letting go of his hand and every shriek was the evening news: "This just in, folks. Tim let go of his brother's hand." If he didn't wake up, his hollow yelps would pierce Papa's Vodka stupor and Papa would beat him. Mama tried once to stop the beating but Papa threw her against the closet door and broke her collarbone. So she stayed in front of her shrine on knees bruised from overuse, sobbing and pray-ing. I hid under the covers while Papa pounded on him, wishing I'd taken a bigger sip of Vodka so I wouldn't be listening in terror to his curses and the thud of his fists on Teddy's little body and Teddy's strangled-dog yips. I held my breath until it burst through my clamped lips in noisy gasps that I smothered with my fist. If Papa heard them he'd start pounding on me.

When I was twelve Papa went into the hospital. His skin had turned lemon yellow and the whites of his eyes were the color of orange peels. He walked like a pregnant woman, swollen belly pushing forward and wide-set legs struggling to carry the extra weight. The doctor said it was cirrhosis. He said there was nothing he could do and sent him back to us. Papa told us good-bye with eyes black as the scorched grass on the California hills, put himself on a bus and went home to Mexico. He didn't want to die here.

Mama stopped crying then for the first time since the day Teddy'd come back. She could hold her little boy without fear now, comfort him and make his nightmares go away. But by then Teddy'd already been in juvenile hall twice, once for setting a fire in a wastebasket at school, once for throwing a rock through a toy store window and stealing a robot. He'd found Papa's Vodka, too, and helped himself to it from time to time. It didn't give him the peace it gave me. It made his nightmares worse. He'd wake up with rivers of sweat gushing through his pores and a scream throttling him. He'd stare at nothing for a while and eventually get up and play Nintendo games until the sun rose and exposed the forbidding corners of our room.

Drugs dropped into his life when he was eleven, and they took care of the nightmares. First it was pot that Señora Ramírez' teen-aged son Steve shared with us over the back fence. I liked it all right but one toke and Teddy glowed. He went once with Steve to buy it and after that he made his way to the dealer every day, stopped there in the mornings on his way to school and never got any farther. When he was suspended for not showing up he started snorting cocaine. He tried everything, speed, crack, heroin, ecstasy. He didn't care what it was and he didn't hide what he was doing from Mama. The tears she thought had dried up now eroded channels in her cheeks. She realized that hugs would not help her little boy and God wasn't answering her prayers, and she didn't understand why. But she never stopped praying and she never stopped loving us.

I stopped praying the day Teddy disappeared. I knew there was no God. He would never let this happen to a child, never do this to a mother who prayed to Him as devotedly as Mama did. The idea came to me that maybe we all have to carry a cross to prove our devotion, that maybe God wants more than prayers and going to church. I snuffed out that idea as soon as it shuffled into view. It was way too deep for a kid to try to make sense of.

I think about it all the time now. I look at the TV news and the people in the doughnut shop and the people on the bus and it seems that everyone is stumbling under the weight of their own heavy crosses, splinters piercing their skin, blood from their thorny headgear blinding their eyes. When I think about Teddy, it seems to me that if, instead of giving in to our anger and guilt, Papa and I had been able to follow the commandment of love, which was what Mama tried to do, things might have turned out differently.

I call on God a lot now. I don't really pray and I can't bring myself to enter a church, but I believe there is a God. I can't figure Him out at all but I guess that's why He's God and I'm not. All I know is that Cleo is in my life for a reason, even though neither he nor I want him here. Maybe I can do for him what I couldn't do for Teddy.

I still feel responsible for what happened to my brother. But I stopped drinking after the accident. I had my broken body as payment for what I'd done; I no longer had to be mad at myself. But my anger didn't go away. I felt like I'd paid back way more than I needed to. Did he have to take my whole future? Why not just break my leg? I'd atoned for the sin of losing him. I didn't owe him anything. Now he owed me. He seemed to be unaware of this and neither made apologies nor offered condolences. All I got from him was that sneer he'd chiseled into his face, and he stayed away from my miserable world, stayed trapped inside his own life, either high or behind bars, so I couldn't confront him. My rage dove into my body, percolated in my veins, feasted on my heart. I buried myself in a dead apartment with dust-tinted windows, shriveled potted plants, barren walls. I eked out half a living on my computer, focusing my attention on an electronic multitude that couldn't see my deformity. I slammed my door and shut out a world that made fun of cripples.

And as my brother was leaving this earth Cleo showed up in my life.

Did Mama send him?

I hadn't kept my vow to love Teddy and help him out.

Maybe she'd sent Cleo to be my second chance. My redemption.

I know I should try to find him. I really don't want to. Maybe next week.

I did everything I could to get him away from her. Lifted fancy men's clothes from the stores in Union Square, leather jackets and boots, silk underwear. Fucked him every imaginable place in the city---on top of the Palace of Fine Arts, down in one of the BART tunnels with the rails cold and gleaming on either side of us, on a cable car crammed with tourists---everywhere just to give him a thrill and make him understand that I was his soul mate, not her. I fucked every dealer I knew every day of the week to get him as much speed as he could stand. But she was all he talked about. How sexy she was. The shape of her butt. Her scent. Her huge boobs. Whenever he talked about her boobs he pulled up my shirt and flicked my nipples with his fingertips. That stung.

Sometimes he cried and then he'd punch me. Or kick me. I had so many bruises I looked like a Dalmatian. Then he'd fuck me over and over, starting in moonlight and not stopping until the sun was high over the San Francisco skyline. But when the speed ran out he went home to her.

I started making things up. I told him I saw her fucking Cam up in his room. He ran up there and bashed open the door. Cam was lying on a naked mattress talking to himself. I watched from the doorway. Cleo grabbed him by his shirt and lifted him off the bed as if he were as light as a newspaper. I don't think Cam weighs more than a hundred pounds. He's a kid, and even though he's taller than me he forgets to eat most of the time. Cleo pinned him to the wall. "Where the fuck is she?"

"Jim," Cam said, "ask this lunatic why he's in my room yelling at two in the morning."

"There ain't no Jim in here!" Cleo barked. "You're the lunatic! What did you do with my Annie?"

"Jim, you know anyone named Annie? I sure don't."

"My wife you cuckoo bird! My wife."

"I thought she was your wife." Cam nodded toward me.

I am.

"She ain't nothing but a fucking bitch in heat."

"All I ever see is you and her. No Annie. If you're that concerned about Annie maybe you oughta to be with her. Ain't that right, Jim?" Talking to a vacant spot next to him. "What? You saw his wife with Chris? You sure?" His foggy gaze wandered back to Cleo. "Jim says she's smoking crack with Chris. Go ask Chris about her."

Cleo dropped him on the mattress and sprinted out the door, shoving me out of his way. I snickered and scrambled after him.

"Chris!" he bellowed as we ran up to the cardboard box. "Chris!"

"Hey, man, shut the fuck up! I don't need no one knowing I'm in here." Smoke, blaring as the lights on a theater marquee, curled out of the slits in the box.

"You get my Annie out of your fucking box."

"Who the hell is Annie?"

"My wife."

"I thought you was married to that skinny ho Sylvie. That's what you say to everyone. She you wife."

"She ain't my wife. My Annie's my wife. You got her in there smoking crack with you." He kicked Chris' box. "You get her out of there right now!"

The box flew back and Chris stood up. His eyes were solar flares and his gray dreadlocks quivered. A machete gleamed in his hand.

"This a box, man!" he yelled. "A fucking box! There ain't room for no one but me in this box. You see that? Come here, take a good look." He stepped closer to Cleo, brandishing the machete. Then he saw me in the shadows, trying to muffle my laughter with my hand. "Oh, you with her." He went back to his box and righted it. "I may be a crackhead but I ain't stupid. You stupid, Cleo. You fucking the slimiest ugliest ho in the city and believing her lies, running around asking everyone 'Where my wife? Where my wife?' You don't deserve no wife. Get your stupid ass outta my face." He sat down and pulled his box back over himself.

Cleo took off. By the time I had stopped laughing and my feet had started moving he'd disappeared.

He went to jail for a couple months around Thanksgiving-Christmas. That's when it happened. I fucked everybody that would, and that's a lot of dudes, believe me. I'm long-legged and slinky and coppery-tan and every man's sexual fantasy. And I didn't use condoms, not once.

I told him it was his but he still didn't leave that redheaded pretender. Couldn't keep his hands off me once I got a little tummy bump and plum-sized boobs, but he wouldn't leave her.

M an here I am back in the hospital. Got clean white sheets and the nurse comes in every couple hours and shoots me full of dope. Started puking again and pain like a hundred screw drivers turning and turning in my gut. I was squirming like a snake trying to scrape my own belly off me and rolling around in my own stinking puke. No one wanted a piece of me that day and no one would give me nothing. No one but Sylvie. I don't got nothing to pay them with cuz that fucking doctor stole all my diamonds and that wheelchair creep helped himself to all my gold buttons. Pete has all the crap I stole from him but he wasn't at home. Said he's going to hold them against what I owe him he's going to keep on giving me shit as long as he still has them the rosary and the gold cross with Jesus dying on it. Expensive crap man. My belly felt like a knife was slashing holes in it and my leg oh man my leg! Hot as fucking hellfire I smelled sulfur and I knew it was satan himself sitting there on my feet stabbing them with his pitchfork and now I'm here again. Sexy nurses here. Everybody gets high they just don't want to admit it. After I get out of here I'm going to come visit. Going to bring them some shit. I know they all use it like my Annie acting like she's such a saint and high all the time those big pupils. Fuck. And now I gotta shitbag on my belly. The doc's right here in front of me he's trying not to laugh. He's the same one who stole my diamonds don't they got no other docs in this place? He's gotta big smirk on his face thinks I'm so fucking funny. Tells me he had to do it he says it's only for a little while. Gotta let my gut rest. Guess the diamonds he stole from me ripped a bunch of holes in me. I say to him "Doc I can't have no shitbag on my belly. I live on the street. My wife kicked me out and I can't go around like this."

"You have a wife?" he says his Groucho Marx eyebrows shooting up off his face and slapping the ceiling.

"Yeah. Something the matter with that?"

He shrugs.

Don't he think I'm good enough for a wife? "She's a whore," I say.

"I'm sure she is."

Does he know her? Maybe he fucked her too.

"By the way," he says. "When we cleaned your leg wounds."

"Yeah?"

"You know you signed a consent form authorizing us to do what we felt was necessary."

"So?"

"After we excised the rotten intestine we examined your legs. You had gangrene."

"Come on Doc. You ain't speaking English."

"Gangrene will kill you if it stays in your body. We had to amputate your left leg below the knee. It was the only way to keep you alive."

"You had to do what?"

"We had to amputate."

"You saying I don't gotta leg?" I fling back the covers and see a neat beige ace wrap squeezing my left knee and down below it there ain't nothing but empty on the bed. My right leg's all decked out in bandages from toe to thigh but down below my left knee there ain't nothing but white sheets giving me the evil eye. I bellow the way Ferdinand did when he sat down on that bee. Leap out of bed to kill that fucking doctor and fall flat on my face and the IV pole crashes down on top of me. I scream and the fucker walks out and the nurses rush in.

Those nurses ain't sexy no more. They're old and ugly and their hands pinch me when they lift me up off the floor and put me back in bed.

I 'm hunting for that fucking doctor. First he steals all my diamonds and then he sticks a shitbag on my belly and then he
chops my leg off. Does the fucker really think I'm going to let
him get away with that kind of crap? I do wheelies down the
hall and the nurses skitter out of my way giggling their heads
off. I'm going to find that fucking doctor and kill him. Took
Nurse Nancy's scissors out of her pocket when she was changing
my dressing. She didn't notice that was yesterday and she still
ain't said a word. Going to rip his gut open just like he did to
me bet he stuffed my diamonds down his own throat. I'm going
to rip his gut open and take all my diamonds back. There he is
sitting at a computer what the fuck do these people do all day?
Surf the web?

"Hey Doc!" I rush at him wheels spinning so fast they burn
my hands grab the scissors off my lap and point them at his heart
and fuck! He's out of his chair in half a second and he kicks the
scissors right out of my hand. They fly up to the ceiling and when
they come down he grabs them out of the air and pushes them up

against my wind pipe. "Doc!" Those scissors ain't letting no air get past them. "Just kidding! Doc!"

"Black belt in karate," he says. "That's what I do when I'm not here."

He sits down at his computer again. I race back to my room.

"Goodness, I'm late!" I scurry out the library door. I'm on my way to meet Joe at the San Francisco Club. This has become a weekly date of sorts—first the meeting and then dinner together afterward---and on Mondays I find myself holding my breath as I watch the hands on the clock meander their way to five p.m. Snapshots of him creep into my awareness with increasing frequency---the way his cheeks crinkle when he smiles, the little stars twinkling in the dark skies of his eyes when he teases me.

Bit by bit I am uprooting the terror that Cleo imbedded in my soul. Church should have helped. It was a warm familiar nest. But veils of shame separated me from the rest of the congregation. The speed he'd forced on me had warped my soul to the point where I heard everyone whispering behind my back. My brain churned with my secret. I would drop my eyes to their shoes, holding my breath and waiting for the moment when someone would say "Didn't I see you and your husband on the street the other night, screaming at each other? You were as high as a kite." Nobody ever did. They showered me with their usual love. And they kept their noses out of my business. Ignored the bruises on my face and my red puffy eyes. Even Pastor Brown, who knew what I was going through. An invisible part of me squirmed nervously as the sermons flapped past my ears. A dusty film coated my tongue as I drank the coffee and ate the cookies provided by the Mary-Martha Ladies Auxiliary and explained that my husband wasn't feeling well and, with their prayers, would be in church the next Sunday. I'd see a faint flutter of a lash, a slight pucker at the corner of a mouth, a sly quiver of an eye. Did they know? Had Pastor Brown told them? Blood would flood my face as I mumbled hasty goodbyes and shrank to the door. Thank God they were too polite to say anything. Eventually I stopped going.

Almost two years later I stood on the church steps one Sunday morning with Joe at my side and wondered how I would explain my long absence and the new man with me. Wondered why I'd thought I could walk through an inanimate door and find forgiveness on the other side. I no longer believed God was in there. If He was, wouldn't He have rewarded me for my years of faithful church attendance by curing Cleo?

In retrospect, I think I wanted the people at church to take me down from the cross Cleo'd hung me on, and they couldn't. They left me hanging there and went on with their own lives. When I finally worked my hands and feet free of the nails pinning me to that rugged wood and fell to earth, I realized that I had always been the only one with the power to take myself out of the grasp of those splinters.

"I can't do this," I said that Sunday morning, staring at the church door.

We strolled a couple blocks to a coffee house and sat outside at a tiny glass-topped table. The sun warmed our faces and steam curled from the cups in front of us. Johnny, an elderly man I'd seen at the San Francisco Club, shuffled by in his cracked brown leather shoes. Joe called out a greeting, inviting him to pull up a chair and join us. I got a whiff of sweaty armpits and never-washed socks, street odors cemented into wrinkles, clothes grimed with reminders of dropped food. I moved my chair away an inch.

Joe didn't seem to notice the reek.

"What would you like, Johnny? My treat."

"You pick."

"Mocha? Cappuccino? Espresso? Vanilla latte with strawberry syrup?" Joe rolled his eyes at me.

"Just a plain cup of coffee. Can I... can I get a muffin, too? Any kind."

"Sure. Banana bran muffin. Get your potassium and your fiber. How's that for a kicking way to get your day going?"

"Thanks, Boss. Is this your lady?"

"No," I answered quickly, feeling my face and neck turn pink. Is that what people think when they see us together? "We're friends. I'm a librarian. You may have seen me at the library."

"No, Ma'am, I don't go to the library. Except to use the men's room. Me and books, well, we don't get along too good."

"Books are wonderful things, Johnny! You can learn about places you've never seen and discover different ways of thinking and doing things. You can curl up with a book on a stormy night in front of a good fire, let your mind fly away to some other time and place and forget your troubles for a while."

"I guess that's what I used booze for, huh, Boss? Guess I never heard of nobody getting busted for driving under the influence of books."

"Why don't you come see me at the library? I'll bet I can find you a book you'd love to read."

"Well, Ma'am."

"My name is Annie."

"Well, Annie. Miss Annie. That's real kind of you but the truth is..." He took a deep breath. "I ain't never told nobody this. No one at AA, not even the Boss here knows it."

We waited. The spoon in Joe's hand went round and round in his coffee cup. I wondered what the big pronouncement was that was so difficult to say. A criminal record? Most of the people at the meetings had one. Joe had one.

He took another deep breath. The spider veins in his cheeks leaked fine ruby dust into his spongy face. "I can't read. There, I said it. That's how come I failed my programs, because I can't read and I never told them. I just didn't do the book work."

"How did you get through school?" I asked.

"I didn't, Miss Annie. I quit after third grade. It was too hard for me, and my dad needed me on the farm."

"You can learn to read. It's easy. I'll teach you. I'm not a teacher but I can help you with that."

"You'd do that?" For the first time his eyes met mine, faded blue irises quivering in a sea of yellow-stained whites.

"Certainly. Does that sound like a good idea to you, Joe?"

"I'm sure there are more people at the meetings who'd like to learn to read, right, Johnny?"

"Yeah, there's a lot of frauds like me there."

"They'll let us use a room at the Club for the class. Maybe we could hold it right after the meeting."

A vague worry about what I was getting myself into swam with gray fins and sharp teeth behind my navel. Along with the worry was a thrill of excitement: I could do this. I could help someone's life be better. Even if I hadn't been able to help Cleo.

At our first class we had three students. The second one had eight. The third one was overflowing and I turned away all but the first ten, promising another class later in the year. Joe was my assistant and after the classes we still went out to dinner, lingering longer and longer over the meal.

"I am so late," I tell myself as I fly down the library steps. It's a good thing the meeting is nearby.

"Annie!"

I stop. Who called my name? I turn around.

A pair of smudged homeless men sits on the steps I've just run down. They're passing a joint between them. One of them waves. He is an old man with blond-streaked gray hair and a sunburned face folding in on itself and carpeted with a gray-tarnished auburn beard. His waving hand is skeletal. One leg ends in a dirty running shoe missing its lace and the other is an empty space camouflaged by jeans. A crutch leans against the step. Have I seen him before? Maybe at a meeting? I don't think so.

I run on. He must've been calling someone else.

When I reach the San Francisco Club I crash into a hulking brick wall of realization. That was Cleo! He looked awful. Tears form in my eyes but they evaporate as another realization hits me, smashing the brick wall into terra cotta crumbs and letting an ocean of sunlight surge over me: I didn't feel a thing when I looked at him.

After dinner I kiss Joe for the first time. A long kiss.

He exhales and his lungs can't remember how to draw in the next breath. They lie flat and empty alongside something in his chest that crunches like shattered glass and radiates pain down his arms and up his neck. He sits on the steps, his solitary foot captured by quicksand, his eyes pasted to Annie's back as she rushes away from him. His mouth opens and closes in dead air and that broken glass in his chest hurts too much for him to try to call her again.

She didn't recognize him. The words dangle in front of him in foot-high letters everyone can see. YOUR ANNIE DIDN'T RECOGNIZE YOU. The letters goose-step, I's dotted with smirks, O's carrying bayonets, until they are hidden behind a thick fog that seeps from under his eyelids, settles on his cheeks, packs slime into his nostrils and tangles in his beard.

"Hey, dude, that was cold. You sure you know her? Can't think why a babe like that'd wanna know a old geezer like you." The crumpled man wielding a joint between two fingers blows a wad of snot out of his nose.

"That's my wife man and you can shut your fucking face."

With a grunt he pulls himself up, squeezing the crutch under his arm, and hobbles into the library to the men's room.

I ain't going to cry. But she sure looked good those sparkling green eyes lighting up the whole street and that big round ass bobbing up and down when she ran.

He looks at himself in the mirror. "Fuck!" A quick hop to the next sink and he looks in the mirror again. "What the fuck's the matter with this mirror? I ain't a day older than thirty-five. Or is it forty-five? It don't matter. That beat-up old man ain't me." He whirls around, catching the edge of the sink before he can lose his balance. "Nobody's in back of me."

His eyes paw the face in the mirror, trying to dig out a recognizable piece of himself from under the layers of dirt and whiskers. A dam breaks and water gushes over the cheeks, streams through the gray-splotched copper wool hanging from jaw to collar and drips onto the shabby Giants jacket. He feels the tears slide down his own face, hot and metallic, and hears little taps as they fall on his jacket.

"Fuck." Great hiccupping sobs splash out of his mouth, bounce off the mirror and knock him to the floor.

I done this to myself. She was right. She was so fucking right.

I gotta get her back.

He washes his face. His eyes peek through a fan of fingers to see if washing has improved his reflection. The same deflated old man bristling with gray and auburn chin fleece glares at him.

How am I going to do it?

I thought I was fooling her and she was on to me all along. She knew what I was heading for and she tried as hard as she could to stop me and I kept right on going laughing my fucking head off like I was some kind of hyena. Just like she always told me when I see a sign that says "Cliff Ahead" I keep on running until I fall right off the edge. What the fuck's the matter with me? Here I am all smashed up at the bottom of the cliff a broken old man and there ain't no one's going to give me a hand and help me get up.

"Hey man you got some change you can spare? Sure could use a cup of coffee." He stands across the street from the library and banters with passersby, points out his missing leg, tells a sad story about a car crash and how he's waiting for his disability payments to start. About how he's an engineer and he's lost everything because of a drunk driver.

Panhandling isn't allowed on the library steps.

A couple hours later he has two hundred dollars in his pocket.

Man people sure feel sorry for me when I look like crap. Maybe I ought to stay like this. But then my Annie ain't going to come back to me. I gotta stay steady. Never been good at that always seesaw back and forth make my own self dizzy. Gotta decide what I want my Annie or a shitload of money from panhandling. If I panhandle I can stay the way I am. If I want my Annie I gotta be good gotta go to work gotta tell the truth. Gotta get clean.

He thumbs through the wad of bills. I could buy a lot of hits with this.

He puts the money back.

He sits on the library steps, head on his knees.

The money whispers from his pocket. "Stick me in your arm Cleo come on you know you want to." And Annie appears, arms reaching out to him.

He stretches out on the prickly grass of the library lawn and watches cotton ball clouds sauntering across a light blue sky.

If I was high right now I sure as fuck wouldn't be laying here looking up at those clouds. I'd be in a dumpster somewhere digging for gold and diamonds I wasn't going to see when I was clean.

It takes him an hour to make up his mind.

He heads toward Pete's.

S omeone is pounding on my door.

"I'm coming." I push away from the computer screen. It sounds like they're pounding with both hands.

"I'm coming. Jesus and Maria."

I open the door. "What's up?"

A grubby hand shoves Mama's rosary and gold crucifix in my face. My eyes migrate from the hand to the frayed black jacket sleeve and up the sleeve to the head bobbing above it.

Cleo. He hovers on the doorstep looking ready to go airborne. I see one shoe and one hollow jeans leg and one crutch. His eyes tap my cheeks and chin and then shy away as if they're afraid to stay focused on me.

"Here," he says, tossing Mama's things in my lap. "I'm sorry I took them."

I can't take my eyes off him. How long has it been? A month? Two? In that time he's lost a leg and his face has creased up like a badly ironed shirt. He's gotten thinner, if that's possible. And there is a distinct odor of shit clinging to him. My first thought is wow, God does punish people for their sins, doesn't He? Then I choke on that thought, bright yellow shame spotlighting memories of bashing my terrified baby brother in his bed, the tiny hand I'd let go reaching through the barrier of time to pinch my dead spinal cord.

"Thanks."

"I forgive you" he says.

"Forgive me?"

"For stealing all my gold buttons."

"Gold buttons?"

"Yeah you took them out of my pocket when I was sleeping here."

"What?"

"No?"

"You're looney, dude."

"No gold buttons. You saying I made it up? Like the doc telling me my diamonds were gravel? Whatever. I need your help so I gotta believe you. Ain't gotta choice."

I back away from him.

"Wait!" Cleo sticks his crutch in the door.

"What do you want?"

"You gotta help me. I can't do this by myself."

"What makes you think I can help you?"

"You're the only guy I know who don't use and who's still talking to me."

"I'm not talking to you because I want to."

"You're good people. That's how come I believe you when you say you never took those gold buttons."

My second chance is staring at me. I'm not ready for it yet. I don't want to let Cleo into my apartment so he can take something else, don't want to let him into my life to cause damage the way Teddy did, don't want to open my heart to him because I know he will ultimately break it. Redemption comes with a high price. I don't want to let Mama down again but I don't feel up to paying that price today.

My gaze fixates on a breeze twirling potted daisies behind him. I suck on my lower lip. Close my eyes and count to ten. Open them. Cleo is still here, blocking out daylight and steeping me in night-damp shadow.

"What do you want me to do?"

"I don't want to use no more but I don't know how to stop by myself. And I gotta get off the street cuz that shit's everywhere. I don't know where I'm going to go or how the fuck I'm going to do it but I gotta stop getting high."

"Why?"

"Look at me man. I'm ugly. It's that shit that's made me look like this."

"And how did you come to this realization?"

"My Annie." Two blobs of light dribble down his sunken cheeks, fasten in his ratty beard. "She didn't recognize me."

"Your girlfriend?"

"My wife man. My other half. My better half. We ain't been together in a while but if I clean up my act she's going to take me back. She's my soul mate man."

"Why now? Why didn't you want to be clean before? I assume your drug use caused her some distress when you were together."

"No man never. She just got herself another guy that's all. I handled her with velvet gloves. I was always good to her."

"I find that hard to believe, dude. I've seen you kick a dumpster for hours."

"I was a good husband. Treated her like a queen. But I left her all alone when I was out getting high and I guess she got lonely and hooked up with someone else. Man I'm only forty or forty-two or something and I look like I'm eighty. I gotta get off the street and take care of myself and start giving back. I took too much from everyone. Gotta start shouldering the load you know what I'm saying? Get healthy and clean and turn back into my good-looking self."

"What if it doesn't work? What if she still doesn't want to get back together with you?"

"She will. I know her man. I just gotta get clean and then I'm going to look in those sexy green eyes and she's going to fall for me all over again."

"You can't stay here."

"I gotta get off the street. That shit's going to eat me up and shit me out and I'm going to die in a fucking gutter somewhere."

I wish he'd go away. I wish I'd never rescued him from that damn dumpster.

"When did you use last?"

"I got out of the hospital a week ago. Smoked some pot and did a couple lines. Saw my Annie yesterday. So yesterday. Ain't even smoked pot since yesterday."

"I can help you get into a program but you have to have been drug-free for seven days."

"There's no way I'm going to stay clean out there."

"I'll make some phone calls. Maybe you can go into detox and from there they'll put you in a program. Come in. You need a shower. You stink. If you touch anything here without my permission I will put you in a jail cell. You got that?"

"I ain't got no bags."

"Bags?"

Cleo lifts up his jacket and lowers the waistband of his jeans. A plastic bag filled to bursting with shit dangles from his belly, half pulled off.

"Oh Christ," I mutter.

One rainy day she came home early and I was still in their house. We were high and gabbling gibberish. Making up words. We are soul mates, you know; it was angels who brought us together. Because we are totally in tune with each other, like one soul in two bodies, we understood the words we were making up. She stood like an ice statue, lips blue and fingertips translucent, the corners of her mouth frozen in a moronic smile. She couldn't figure out what we were saying.

I said to her "I fucked trucked Cleo Deo today play. He's leaving sheaving you and he's going to marry carry me." I casually pulled up my shirt and rubbed my tummy-bump. I yawned.

She didn't make a sound. Her eyes rolled around and around, avoiding my tummy and my beautiful pregnant boobs.

Then our sweet secret conversation ended, because Cleo said "What the fuck are you talking about? I brought you here to get you out of the fucking rain and give you something to eat and you're standing here telling my wife lies about me? Get the fuck out of my house!"

"Cleo Deo!" I protested, but he pushed me to the door.

"I ain't going to let her hitchhike back downtown," he told her. She still hadn't said a word, but I saw a glimmer of dampness in her eyes. "It ain't safe. Give me the fucking car keys. I'm going to drive the bitch up to Market Street and drop her off and then I'm going to come right back."

He kissed her on the cheek as he took the keys from her hand. She was catatonic. If he'd lifted her leg in the air I'm sure it would've stayed there. Why was she acting like that? If she'd been me, she'd have been cursing and hitting him. Or hitting me. Of course, I'm not a lady. I don't pretend to be. She was a real lady.

He stopped the car a block from the house and slapped me.

"How come you fucking told her that? You want her to divorce me?" He slapped me again.

"Why don't you lose snooze her, Cleo Deo? You know you love me flea. That's what you said head. I'm your real seal wife life. I'm making baking a baby for you stew."

He slapped me a third time. "I never said I love you. And you ain't my wife. You're a fucking skank. And who knows who that kid's dad is." And then his mouth was all over mine and he fucked me right there in the car a block from their house. In broad daylight.

After the door closed behind them I sat down. My coat was still buttoned. My hand was still in the air waiting to drop the keys into the handbag that was still hanging from my shoulder.

It had happened so quickly I hadn't had time to react.

She was the girl he spent his time with, a towering pitted husk with spiky green hair. And pregnant. And barefoot. And reeking of female hormones, the scent put up shoots and blossomed in her footprints on the carpet, trailed behind her like a wedding train.

That was the first time I'd seen her. I'd found condoms in foil packets lounging like mints on the pillows, and a syringe, a drop of blood congealing inside and the needle poised to prick me, on the floor behind the toilet. A tampon wrapper in the bathroom wastebasket, a burgundy smear on the sheets. When I asked him he always said he'd brought her home to feed her. He assured me that he didn't even like her. Then why was I greeted with condoms when I walked into the bedroom? Why were used syringes hiding like snakes in the bathroom? Because she was crazy. She was supposed to be on psych meds but she refused to take them.

Oh.

They left at exactly four-forty-six. Underneath the milling horde of screams in my brain I heard a low rumble, a premonition of an earthquake, a volcanic eruption, a tidal wave.

The rumble increased when I checked the time. Five-thirty. Did I hear the car pull up?

I peeked out the window. The driveway was empty.

Six o'clock. Market Street was only a few minutes away.

Seven o'clock. I paced. How many evenings had he left me sitting here by myself and then come home and accused me of having a lover?

And he was the one with a lover. A pregnant one. Was it his?

I wanted so badly to get pregnant, even though the doctors insisted I couldn't. God can do anything, I told myself. We had sex every working day and on our days off twice a day or more. Every time I begged God to make this the lucky day. But my womb stayed complacently empty, and this girl that he brought to our home when I was at work and obviously made love to, probably in our bed, was pregnant.

The rumble erupted and blew a hole in my face, turning my mouth into a gaping lipless O. Banshees in tight V formation shrieked out of that O.

I grabbed a pillow off the couch and threw it at the wall. I hurled another one. The lamp fell with a crunch and the room went black.

I ran to the bedroom and yanked his clothes off their hangers. Bolted down the steps and into the garage and out the back door carrying a load of shirts and sweaters and jeans so big I couldn't see over it. Every one of them was a gift from me. I screamed as I dumped them in the garbage can. I panted, scalding air blistering lung tissue, as I ran back and forth, a train on a track, until the closet was empty.

"She's not even pretty!" I screeched. "She's ugly. A scrawny Amazon with green hair and a scabby face! Ugly!" I dropped the last armload of clothes on the back walk, dug my heels into them and tried to rip them apart with my feet.

"You are one foolish woman," I shouted at myself when I'd given up on the clothes, leaving them whole but rippled with heel prints, and I stood in my tomb-quiet living room. "Foolish! You have a Master's Degree and you're still nothing but a goddam fool!" And then a mudslide of words no Christian woman should ever say flowed over the floor and halfway up the walls and I was neck deep in the filthy language I had absorbed from Cleo. I struggled to keep my nose and mouth above the rising slime that was filling my home.

"Why, God?" I shrieked. "Why? Why?"

Clothes I'd dropped trailed from the bedroom and out the back door. His favorite shirts rankled in the garbage can, mounded with scraps of dead food, defiled by his aftershave, his cologne, his toothpaste. His baseball cards were melting to pulp in his shampoo. I had smashed his favorite CDs, jumping on them with fury.

The force driving the destruction of his belongings vanished, leaving me exhausted and wheezing.

Shame crept from my toes to my heart.

God had tested me. I had failed the test.

I wondered if I could salvage anything. After all, he would come back eventually. And want to know, with a hurt look on his face, why I had done that. And, no doubt, use his damaged possessions as an excuse to knock me into the wall.

I ripped the sheets off the bed and threw them away, cringing fingers shielded by rubber gloves. I couldn't bear to touch the sheets her scabby skin had touched.

I dozed on the couch. I couldn't lie in that bed yet. I was too tired to eat, too tired to brush my teeth. I was still wearing my coat and my handbag was still slung over my shoulder.

I awoke at one in the morning. The silent house was a hand clamped over my nose and mouth. Panic hacked open my chest and reached its arctic fingers into the bleeding gash and froze my lungs. They couldn't move. I had to force myself to myself breathe. In---out. In---out. The panic hacked deeper and its hatchet-blade went all the way through my heart and out my back.

"Oh God," I pleaded. "Please get me through this, dear Jesus. Please tell me what to do. I need Your help. I need Your help. I need Your help."

Somehow the night passed as I prayed. I took a taxi to the library in the morning. "I need Your help" was the rope around my fingers that kept me from being sucked into the whirlpool that my life had become. It eased my agony enough to let me do my job.

T hat whole next summer I looked like a glossy supermodel with a watermelon under my shirt. He took care of me as if I were his little baby. He begged and stole to get me enough food. Found places for us to sleep so we never spent the night on a stranger's steps. Sometimes it was in someone's room on a dirty carpet with no pillow or blanket, but he'd lay my head on his chest and hold me in his arms and I'd be warm. The tick of his galloping heart lulled me into lala land. I was so happy.

I think he'd had a fight with that redhead and she'd finally thrown him out. Maybe because I was preggers. He never talked about it and that was fine with me. He was mine now. I lifted a wedding ring from Kay Jewelers and one night when we cuddled on the damp beach and gray fog wisped across a full ivory moon he put it on my finger. I flaunted it at everyone.

As my tummy bump grew we talked to the baby. I told him (I knew it was a boy) how great his daddy was, how his daddy was going to take care of us, get a good job and rent us a big flat. I told him he'd have a sister one day, and a puppy of his very own. And we'd always have good food and lots of cookies. I knew how to bake cookies. I would bake for him.

Cleo wanted a daughter. He decided to name her Elizabeth after his grandma. Since I knew it was going to be a boy I didn't care, although Elizabeth was hella boring. I wanted something livelier, something that would tell people how we lived our lives. We joked about naming a boy Speed or Point and I thought a daughter could have a prettier name like Crystal or Heaven. We knew we weren't serious, but we began calling the growing baby Dopey. He always kicked more when we called him that. I don't know if it was because he liked the name or because he didn't. I don't think he knew what it meant.

One of Cleo's stupid friends must have said something to him, because one day he decided he didn't want me to get high anymore. He said it wasn't good for the baby. That's bull! If it's good for me and him, it's good for the baby. Did he love the baby more than me? I had to be first. I had to be the most important thing in his life. He had to love me so much he would rob for me, kill for me, die for me. A baby is just something you make. It must never take my place in his heart.

One night he left me out on the street when he went to someone's room to get high. Left me out on the street because he was worried about the baby. For reals! I lay down on the sidewalk and started moaning. People came. I told them I was in premature labor and would they get my husband out of that hotel.

They got him. His face was tomato red and his mouth was a thin straight tightrope, but when he saw me writhing on the ground he dropped to his knees and bent over me.

"Sylvie baby what's the matter?" He cradled my head in his arms, a layer of stale tobacco breath settling on my face.

"I think sink I'm in labor saber," I sobbed. "I think drink I'm going to lose choose the baby."

"Let me call you an ambulance." He gingerly laid me back down and folded his jacket under my head. He didn't notice when I lifted his wallet from his back pocket.

He stood up to find someone with a cell phone and I rolled over and crept away. I was on the next block before he realized I was gone.

"Hey!" he shouted, sprinting after me.

"You think stink you're going to get high pie without me free?" I shouted back. I waved his wallet in the air. "I'll show you who you're messing stressing with." I dribbled the bills down the sewer. It was a couple hundred in twenties. I kept his ID and chucked the wallet in a dumpster, pictures of his precious redhead included. I ran on, gigantic tummy bouncing up and down.

I looked back. I didn't see him.

I stopped, panting, my thighs burning and my belly screeching like it was tearing loose. Running when you're six months pregnant and big as the Queen Mary is not easy.

Where was he?

I didn't care. He'd be back. I knew his heart. His heart was mine.

I sold his ID to a dealer friend for a hit and a fuck.

C leo stayed away from her all summer. I knew he thought
about her. Sometimes he groaned her name in his sleep, and
it made me so mad I'd leave for a while and shoot whatever kind
of dope I could find and fuck whoever I had to, to get it. I didn't
save any for him. He had to get his own since he'd decided that my
getting high wasn't good for the baby.

One night in September I smoked crack with Chris. He let me
sit outside his box and passed his pipe to me through one of the
slits in the side.

"More snore," I demanded when it was gone. I was already
so high the world was drenched in glitter but I wanted to be
higher.

"Fuck!" he shouted, but he lit another rock and handed me the
pipe.

I felt Dopey kicking and kicking. He was tearing the shit out
of me. "Stop hop it, you fucking kid did!" I yelled at him, slapping the little bouncing knobs that were his feet. "You're hurting
skirting me." I thought baby kicks weren't supposed to hurt but
his feet were ripping me apart. Every kick was an axe slashing
through my insides. A river of blood gushed from between my legs

and submerged my feet as I squatted on the sidewalk. "Chris!" I screamed.

Forget about rhymes, I was dying.

"Goddam!" Chris said when he emerged from his box. I was doubled over and grunting. He called 9-1-1 on his cell phone and then he disappeared back into the box and it tiptoed discreetly down the block, crossed the street and parked itself on the far corner.

I was lifted off the street by the paramedics, blanketed onto a stretcher and rushed to the hospital, siren blaring, pain blasting up from my belly and out of my mouth, echoing the siren.

"Tim! You gotta get me out of this fucking place!"

"Dude! It's three in the morning."

"You said it was okay for me to call you any time."

"You've called every hour since midnight. I'm not getting you out of there, Cleo. You can do this."

"No man I fucking can't. I been awake all night every night since I been here. And they won't let me go out and smoke and we ain't allowed to smoke inside. I'm going crazy."

"How long did you say you've been doing speed?"

"Since I was seventeen."

"So that's...how old are you?"

"I don't know. Forty forty-five. How come you want to know how old I am?"

"If you're forty years old and you've been using speed since you were seventeen that's twenty-three years, Cleo. More than half your life."

"What's your point?"

"For twenty-three years you've only slept when you came down off a high. Your brain doesn't know how to sleep anymore."

"I was clean sometimes."

"Did you sleep then?"

"Yeah. It wasn't like this. I was clean for all those years I lived with my Annie. I fell asleep with her in my arms every night. But I never slept all night long. Even when I was a kid I woke up every couple hours and had to work real hard to make myself get back to sleep, peeked in everyone's room to see if they were all still there, make sure the closet door was locked. Crap like that."

"You should be able to learn to fall asleep."

"They won't give me no sleeping pills."

"Of course they won't. You're in drug rehab. They aren't going to give you any chemicals. You've got to learn how to deal with your problems, and you will. I know you will. You just have to be patient."

"Patient? Me? I don't got time for that. Get me out of here now. Now! Call whoever you gotta and get me out of this prison."

"You're staying."

"I'm going to leave as soon as they unlock the doors in the morning."

"And do what?"

"Smoke."

"And?"

"I don't know."

"Yes, you do."

"I'll be free I'll be breathing fresh air again man. No walls to box me in."

"And what will you do when you're free?"

"Go over to Pete's and bum a hit off him."

"That's right. That's exactly what you'll do if you leave there. Is that what you want?"

Silence. A full minute of mute night on the other end of the line. Finally he says "No."

"No?"

"No. I don't want to use that shit no more."

"You're sure?"

"I'm sure. I gotta get my life back together so I can get my Annie back."

"Then you'll stay?"

"Yeah. My crutch has been poking holes in the fucking rug all night. It looks like I got gophers in my room."

"That's better than getting high, isn't it?"

"I guess."

"Cleo?"

"What?"

"Please don't call after midnight unless you're dying."

"I am dying man. That's what it feels like."

"You're not dying."

"Maybe I'm just coming back to life. Like when your leg's been asleep. It don't feel too good when it wakes up."

I don't expect that much wisdom from him. "Deep, dude. Real deep."

"Yeah. I ain't as stupid as you thought huh."

✂ ✂

Aw man! There's my fucking dad how come he's here in the middle of the night? Going to fuck me again Dad? Like you did when I was a kid? Yes you did don't lie to me. Is someone banging on the door? No I'm hearing stuff. Don't want no one to come in right now. And she just stood there rolling her eyeballs. Didn't lift a finger to help me. Didn't tell you to stop. She hated me you knew she hated me cuz I told her I loved my real mom and she would never be her. You knew and you didn't give a fuck. You let her hit me you laughed while she was busting my face and then you locked me in the closet for two whole days. Didn't bring me no food. Who the fuck's knocking on the door? All the guys are asleep. Didn't even let me out to piss I pissed on myself in the dark there were monsters in that closet. Monsters. I saw their red faces with their black pointy horns and their skinny tails slashing around in the air like whips. I prayed to Jesus like they told us to when Mom took me to Sunday school but those monsters didn't go away. They sat in the corner and mumbled. I didn't understand them. I heard "little boy" and "eat him up" but I didn't understand all the other words. They crawled closer and closer I saw their hairy toes gliding towards me and I heard their long toenails scraping on the floor and their mouths were as big as caves with bloody fangs hanging out and they were slobbering all over me. How come you didn't beat them up Dad? You were as strong as Superman and you could smash them to pieces. Maybe someone ought to come in. Chase my dad away get me off this roller coaster that ain't going nowhere. You could save me how come you just let me stay in there? I was so fucking scared I shit on myself. And you let me stay in there for two whole days pounding on the door and screaming to get out and when you finally let me out what did you do? You fucked me and she laughed. Is it cuz I was bad? Chased the cat and it got stuck in a tree. The fire department had to come and get it down. Tried to wash clothes for my new mom and all the colors ran. Took a dollar from her purse to buy me a popsicle from the ice cream man. Is that how come you were going to let those monsters eat me up? And I was so stupid always asking you stuff. How come the moon ain't always round Dad? How come clouds don't fall out of the sky? How come boats can't fly? "You're a stupid piece of shit" was all you ever said. I was sorry I was so bad and stupid all the time I didn't want to be but you didn't need to throw me out of the house. I was ten years old still a little kid. I wanted to grow up and be just like you. Look at me now all my clothes are the same as yours. White tee shirts black jeans and steel-toed work boots if I can get them. I sat there in the freezing cold snow and cried. It was winter Dad snow on the ground and when I sat in it it was over my head. I didn't know where to go my real mom was dead my gramma lived in a different town and the neighbors called the cops and you told them I ran away. You lied to them. I gotta stop all these thoughts they don't do me no good. All that crap is in the past now. I love you Dad even if you hurt my heart crushed it under the heel of your boot that's what you did. I gotta go out and smoke. I ain't going to get high I gotta hang on to my Annie she's the only good thing I ever got in my whole life but I gotta get some sleep and all these thoughts rain down from a hole up there in the ceiling and my brain's a big empty bucket and all these bad memories are filling it up and it's making me crazy. They gotta at least let me go out and smoke.

"Hey Matt," I hiss from the top landing. The night counselor's watching TV downstairs in the living room.

He comes to the foot of the stairs rubbing his eyes and yawning. Seems like I'm the only bozo in this fucking place that ain't asleep.

"What's up, Cleo?"

"Man I gotta go out and smoke. I can't get to sleep and I got all these bad memories jabbing at me."

"What kind of memories?"

"My dad. Crap he did to me."

"Come on down and talk. You want some hot chocolate?"

"I want to go out and smoke."

"I can't let you out at night, Cleo. You know that. Tell me about your dad. Where does he live?"

"North Dakota."

"That's a long way off. You miss him?"

"Fuck no."

I lie in bed, eyes fighting to stay open because I know the phone is going to ring soon and there's no point in dropping off to sleep. Cleo has called me every night since he started his program. Every night, every hour, all night long. I thought they had rules in those rehab places. I peer at the glowing numbers on the clock. Midnight. He should've called by now. Maybe he's going to sleep tonight. Or maybe he's run away.

My thoughts stumble. The weight of being awakened repeatedly for the past few nights pulls me deeper into the bed and I nod off. I jerk awake when I hear my name. Teddy's voice. I look around. Nobody. I glance at the clock again. Three. Was I dreaming about Teddy?

I settle back on my pillow and disconnected scenes stutter through my sleep-depleted brain. Teddy is digging in the back yard. Cleo is digging in the back yard. His amputated leg is propped against the fence and his crutch is the shovel he digs with. He and Teddy are burying toys. Papa slaps Cleo, and Cleo's leg jumps up and kicks him.

The sun smears the walls daffodil yellow. There were no phone calls all night. I bolt up, balance on the edge of the bed with my dead legs dangling and dial his house.

"Hello," I say when a counselor answers. "How is Cleo? Did he sleep last night?"

They put Cleo on the phone. "Yeah man I'm good. I didn't want to bother you. I figured I been giving you a pretty tough time and you needed a rest."

"Did you sleep?"

"Some. They're painting and they let me paint the kitchen. I did the whole fucking thing. Took most of the night and then I slept a couple hours and I'm good to go. Everybody says I did a real good job."

"That's great, Cleo. Really great." I hang up and lie down again, lifting my legs onto the bed with my hands.

What a mother hen I've become. I can't sleep when I don't hear from my baby chick. Damn!

W e sit at the back of the meeting room. My knitting needles click softly as I work on a black and red muffler for Joe.

I'd stopped knitting when Cleo's love turned rabid. He said I was too involved with it and I ought to be focusing my attention on him. When I put it away he ignored me and watched TV. Football games. Cop shows. Or he was gone. Mostly he was gone, and I was afraid to pick up the yarn and needles in case he should suddenly come back. I sat like a boulder on the couch, apprehension chipping me into gravel, staring at ghosts of cops chasing memories of criminals across the television screen, unable to pick up the remote and switch to something I liked.

Now I am knitting again.

This is a speaker meeting. These are the most interesting of the NA meetings, but the traumas recounted by the speakers upset me. I compare Cleo's life with theirs to see if there are similarities, and there are. He was abused terribly. His family chopped his heart into little pieces. But wouldn't someone try to fix their heart? Wouldn't they let go of the pain or at least accept it and move on at some point? Who hasn't had pain in their life?

A woman is telling a story of sexual abuse. Her father.

My thoughts flit back to the kitchen table of my childhood and I see my dad, sandy brown hair neatly parted on the right side of his head, perpetual sandy fuzz on his upper lip, sand-colored eyes, bending over my shoulder to inspect my homework. He taught me to slow-dance when I was ten. Stood me on his feet and waltzed me around the living room. I was going to my first school dance. At that age the thought of being held by a boy puffed out my cheeks in disgust, but my dad suggested I learn how "just in case."

He never made me feel that I was a woman first and a person second. But he made sure I got my homework done, and when my first crush ended with a rude remark and stinging humiliation in front of everyone in my sixth grade class, he gave me his hanky to dry my tears. Through watching him struggle to achieve his dream---working construction to support us while he went to college part-time, finally earning his degree and his teaching certificate and a position at Lowell High School as a biology teacher---I learned that there's always a way to make things better. He taught me without ever putting it into words that what determines my fate is my will, not my body.

How different from the story this woman is telling. Her dad sneaked into her room night after night, at first reaching his fingers inside her diaper, and when she was older pulling up her nightgown and tickling her big-girl potty-trained self. The touches changed to slow caresses and his fingers moved inside her. He'd whisper how much he loved her. More than he loved her mother, who was so mean to him. He made her promise to never tell about their secret nights because her mother would be jealous and throw her out. He bought her the prettiest dresses, the sweetest dolls. Always had a piece of candy for her. Her bigger sisters were jealous of the attention at first but then their eyes turned shameful when they looked at her and she began to think that maybe he shouldn't be doing that. She knew he didn't do it to them.

She wanted to ask her mother if it was all right. But Mom would put her out on the street, and she might starve to death out there. She couldn't squeeze out a word.

When she was eight her mother divorced him for her own reasons, but she could never bring herself to tell her what he'd done.

One morning, waking up face down in an alley after sleeping off a crack high, her grime crusted eyes saw a mama cat stretched out on a scrap of cardboard, grooming her newborn kitties. She remembered her own baby, abandoned in a hospital nursery when she ran off to score another rock, thick clots from the birth drooling down her legs. She crawled out of that alley, stumbled miles to the docks and jumped in, her guilt more than she could live with, but the chilly bay water washed her clean and her numb legs kicked her up to the surface.

She hunched in a back corner of the NA meetings for months, afraid to make a sound. One day her story refused to remain unspoken and word by agonizing word bled out of her mouth. She found a sponsor and cried her way through the Twelve Steps. And then she told her mother.

Her mother bawled like a baby.

How does it feel to have the person who should be protecting you from the evils of the world become one of those evils?

She describes years of prostitution, getting high on crack and selling her body to get more. Sometimes ten or fifteen five-dollar tricks a day, just to turn her confusion into a short moment of oblivion. She was twenty-five years old and fifty pounds underweight when she was handed an AIDS diagnosis.

I shiver. I take the two feet I've completed of Joe's muffler and gather it around me. I picture her as a small child in a white lace dress with a red sash, a red flower tucked over one ear, a big wide grin on her face; and I see the hands of her father wiping away her beautiful smile one touch at a time until no one could remember it was ever there. The young woman whose story she is telling, the one with the wild unwashed hair and mismatched shoes, shrieks in my mind in a crack rage, as crazy as Cleo, the entire purpose of her life being to erase her shame with a drug that resembles a dirty old tooth.

Oh God, this is too much sadness. Where are You when people need You? Why couldn't You have saved that little girl so she wouldn't be here now cutting holes in our hearts with her story?

Joe's arm settles to my shoulder.

"I don't know why I keep coming here with you. I'm not an addict. I don't need to hear this."

"I know. Do you want to leave?"

"No, I'm already here. I'll stay." A tear rolls down my cheek.

The baby was black.

"I ain't taking care of no black kid!" he yelled.

"I thought sought it was yours chores."

"I never fucked you so how's it going to be mine? But I was still going to take care of you and a white kid."

"It's love shove that makes a family. Not snot color. And you've spent weeks leeks fucking bucking me. I know you shoe didn't forget pet that."

"Bull shit. I ain't fucked no one but my Annie and I ain't feeding no black kid. You go and find his dad and get him to rent you an apartment."

"He raped taped me. I told you flew. Last past Christmas. Big black shellac dude rude."

"You're a fucking liar."

"Look who's talking caulking! You've lied died to that redheaded bitch snitch about me knee ever since you met bet me."

"I never lied to her."

"Bet you never told sold her I was your real steal wife life."

"You ain't my real wife."

"Then why sigh do I have this ring sing?" I waved my left hand at him.

"That ain't even a real ring!" he shouted. "It don't mean a fucking thing."

The nurse had brought the baby in for me to feed, and I held him to my swollen boobs, ducking my head so Cleo couldn't see how angry I was. The baby's little mouth tugged at my nipple. I felt the tug all the way down to my baggy vagina. It felt good.

"This kid did's making me horny corny." I put him back in his plastic bassinet. He bleated in his tiny newborn voice. "Come here spear." I pulled the sheet down, spreading my bare legs.

He spat on the bed between them, his face snarled like uncombed hair. "I left an angel for you. Every bozo in the city must have warned me but did I listen? No stupid me I thought I could take care of two women at the same time and juggle them back and forth like I was juggling two balls. And who's the bozo who got juggled? Me. I lost my Annie and I sure as fuck don't want a piece of shit like you." He strode out the door, punching the air with purple fists and vomiting profanity on the polished linoleum floor.

"Cleo!" Panic wrenched my words back into normal English. "Cleo! You're my husband! Don't go. You said you wanted this baby. That's why I had him. For you! If you don't want him we can give him away. We can sell him. I need you. Don't go."

The baby howled. I whimpered. I hadn't expected this.

The nurse came in. "Did you try to feed him?" she asked, covering my bloated boobs and blood-tinged thighs with the sheet.

"He won't eat. I'm tired. Can you bring him to me later?"

"Of course, honey. You get some rest. Do you need a blanket?"

"No, thanks." I burrowed into the pillow. She wheeled the bassinet out.

Cleo didn't come back.

I sneaked out an hour later with a bag of sanitary pads under my shirt.

I knew they'd find a home for the kid. That's what they do with abandoned children.

I couldn't find Cleo. Nobody would tell me where he was. I ran from one street to another, checked all our favorite hangouts, visited all our friends, but he wasn't anywhere.

Now who would protect me?

T he meeting ends.
I stay in my chair, hands slack, yarn on the floor. Eyes seeing nothing. Joe stands.

I get it, at least part of it. I finally get it.

Since the time Cleo relapsed and shoved me through the drug-induced rifts in San Francisco's tree-lined avenues and down into the magma seething below them, I'd prayed to God for guidance. I'd asked Him why? Why are You doing this to me? What have I done to deserve this?

I'd wallowed in my bruises and shed battered bloody tears until I had none left. A desolate road stretched ahead of me. I didn't know where it led. I'd forced myself to keep walking, tattered feet stammering forward. Sand blew across the scorched asphalt, lonely as the first day of creation, and vultures hulked on Joshua trees waiting for my last gurgling breath. But dying wasn't an option for me, and I wasn't going to spend the rest of my days reopening my wounds with a scalpel of self-pity. I had to follow that road, footprints dredged with shards of blood, into an unseen future.

That is the difference. I don't know how to blunt my pain by destroying parts of myself. That's what a horse does. My grandfather had a ranch. One day when I was quite small I saw him leading a horse around the corral, around and around and around. "Whacha doing, Grandpa?" "Horse has colic, Anarooney." That's what he called me. "What's colic?" "Gas stuck in his gut. If I don't keep him walking he'll kick his belly to get rid of the pain. Could kick himself to death."

"Are you all right?" Joe asks.

I flash him a wide smile. "I'm so fine you wouldn't believe it."

"I do believe it. You're quite fine." His face ruptures in a big wink and he takes my elbow and guides me to the door through mingles of people with cookies and coffee cups in their hands.

M y eyes are trying to read his lips. I can't figure out what the fuck he's saying.

"The first step, Cleo. What is the first step?"

"I don't fucking know and I don't fucking care."

"No swear words. Remember the rules."

"I don't know and I don't care. Better?"

"I just told you what the first step is."

"Powerless. You said powerless." Baseball. The game's started. I want to go and watch the Giants.

"That's right. Powerless. What does that mean? If you say you are…"

Miguel ought to take that cap off his head. Red cap makes him look like he's in a gang.

"Cleo."

"What?"

"What's going through your brain right now?"

No gang colors allowed I wish my Annie was here to see me see all the bull shit I'm going through for her. I want to go and watch the game sneak over the fence and just be there man hustle a hot dog and a beer and hear all the people roaring.

"I don't know." Why is he only asking me? Ain't that discrimination? Look at that sun pouring through the window. Rays of twenty-four carat gold. Wish I could sell that I'd be rich. Then my Annie'd come running back for sure. She wouldn't give a fuck if I was high.

Stupid counselor's making a shadow on the floor and it jiggles every time he opens his fucking mouth.

"Can someone tell Cleo what the first step is?"

"We admit that we are powerless over our drug of choice." Wayne. Show off I knew the answer. He should have asked me oh he did ask me. What time is it? The game's already started. I could have been out at Pac Bell Park no it's AT & T Park now. How many times are they going to change the name?

I don't know what powerless means I don't know what power means. I just want this fucking group to be over.

"You're stupid Cleo."

"What did you say?"

Toenails screech like chalk in back of me.

"Stupid stupid stupid too stupid to bother with."

"What the fuck man!"

"Powerless, Cleo. Pay attention." The toenails click out of the room and I hear the soft bump of a door shutting.

I know what's going on. I been clean two weeks and don't they get why I gotta use that shit? It ain't to feel good like everyone thinks. I gotta use it to keep those monsters away. Even when I was with my Annie and clean as a whistle I had to smoke a little pot. I sure couldn't let her know how fucked-up I am. It helped some not as good as shit I can't think straight without it I go around and around back to my dad and back to the closet and let all those monsters out and then they're chasing me down the street and I'm screaming for help I can't explain it to no one cuz they all use those big words and I don't know what they're saying and I feel about two inches small. They're all so smart and I'm so stupid.

Every person I ever knew saw how stupid I was. Everyone except my Annie. They spun me around like a top. My mind runs here and there and hauls me along with it. Baseball to my Annie to my dad and he wants me to focus on a step? Step ladder? Ladder engine? Fire truck? Pick-up truck I want a Chevy pick-up pick up a girl and what do I want to do with her? You know. Man I gotta stop this fucking brain-spinning. I want to learn this I gotta learn this. Powerless. I know what it means the relationship between me and my brain. God You made a big joke when You made me don't know why You got it in for me. I'm powerless to control it without filling it up with shit. I'm just a shit-head. Really.

"I'm powerless," I say. Oh it ain't my turn.

"Cleo. Follow the rules. Wayne was talking."

"Sorry." Can't do nothing right. I wonder what's the score must be in the third inning by now.

O n a dazzling day in early June, Joe and I watch his son walk
across a stage and receive his diploma.

"I can't believe it!" Joe crushes him in a bear hug.

"You graduated and you didn't think I could? Come on, Dad!"

"Come on, Dad!" I chime in. Laughter soft as dandelion fluff
tickles our noses, ears, necks. The sun gushes through a fissured
sky and a brisk breeze finds its way to us from the Golden Gate,
plays with the tassel on David's cap, flicks the hem of my long skirt
and whisks around my leather-booted ankles.

"Why aren't you like the others?" I ask Joe that evening after
we've returned David to the apartment he shares with three other
medical students, all new doctors now, and Joe and I sit in his car
in front of my house.

"What do you mean?"

"You got away. You won. I know you said your son saved you,
but a lot of these addicts have children and that doesn't stop them.
David's mother. She kept on using."

He shrugs.

"You have to have an idea. How can you help them if you don't
at least have a theory to work with?"

"You're right. I do have a theory. I had a mother who loved me."

"Are you saying addicts aren't loved by their mothers?"

"No. I'm saying someone has to love the child. It doesn't matter who, really, as long as it's someone who's important to him. Someone has to stand up for him and teach him that he's valuable. A child doesn't know that unless someone tells him. A child thinks whatever his parents do to him is what he deserves."

"So your mother loved you."

"And I loved her."

"And your father?"

He hesitates. We've never spoken of his childhood. We've discussed his travels, his son, my childhood, my dog, his motorcycle, his rides to Sturgis, his job, my job, my mom and dad, our opinions of the government, our views on religion. Embarrassingly, we've talked about Cleo many more times than we should have. He's never mentioned his parents.

"My father was an alcoholic."

The lines on his face melt and run down inside his collar. A frightened little boy peeks out of his eyes.

"We lost our house. We moved into a two-room apartment. My mom had to start working. This was back when mothers were supposed to stay home. People looked down on us. Called us white trash."

He stops.

"You don't have to tell me."

"I've never talked about these things. Not even when I did my program. It's time to get them out. They're buried but not dead. Every time I look at my son I remember the vow I made the first time I saw him, that I was not going to be like my father."

"Let's go inside. I'll make some coffee.

We sit next to each other on the couch, shoulders and thighs touching. A small table lamp in the corner preens quietly in its circle of yellow light. Shadows blot out the rest of the room.

He stares straight ahead. "I was an only child. My mother got pregnant several times but each time he beat her until she miscarried. 'No more brats!' he'd yell. This was before birth control pills. Remember, I'm an old bastard. 'No more brats. This one's bad enough. I don't even think he's mine.'"

A drop of water trickles from one eye, shines silver in the dark room, dawdles down his cheek.

"Stop." I lay my head on his shoulder. "I don't want to hear any more."

He continues as if he hasn't heard me. "She always stood up for me. Dried my tears when he was through slapping me around. Sometimes he hit me with a belt. For stopping to play on the way home from school. For not eating dinner fast enough. For eating too fast. For getting an A-minus on my spelling test. She wanted to leave him but women didn't do that in those days. It was ''til death do you part' and 'for better or for worse,' no escape. There was no place for us to go, anyway. Her family was all dead."

He pauses. Seconds amble by. The lamp on the table brightens. His voice finally scratches on. "He killed her when I was twelve. She was hiding me behind her to make him stop punching me. He struck her so hard she fell and hit her head on the base of the brass floor lamp. He didn't realize she wasn't moving. Kept screaming at her and kicking her in the face. Blood was oozing from her nose. I slid away and he was too busy to notice. That's the last memory I have of her. Dead on the floor, blood on her face, and my father kicking her. She saved me, but then I was out on the street with nowhere to go. I jumped a train and made my way to New York City. Was befriended by a couple of junkies and did my first hit that same day. Met Marina, David's mother, a few years later and we decided to come to San Francisco. Started mixing crystal meth with the heroin so we could pretend we were normal. Eventually we skipped the heroin and just shot meth."

I take a sip of coffee. His cup is untouched.

"I thought about my mom when I brought David home. How proud she was of my schoolwork, what big dreams she had for me. Always told me how smart I was. She knew I was going to be some kind of scientist. We talked all the time, I told her everything that happened in my life. And she told me every day how much she loved me. She swore we would get away from him. We would make a good life for ourselves without him, somehow."

He turns to me, his usual broad grin puckering his cheeks. "There. Now you know everything about me, my history and my theory. And I know I'm right."

"Make love to me," I whisper.

"No." The heat in his eyes ignites the air between us.

"You don't want to?" A torrent of fire skids down my throat, scorches something in my chest.

"Of course I do. But not now. Not because you're feeling sorry for me."

"I feel close to you. Not sorry."

"It has to be because you love me."

"I do love you. You've given me a life again. I will love you forever."

"That's gratitude. Not love."

"But..."

"Goodnight, Annie. I'll wait until you know what you really want."

"But..."

The door ticks shut behind him and the soles of his shoes tap down the stairs.

I should feel hurt but I don't. I'm elated. I'd locked myself in a tower stronghold after Cleo's terrorizing attempts to love me, and now the tower is unlocked and the drawbridge is down.

I'm not afraid to let a man get close enough to touch me.

I want to be touched.

By Joe.

I can't find him.

I've been hunting for him forever. I get to someone's room and they tell me he just left. The same thing happens everywhere I go.

I know he can't still be mad about the baby. He knows how much I need him. I have to fuck these jerks just to get money for food and half the time they don't even pay me. We get high and we fuck and they disappear and when I come down I'm as hungry as ever. I slip bananas and oranges or a small carton of milk into my pockets at the grocery store but that isn't food. I want a hamburger or a pizza. If you don't pay at McDonald's they call the cops. So my ocean-sized hungry stomach stays hungry. I was never hungry when he was around.

"Hey, Cam Spam! Where's Cleo Deo?"

Tall and gangly as a flagpole, Cam slides his eyes earthward along his narrow nose to peer at me. His slim frame casts a pencil-wide stripe of shadow down the center of my face.

"That's a totally messed-up thing to call me."

"Don't you like dike poems?"

"Spam ain't poems. Spam is unwanted animal parts, intestines, horns, hooves, snouts, ground up and made into a loaf. Ain't that right, Jim?"

He's talking to someone who isn't here. He isn't going to tell me anything.

There's Pete. Hooray! "Pete Sweet!"

"Hi, crazy girl! What do you want?"

"Cleo Deo. Have you seen bean him?"

"Not in a while. I heard he's in a program." He bites into a big red apple and sprays me with crisp fruit-scented droplets. My mouth waters.

"Oh, please tease! Give me a bite kite. I'm so hungry I'm going to start chewing cooing the sidewalk soon tune."

"Okay." He leans over and bites my neck.

"What are you doing mooing? Not that kind mind of bite mite."

"I vant to drink your blud." He bares his teeth, raises his eyebrows and widens his eyes into big white circles that border his lead-colored irises.

"You're sick thick."

"I know. You want some of my apple?"

"I'll let you fuck pluck me for one tiny bite kite of your apple dapple."

"Sylvie sweetie. You know I'm not into women. Here, go buy a happy meal." He hands me a five-dollar bill.

"For reals deals? Thank shank crank you! Find out where square he is, okay play? Which program pogram? I'll go see free him."

"Sure, crazy girl. Sure."

I can't believe I'm sitting here hoping he'll call.

At first I didn't want him around. He begged his way into my life and phoned me all night every night until I was teetering on the precipice overlooking madness. My sleep-bereaved brain wanted me to strangle him.

At some point he slid his street-worn hands into my chest and wrapped them around my heart and my heart got used to his touch. Now I'm sitting here like a lovesick fifteen-year-old girl waiting for the phone to ring.

They finally gave in and started him on some kind of medicine. He was driving everyone insane. Awake all night, unable to pay attention. Always interrupting. Couldn't stay focused.

I don't know what's wrong with him.

He's not stupid.

I am. Why did I let myself get so involved? I like being alone. I can forget I'm in a wheelchair. If I'm not with someone whose feet are carrying them around the way they're supposed to, I don't think about the unyielding pressure of the sidewalk when I step on it, the sun-drenched brown earth with tickling shoots of new grass under my bare feet in the spring.

After the accident I quit my job. I couldn't go back to the working world and suffocate in the pity of my co-workers as I rammed my black leather chariot with the big silver wheels into their desks. I was twenty-nine, too young to be stuck in one of those. And Rosa, my girlfriend. She left me. I can't let myself think about that, how it is to be with a woman. It will never happen again, so why make myself miserable?

I wish he'd hurry up and call. He's been there four weeks and now he's allowed to have visitors on Sundays. He's supposed to let me know when to come over.

I haven't seen him since he went into his program, and I barely know him. But we've spent so much time on the phone I feel as if he's my best friend. A crazy friend, that's for sure. Whines and complains or else he's completely giddy. But he's the only person I've really talked to in years.

I need to get out more.

W e walk from the Opera House to his car. Wispy clouds
scuttle across the dark gray sky above Van Ness Avenue,
obscuring stars dimmed by city lights.

"What a wonderful opera! The costumes were breathtaking."
We hold hands. It's been a long time since I've been this happy.
Joe makes me feel as if I can do anything. My head is crowded with
plans: I'm going to write a novel. I'm going to go back to school
and get a teaching certificate. Maybe a certificate in drug coun-
seling, too, so I can do groups for all the women addicts. So I can
teach them to keep walking.

As we approach the car a shadow runs up to him, a shadow as
tall as he is with spiked green hair. I know that shadow.

She throws her arms around him. "Joe Snow!"

"Hey, Sylvie." He gently disengages her arms from his body
and steps away from her.

"It's been too long wrong. Is this your lady sadie now cow?"

"What do you want?"

"Hungry dungaree, man. I'm really steely hungry. I already
tried cried to eat my shoes news."

I glance at her feet. Shoeless and wrapped in a blanket of dirt. One great toe is purple and swollen; I'll bet she stubbed it.

"What happened to your room and your job?"

"Oh, you know blow." She shrugs. "Come on, I'll fuck luck you spew for a hamburger, Joe Snow."

"Don't talk that way, Sylvie." He hands her ten dollars. "Take this."

"I'll still fuck stuck you. Like we used juice to. Remember December?" She leers at me and prances off.

"I know her," I gasp. Electric current jolts my heart out of my chest, dangles it in the air an inch beyond my reach. "She's the one..."

He opens the car door for me and I slide onto the seat. "Which one?"

"The one...the..." My eyes flood. "She was in my house. With Cleo. She...He left me for her."

"She's a train wreck, Annie. From what you've told me about him, they're a perfect match."

"And you..."

"Never. She's not my type."

My hands wobble and my feet are ice cubes clattering inside shoes suddenly two sizes too big.

"You..." She said she fucked him. "I'm not the only woman in your life, am I?" My voice booms. I hear the ugliness behind the words but I can't stop them.

"You are now. It's been more than twenty-five years since David's mother took off. I've had girlfriends."

"You've never told me about them."

"They didn't mean anything to me."

"And was she one of them?"

"She was in a residential drug program and I was one of the counselors."

"And you, and you...fucked her." I have never said that word to another human being. It spurts out of my mouth and slaps him in the face.

"I did not." His voice doesn't get louder. It shrinks. It slips out in a fine pencil line, and his eyes blacken into a smoldering pile of charcoal.

"She said you did."

"She's a liar."

"She said Cleo did, and it was true." I am huffing out great gusts of steam that fill the front seat. "You still haven't made love to me. You must have someone else."

"Get out of the car."

"What?"

"Get out."

"I will not get out," I yell.

"This is unnecessary. I won't have this drama in my life. Been there, done that, and I'm not going back there. Ever." He comes around to my side of the car and pulls me out. "I don't date married women."

"I'm not married. I divorced the damn bastard." I'm standing on the sidewalk shrieking.

"Then why are we arguing about him? When you've really divorced him let me know. I like you a lot." He stalks back to the driver's side and the car roars away.

I freeze, unable to raise a hand or twitch an eyelid. My voice has shut off. A single sob bubbles out of my mouth and floats off into the night.

I see her lanky silhouette lounging against a wall, watching. Grime-covered feet on the same sidewalk as mine. She saunters over to me.

"Hey, don't take it so hard card. Dudes crudes are all jerks perks."

I run down the street to get away from her. I hoist my skirt to my knees so I can run faster. My black suede pumps fall off and I leave them behind. I dash the few blocks to Market Street and my thigh muscles scream and my lungs convulse as they cry out for more air. I plunge down the steps to the BART and get on the first arriving train.

I sit in the back seat of the last car. I don't know where the train is going. I don't care.

I s this what I've become? A drama queen? A woman so filled with fear that she has tantrums in public?

I ride the subway until it shuts down for the night. I get off at the last stop. The station sign reads Fremont. I'm in Fremont and it's twelve-thirty in the morning. A taxi back to San Francisco will cost a hundred dollars.

I walk out of the station and sit on a bench.

August nights in the South Bay are warm. I pull up my legs and rest my forehead on my knees. My stockings hang in shreds. My feet are filthy and one great toe is red and throbbing: I stubbed it tearing down the stairs to the train. My ankle-length velvet skirt wraps itself around my legs and keeps out the night air.

I don't understand. I was doing fine. I rarely think about Cleo. Joe is the only one in my mind when I'm awake and he dominates my dreams at night.

Even though he still hasn't made love to me.

Maybe he knew this was coming.

"That goddam bitch!" I mutter to my knees.

I need to go to church. I no longer talk like a Christian and I don't act like one. I act like Cleo, a grown-up baby.

Is it such a thin line between right and wrong, good and bad? I thought there was a chasm the size of the Grand Canyon between us, with me on the good side and Cleo on the other one. One long skinny girl closed up that chasm and put us on the same side. The bad one.

And I didn't use drugs to get there. I did it all on my own.

Then who is the better person?

And I thought I had something to teach the addicts. How to be strong. How to rise above life's miseries.

What a joke. I'm not strong and I haven't risen above anything.

Enamored of the moment is all I was, flattering myself because of the attention Joe gave me. He made me feel bigger than life.

Just because I'm not hooked on a chemical doesn't mean I'm better than anyone who is.

Those women could probably teach me a thing or two.

Take that girl Sylvie.

She's one smooth cookie, let me tell you. Wraps everyone around her fingers, including me. Effortlessly.

And me? An arrogant bitch.

Nothing more, nothing less.

Arrogant.

Why didn't I see it before?

W ow. I didn't have to do that. I already took Cleo away from
her and I don't want Joe. He's too old and he expects people to behave. Not like Cleo who doesn't care what you do as long
as you come back to him. I could've let her be. But it was too easy.
She fell--floomp!--just like that. The look on her face! One second she's a snobby rich bitch with her fancy clothes and diamond
earrings, hanging on Joe's arm with her nose in the sky as if she
doesn't breathe the same air I do, and the next second she's all by
herself and he's gone. Dumped her. And I did it. Boy, I'm good!

I almost feel bad for her.

"You look good, Cleo. I hardly recognize you."

We're munching on chips and guzzling sodas on the patio behind the big Victorian that houses his inpatient rehab program. It's a bright August day. The sky is clear blue with no hint of fog. Sparrows flit among the trees that edge the patio and some perch on branches and twitter, ignoring us. Pigeons hobble around our feet, their heads bobbing and their eyes to the ground as they hunt for crumbs.

"You saying I used to look bad?"

"You had a worm stuck in your mouth the first time I saw you."

"You're shitting me."

"A worm."

"Man!" He crunches on a mouthful of chips. "That dope they give me it's really shit. You know that? I'm in a drug program and they're forcing shit down my throat." He throws his head back and bays.

"You're kidding."

"Yeah man. But it's a tiny dose. I used to shoot six or seven grams a day if I could get it. This shit's only a couple milligrams.

But I can think now. Listen to this: e=mc squared. ab + cd = abcd. And how about this: Antidisestablishmentarianism. I can spell it too: a-n-t-i-d-"

"Stop!"

"i-s-e-s-"

"Cleo!"

"You don't want to hear me spell it?"

"No! You're doing great, but that kind of stuff won't get you far. What are you going to do with the rest of your life?"

"Get a job."

"Okay. Maybe I can help. What can you do?"

"I can talk anyone into buying anything. I'm a salesman. Or some people'd call me a conman. Depends on how you look at it." He bays again.

"You want to be a salesman? You mean a car salesman, or a door-to-door salesman?"

"That sounds like a drag man."

"It sure does. What else can you do? What did you dream of doing when you were a kid?"

"Porn star."

"You're serious."

"Sure. I look like a movie star and I like sex. Sounds like a great job to me." He snickers.

"What about going to school?"

"School? Like college?"

"Or a trade school. Learn how to do something you can get paid for."

"Man I hated school. I was always in trouble. Never graduated. Don't even gotta GED. I ain't going back there. Come on. Let me show you around. You're making my brain jump through hoops. I just learned how to think a couple days ago. Ixnay on the estionsquay okay?"

He takes off for the ramp that leads to the back door, streaking ahead of me on his one foot and his crutch. I wheel after him as fast as I can.

The beard is gone, the clothes are new. Socks are bleach-white. Gym shoe without a fleck of dirt. Head shaved, makes his eyes pop like lighthouse beacons. He looks good. But he's not. Not yet.

Maybe he'll never be good.

‌⚒‌

Monday morning my shoes gouge tracks in the sidewalk as I drag myself to the library. I sit at my desk, motionless as a sack of flour. I shouldn't have come in. I can't face this day. I close my eyes against the light flooding through the windows.

"Annie?"

I pretend I don't hear.

"Annie, what are you doing here?"

I open my eyes. It's Kevin, my assistant. "What do you mean?"

"You're on vacation. Did you forget?"

"Vacation?" I'd taken two weeks off to go to Sturgis. I was going to ride behind Joe on his Harley all the way to South Dakota. I was going to sleep in his arms in motel rooms on the way, sleep with him in his sleeping bag in a tent in a campground in Sturgis. Make love to him until we couldn't remember where we were. That's what I'd planned.

I snag my lower lip in my teeth, nostrils flaring, eyes fogging up.

"Did you two have a quarrel?"

"It was my fault. I was an idiot." I stand up. "I guess I'll go home. I'll see you in two weeks." My face is a block of wood and it splinters when I try to smile.

"Let's get coffee. I have time. You need to talk."

Kevin is in his fifties. Efficient, intelligent, polite. Always perfectly dressed, no fads, no ostentatious jewelry, his clothes immaculate. He shows up early every morning, quickly and quietly does everything I ask of him, and doesn't go home until he's seen me to my car at the end of the day. I don't know anything else about him.

"I don't want to burden you."

"You think I don't know anything about love."

"Do you?"

"I've been with the love of my life for thirty years. Does that count?"

"You have? You never mention her. You never bring her to our Christmas parties. Do you have children?"

We are tucked into a corner in a coffee shop a block from the library. Joe and I have been here a hundred times.

"Him. Not her. Him."

"You're gay?"

"Does that bother you?"

Bother me? I remember the beautifully dressed pair of women---hats, gloves, tailored suits---who sat indecently close to each other in an empty pew at the back of the church one Sunday. The other members of the congregation mouthed silent comments to each other, and there was a faint hesitation in Pastor Brown's hand as he offered it to each of them after the service. They never came back, even though nothing was said openly and never has been in that church. But the Pastor's hesitation trembles in me as I look at Kevin's benign face. I shake it off. Surely someone who's as kind and gentle and hardworking as Kevin would rate higher in God's eyes than someone like Cleo, who was a woman's husband and was heartily embraced by the church even though his reality was brutal and twisted. I don't care who Kevin loves. My church couldn't save me from Cleo. Why should I let it tell me who to like?

"No." I smile my biggest smile at him. "But I had no idea."

"Because I don't drool over the pretty boys who come to the library? Because you've never seen me in leather chaps at the Folsom Street Fair? Never heard me sing along with Cher?" He chuckles as he dribbles milk into his coffee.

"That's a stereotype. I know it doesn't fit everyone. I never thought about it."

"How many years have we worked together?"

"Ten? More? Now I'm embarrassed. I've known you that long and I don't even know you, do I? Is it my fault?"

"Not entirely. I learned early on to keep my private life and my public life separate."

"Why are you opening up to me? I don't deserve it. I've treated you as if you were my servant. A face. Not a person." This has been a horrible week. First I am abruptly made aware that I behave no better than Cleo, and now I am gazing in a figurative mirror and seeing an arrogant self-centered Christian who treats the people around her as if they were furniture. I don't think the Bible teaches us to treat anyone like that, gay or straight or addicted or anyone. I want to slide under the table and evaporate. How can I call myself a Christian? Do I do anything Christians are supposed to do? I'm the most self-absorbed person I know.

"Annie! Did you hear me?"

"No. I'm feeling sorry for myself. Please say it again." The mirror fades and my eyes return to him, begging his softly furrowed face behind the rectangular wire-rimmed glasses to pin me to this space and not let me plummet into my abyss of self-pity.

"I know you love him."

"But I don't trust him."

"Did he do something? We men can be stupid."

"He didn't do anything. But my ex did."

"Ah, a sore spot on your heart. A wound. Is it scar tissue? Or is it an abscess that will heal if you open it up?"

"I don't know what it is. I didn't know it was there. I'm still numb from finding it. We had a big fight." I dab at my eyes with my napkin.

"Have you called him?"

"I'm too ashamed."

"And he hasn't called you?"

"He said to let him know when I'm divorced. I don't know what he means. I am divorced. For two years now."

"But you're still carrying your ex around with you. Some people cling to their bad memories, Annie. They make them the focal point of their lives. You have to let them go."

"How? How do I forget all the things he did to me?"

"You love Joe, don't you?"

"I do. So much."

The early morning coffeehouse babble shelters us from the prying ears of the customers seated nearby. He slowly sips his coffee. "When Mark and I had been together about a year I had a brief fling with a friend of his." His eyes widen. "That surprises you? I used to be a real hunk. Ripped. Thick black hair. Lots of guys were after me."

My eyes dissect him, searching for the hunk imbedded in his puckered slightly flabby face and receding gray hairline.

"Anyway, this friend told Mark. I think I would've told him myself in time, but he told him while it was still going on. I've never forgotten the look on his face when he confronted me. He wasn't angry. But the pain. His eyes." He stares at the wallpaper behind me, a pink tinge edging his eyelids. "It crushed him. I had to leave. I couldn't bear to see what I'd done to him, and for no other reason than a few moments' illicit excitement."

"But you're together now?"

"He's a better man than I am. We couldn't stand to be apart, and he eventually accepted my apology and took me back. And he's never said a word about it. If I'm late, he greets me with a smile. If I forget to call, if I go somewhere with a friend---not a syllable. If he suspects anything, he doesn't say it."

"Have you done anything?"

"I learned my lesson. Being an adult means you honor your partner. You never do something that will hurt them."

"But how did he...?"

"I think it was a leap of faith. He made up his mind when he took me back that he would do everything he could to make this work. He knew that accusations and jealousy take root and spread until they strangle every relationship that allows them in. He refused to give them a toehold in ours." He checks his watch. "I'm late."

"This has to be the first time in ten years."

"Enjoy your vacation, Annie. I hope I helped." He kisses my cheek and rushes out the door.

My fingers touch the spot he kissed.

Maybe there is hope for me.

M y bare feet crunch on cold wet sand as I drift on Ocean Beach, supposedly watching the sun go down but actually so lost in my thoughts that the world around me is a dusky smudge. A breeze buffets the sodden gritty hem of my skirt, scraping it against my ankles. When the horizon turns dark blue I become aware that it is night.

I'm tired of walking but I don't want to go home. It's been a week since our fight. I know he's in Sturgis now with thousands of other bikers. I feel like I'm the left half of my body and he's the right half. My heart is pumping blood through cut arteries out into the sand. I can only take half-breaths. My eyes see only his empty silhouette. Everything else is a blur.

I never missed Cleo this way.

I'm not going to let him ruin the rest of my life. Joe is a good man and he cares about me. I want to be with him.

But I don't know how to trust him. Or anyone.

I trusted Cleo and it was a mistake.

Now I'm standing at a crossroads. All paths except the one I've already walked lead into a dense mist, dripping black tree branches poking through the gloom to impale me. I need to see what lies ahead of me, and I can't. How do I decide which path to take? Joe? Or someone else, whoever that may be? Or no one.

The beach sinks beneath the incoming tide. Waves rush over my feet. When the waves rejoin the ocean they leave behind lacy little bubbles. Lacy bubbles softly kissing my toes.

How come it's always worse at night? That tiny bit of shit they give me keeps those monsters stuck in the closet and my head's clear and I can think now but at night my mind gets stuck. It gets focused and it stays focused and it fucks me all night long. In the daytime I'm a TV remote and I can choose which shows I want to watch but once the night creeps in and the stars start blinking I get stuck on one channel and I can't change it. Last night it was my dad. All night long he stood in front of me. Didn't say he was sorry didn't say a fucking word. Just stood there holding his hands out like he was going to haul me out of bed and take me somewhere. Where? Where you going to take me Dad? You going to fuck me again? Lock me up in a closet? Kick me out in the snow? Hah this is San Francisco it don't snow here. I still don't like her. At least she feeds me when I come see you. That was years ago I only been back once since I was ten. Went to see you when I was twenty-five. I think. I guess she's good to you huh Dad? That's what's important. She's good to you. I don't gotta live with her so it don't matter if she don't like me. That was last night. Tonight it's my Annie. How come she left me? I tried so hard to be good to her. I went to work for her. I never worked a day in my whole life before and I gotta real job for her. Cuz I love her don't she get that? I sleep a little bit and when I wake up she's right next to my bed and that scent of flowers that always comes off her skin wraps me up like a blanket and she's smiling at me. Sun's gleaming in back of her red hair and it makes her look like a sunset over the ocean green eyes and skin like white sandy beaches. I get crazy when I get high. So I gotta stop getting high. Five weeks clean. Every day's a belly full of fire and the fire's a shroud wrapping around me and burning me to ashes cuz I want to get high so fucking bad. Can't think of nothing else. Sit in group and can't think of nothing but getting high going over to Pete's and getting some shit from him and getting high. And here she is smiling at me. Her smile's a big bucket of ice water. It puts the fire out and instead of thinking of shit I think of her. Think of those tits as big as full moons shining down on me big enough to hide me from those monsters and when I'm fucking her I'm not even on this planet no more I'm in heaven somewhere. Maybe that's where God is. Maybe He sent my Annie to take me to heaven. I sure don't deserve her. "What did you see in me Annie?" I ask her even though I know she ain't real and she ain't going to say a word. "I never done nothing good in my whole life. You think you were going to make something out of me? I was the kid who got expelled from kindergarten did I ever tell you about that? Put ink in the fish tank and all the fish died. I thought they were going to turn black but they all died and I got expelled. I never been nothing but a piece of shit. And you were smart and sexy and had a lot of money and there wasn't nothing you needed from me. You already had it all. You made me feel like I was nothing and now you're here and I love you so much but I'm just a piece of shit Annie." Her hands unbutton her blouse and take it off and unfasten her bra and let those sexy big tits loose and they say "Bury your face in us Cleo we're going to hide you." Oh man the shower gotta go take a shower. I burn like hell from wanting shit and my Annie sets me on fire too. How am I going to make it through this?

"Hi, Judy."

"Annie? Is that you? Gene, Annie's on the phone! Are you all right? Is that bastard gone? So you can talk? I'm so glad you called!"

Her voice vibrates in my ear.

"Yes," I say. I don't know which question I'm answering. They're all "yes" questions.

"How are you? I called you so many times but you never called back. I figured he was giving you a hard time. But it helped us, can you believe it? My Suzy was dating a kid—real bad news but would she listen to me? Of course not. The kid was into pot and ecstasy and everything else---Suzy wasn't, she told him she didn't like that stuff and he never made her use any of it but she was there when he was doing it and I was afraid she would get busted because of him. My daughter in prison at the age of fifteen. I was so worried. Every time she went out with him I paced the house until she came home. I wore out the carpet, we had to get a new one. And I couldn't forbid her, you know, she has to learn to make the right choices herself, not always expect me to make her decisions. Anyway, after that bastard came over that night and dragged you out of here, screaming the way he was and threatening us, Suzy broke up with the kid. Broke it off all on her own. I was so proud of her. She said now that she'd seen how bad drugs were she wasn't going to date anyone who was even curious about them. She's going to be a freshman this fall at UC Santa Barbara. Wants to be a marine biologist. But how are you? I panicked when we didn't hear from you. I didn't know if I should call the police or what."

"I didn't want to get you involved. I thought he might go back to your house and do something we'd all regret, so I stayed away." I'd cut myself off from my friends. He didn't want me to see or call them. He was afraid I would leave him for one of their husbands. I was afraid that if I got in touch with them he'd go to their homes or their jobs and hurt them. I had to let go of them. When Cleo ruled my world it shrank to the size of a coffin. He and I were the only people in that cramped space, inhaling each other's second-hand air, sloughing off each other's skin. Work and church became places where I hid behind a plastic smile and hoped no one would notice the fear in my eyes. As much as I hated to be at home with him, it was better than being out in the world wearing a mask with rosy cheeks and red upturned lips, terrified that the next gust of wind would blow it off and send it bouncing down the street, exposing me.

"Is he in jail now? It's been three years. Gosh, has it been that long? Suzy was a sophomore in high school then."

"I divorced him two years ago."

"Good for you! I know that wasn't easy. I know you wanted to hold on to the marriage, especially after that first jerk you married. But it's for the best, you'll see. Someone really nice will come along and you'll forget all about him. Or is there someone already? You're such a knock-out. I would think men would be falling all over you, honey."

"I have a difficult time with that."

"Why? Too many to choose from? Can't make up your mind?"

"I think I've lost the ability to trust."

"Now Annie, not all men are like him. There are good men out there all over the place. Look at my Gene. He's the sweetest, gentlest man you could ever meet. Sits home with me every evening, helps with the housework, never loses his temper. Won't even kill a fly or a spider, he just shooshes them out the door."

"He's an alcoholic."

"He drinks a little too much. But he goes to sleep when he drinks. He's not one ofthose holy terrors who scream and fight. We've been married twenty-three years and he's never raised a hand to me. Never. You have to choose your battles, Annie, honey. What do you want? A man who drinks a little but worships the ground you walk on or a man who is sober but treats you like a slave? You have to figure it out. You can't have everything. By the way, we're having a birthday party for Suzy. Her birthday's in September but she'll be in Santa Barbara then, so we're having her party before she leaves. Why don't you come? She's always saying how much she misses her Aunt Annie. You dropped out of our lives and left a big hole, honey. A crater. We've got to get together and fill it up, we've got so much to catch up on. The party's this Saturday. Come over any time and we can talk, maybe you can help me get things ready. We used to do everything together, remember? Parties, barbeques, picnics on the beach. The whole gang of us, Gene, and Mary and her husband, and Midge and Debbie the twins. We've been friends since high school, more than twenty-five years. Can you believe it? I've missed you so much."

"I can't come this Saturday. I have a prior commitment. But tell Suzy I love her and I'll call her later."

I hang up, ears buzzing from her high-pitched chatter, and then I realize: I lied to her. I'm not doing a thing on Saturday except feeling sorry for myself. I couldn't bear the thought of listening to her blabber for a whole day, so I lied.

Is this Cleo acting in my life again? Am I ever going to be myself? I never lie. Not to anyone. Not in my entire life. The kids in elementary school called me Georgia Washington because I never lied.

Now I'm a liar. Like Cleo.

I could've said "I don't feel up to it," but instead I lied. It was that easy.

So evil infects the people around it, chips away at their hearts the way a cancer chips away at a body. Shows up in their character when they least expect it.

Then how do we spread good?

Joe could help me figure this out, but there is a tree flourishing inside me with an enormous pitted trunk and sturdy leafy branches dotted with bunches of purple sour-smelling fear flowers. I can't get past it.

Cleo planted that tree, and it won't let Joe in.

I have to find a way to uproot it.

And she's wrong.
I don't have to decide which evil I want to live with. I don't believe that for a minute.

I want someone who is real. Like me. I am what I am. I'm not hiding wickedness behind a smile.

There have to be men who are like that.

They can't all repay your love by making an omelet of your sanity.

I know she's wrong.

I think my parents sheltered me too much.

As my breasts grew from the size of grapes to the size of lemons and then grapefruits, the necklines on the blouses I was allowed to wear climbed up my chest to my chin.

My dad, my mentor, my guide, my protector, gentle as a baby sparrow, encouraged me to wear cardigans over my blouses.

According to my mom, he had been wild as a teen, disrespectful, rambunctious, disregardful of all rules—school's, Grandma and Grandpa's, God's. Mom tamed him.

So I wore my high-necked blouses and my cardigans to hide my mushrooming bosom. Went to church and prayed as I was taught, followed the Ten Commandments to the best of my teen-aged ability. I made up for the lack of excitement in my life with books. I read fairytales, romance novels, *Wuthering Heights, Little Women, Jane Eyre*. I dreamed of finding my own true love who would whisk me off to his mansion and we would be oh so happy. He would be handsome, smart, kind. Maybe a bit wild: I could tame him the way Mom had tamed Dad. And our love would last forever.

My parents never told me those books weren't true. Maybe they didn't understand how much I had incorporated them into my aspirations.

They didn't allow me to date. All through high school I hung out with my girlfriends, staring at the cute guys and giggling behind fisted fingers, blushing and running away if one of them approached. Mom arranged a date for the senior prom, a neighbor boy. Kent. Had his own car. Dad followed us in his blue Dodge, parked outside the gymnasium, which had been turned into a fairyland for the prom, and waited. Followed us home. I was an obedient Christian girl and I knew he did the right thing. Lips were something boys wanted to kiss and breasts were things they wanted to touch. I knew they weren't supposed to. I didn't know why. The girls at school told wild tales that I didn't believe, and there were those "bad" girls who did things that I didn't believe, either. "Trust me, honey," Mom said. "We know what's best for you."

Rebellion came when I moved away to college. It broke out in my clothes: mid-thigh flouncy skirts, skimpy lace underwear, stiletto heels, flashing collar-bone length earrings, blouses flaunting many inches of non-Christian cleavage.

I sneaked a couple cold kisses with a boy in English Lit but the fear of having to explain them to my parents and the knowledge that he wasn't my true love, he was just a fellow student, made me stop. Ingrained as I was with my parents' standards of chastity and my own fairy-tale inspired dreams, I didn't allow him or anyone to lay a finger on my perfectly shaped huge breasts, but I made sure everyone knew that they were bigger and better than any other breasts on campus.

So when the man who would become my first husband walked into the library that day and ran his fingertips over the soft skin peeking out of my low-cut neckline, my body woke up with a scream and electricity surged through places I hadn't known were wired. I was sure my true love had found me.

I think they sheltered me altogether too much.

M y hands are corpses in my lap. I stare at the computer screen but I don't see it. A sigh starts above the line between life and death in my lower back and shudders its way up my spine, plops out of my mouth and falls to the keyboard.

My living room walls crept closer during the night and the room is now the size of an office cubicle. Four bare walls support dusty bookcases. The sofa is black leather. The carpet is gray. The entertainment center and the computer table are coated with dust. When I open the dusty blinds the sunlight trying to make its way through the unwashed windows is gray.

I pick up my weights. I have to keep these arms strong. I have to be able to get away from any idiot who thinks I'm easy prey when I'm out there on the street.

I put the weights down.

A tidal wave of gray floods my nose and mouth. It will drown me if I don't get out of here.

I escape out the door and roll across the street to the bus stop.

The September sky is a faded blue. A few tufts of cloud glide across it, backlit by the sun. I inhale. Soft warm air gushes into my lungs.

I was fine. Absolutely fine. I loved my life. Had my own company, my own cozy little apartment. Nobody to waste my time. No one to think of me as a pathetic cripple. Then he came along and I just had to let him in. For my mother's sake. And you're gone, Mama. I love you dearly but you're gone so stop messing with my life. I was doing fine.

The bus pulls up. The five or six people at the stop wait patiently for the wheelchair ramp to lower and unfold. My cheeks burn. After ten years of doing this I still can't stand it. I wasn't always like this, I want to tell them as they shift their feet and studiously look the other way. I used to walk the same as you do. But I glue my eyes to the ramp and my mouth stays shut.

I get off at Pier 39.

Tourists ripple in suffocating throngs around me, siphon my breath into their own hungry noses, scarf me down and upchuck me on the other side of the street.

Why on earth did I pick the pier?

Sea gulls circle above me with an occasional squawk. Two street performers, one painted gold, one painted silver, jerk to a techno song blaring from a boombox at their feet. People drop dollar bills into a can next to the boombox.

The sun covers me like an umbrella. People chatter. People laugh.

I propel away from the throngs and across a parking lot and stop next to the water, its aquarium-reek prickling my nostrils.

"Here, bro, take my fries. I don't want them." A skinny teenager in grungy jeans and a faded tee shirt holds out a bag of French fries.

"Sure, thanks."

The kid sits down on the curb next to me, a cheeseburger in his hands. He takes a bite. "I love these birds," he says.

"Yeah?" I don't want to take food from this boy who obviously needs it, but I don't want to hurt his feelings by turning him down. I cram a couple fries in my mouth.

"Yeah. Watch this." He tosses a chunk of bun on the ground. Twenty gulls screech through the air to squabble over it. "That's hella cool."

I throw a fry. More birds join the fracas. The kid laughs. I smile.

"I never seen you here before, bro. You new in town?"

"No. I have my own apartment. I don't get out very often."

"This is a good day to get out. No fog. That fog's hella cold. Eats into your bones, 'specially at night."

"Don't you have a place to stay?"

"Nah. I'm from Portland. Came down here with my girl. Her stepdad got her pregnant and she had to get away."

"Is she okay?"

"Yeah, they found a group home for her and they're gonna help her when she has the baby. I'm gonna go see her later. We gotta figure out what we're gonna do. I mean, she's fine, they're gonna take care of everything. But I gotta go back to school. I see that real clear. No school means I'll be out here panhandling forever. When I'm old like you I'll still be panhandling. That ain't what I want."

"Good for you." Old like me?

"Hey, bro, look at that babe. She's got her eye on you."

I look where he's pointing. A gorgeous woman in her mid-twenties smiles at me. The breeze puffs out her shoulder-length black hair, and shimmering pink lipstick draws my wondering gaze to her heart-shaped full lips. Sunglasses hide her eyes. She is surrounded by a group of women decked out in Capri pants and tank tops in various colors, taking pictures with cell phones: tourists. "I don't think so." Could it be? She's smiling at me, the dude in the wheelchair?

"Look, bro, here she comes."

She threads her way through the crowd, leaving the other women aiming their cell phones at sea gulls and cable cars.

She floats. She's not real. She's an angel. I think I love her.

"Hi there." A soft husky voice. An alto song. A tinge of southern drawl.

"Hi," I answer, and then I see that she's smiling at the kid. Not at me.

"Hi there," she repeats, taking off her sunglasses and staring into his eyes, her irises the steel gray color of the ocean on a stormy day.

"Hi," he answers.

"You're a cutie."

"I...I guess so, Ma'am."

She giggles and I hear harp strings being plucked.

"Can you do me a teeny weeny little favor?"

"Sure."

"Will you have sex with me?"

"Huh?"

"I'll pay you. We're here from a little hick town in Alabama and this is our first time in California. We came here to have fun. So I want to have sex with a California cutie like you."

I can't believe my ears.

"Twenty dollars. Is that enough?"

"I...sure."

"And we're going to take pictures and email them home. Is that okay with you?"

"Take pictures? Can't you ask somebody else?"

"But you're so cute! We aren't going to post them on line, I promise. Do you want more money? How about twenty-five? No? Okay, fifty. I'll pay you fifty dollars. But it has to be on the beach with the Golden Gate Bridge in the background. Okay?"

"Fifty dollars?"

"Please say yes. It means a lot to me."

"Okay." He looks at me and rolls his eyes. "That's enough to get me home."

"Use a condom," I mutter to no one as they are joined by the rest of her chirping friends, all of whom ignore me.

Disgust gags me. Not for the kid: he's got his ticket home. For me. I actually thought she was interested in me, the cripple. After ten years I still haven't learned.

This is why I never go anywhere.

And all this God crap. Well no they ain't calling Him God.
They're calling Him a higher power. I don't get it. I can't
believe in nothing I can't see.

"What about love?" Big shot Wayne with all his starched white
shirts and his fancy ties like he's better than the rest of us. How
many DUI's he's got? Ten!

"I can see love," I answer.

"No, you can't."

"Yes I can. It's people holding hands. Kissing. Having sex."

"That's not love, Cleo," Jeff says. "That's an expression of love.
It's not actual love."

"It's the same thing to me." Jeff's the intellectual of the group.
He's a writer. His room's full of books stacked all over the floor
and he pounds away on his laptop all day long. Ain't published
nothing in years. He's a speed freak same as me. Lost his wife and
lost his kids too ain't seen them since they were babies. They're
all grown up now. Had a mansion and a fancy car. Stuck a needle
in his arm and forgot about them. And the fucker thinks he's got
something to say to me.

"But, man, it was such a relief," Frankie cuts in his face all covered with swastika tats he got on a month-long shit binge, "to finally figure out that I'm not responsible for it all. I don't have to worry about traffic lights taking forever to change, or the fog hanging around too long. I don't have to stop the drug trade across the border and it's not my job to snitch on all the dealers and get them locked up. I only have to worry about what I do. God can take care of the rest. Or the police. Maybe we could call them a higher power."

The guys screech at him. "No way!" "Those scumbags!" "The cops?"

"I guess I could believe in something that makes the sun come up and go back down," I say. "But don't call it God. My wife preaches about God all the time and it makes me crazy. God don't like it if you do that she says. Or you make God angry when you say that. I want to knock her teeth down her throat when she gets going with all that crap."

"She really says that?" Frankie asks.

"She prays every morning. Reads from a little book of daily prayers. And she gets this look on her face. Even if she don't say it I hear it. I know what she's thinking."

"Is she in here?" Jeff.

"Do you see her?" I retort.

"My point exactly. Whatever her manner of belief and her way of trying to get you to believe, she's not here and you are. That should tell you something."

"I don't see you down on your knees praying."

"I pray. Not on my knees but in my heart. I thank God every morning that I'm still alive and I'm still clean."

How am I going to pray to something I don't believe in? Maybe I ought to pray to the sun every morning when it crawls over the horizon. I gotta get up so fucking early when I got kitchen duty I could get down on my knees and kiss the linoleum in its honor if I wanted to. If I pray to the sun is it going to bring my Annie back? It sure as fuck ain't. The only thing that's going bring her back is if she sees me clean and working.

At four in the morning his eyes snap open. The alarm is set for six but at four his eyes are peering through the soldier-shaped shadows standing guard throughout the sleeping house.

Gotta make sure the kitchen's still clean. Latrice the cook she's a great lady. Five kids and her old man's a disabled Desert Storm vet. She smiles and laughs all the time like she don't gotta worry in the world. Cooks like an angel I swear we eat the food of the gods in this place.

He sneaks noiselessly down the stairs, painstakingly choosing the spots to place his foot and his crutch. Mumbles "Careful careful" under his breath. I know where all the squeaky steps are can't wake nobody up.

The kitchen is silent. A night light glows in one corner. Everything is neatly put away. No one is there.

He hobbles back upstairs.

He can still hear the guys chatting and laughing as they make themselves snacks.

Those guys don't give a crap about no one but themselves I always gotta clean up after them. Latrice don't need to start her day with a kitchen full of crumbs and mustard stains, knives and sticky plates and cups all piled up in the sink.

At six the alarm thuds his restless foot to the floor. He hops to the shower without the crutch. His single leg is as strong and sturdy as an oak tree.

Scalding water blasts his body for five minutes. He flicks a towel across his nakedness, hops into his clothes with still-wet skin. "Fucker," he mutters, wrestling with his jeans to pull them up his damp leg.

A heap of white towel catches his eye from the bathroom as he rushes out his door. I'll pick the fucking thing up later gotta go to work now.

The polished wooden banister carries him to the ground floor. His foot gallops off to the kitchen, pulling him and the crutch along with it.

The kitchen is spotless. It's quarter after six.

Gotta fill the big pot with water and get the fucker boiling.

Latrice comes in as he's getting out the silverware. She kisses him on the cheek.

"Hi, baby. You always on time. I sure do appreciate it." She hangs her sweater in the broom closet. "You get any sleep?"

"Yeah a little but I wanted to get everything all set up for you."

"You a sweet man, Cleo."

"Sometimes I guess."

"What you mean 'you guess?'" She stirs oatmeal into the boiling water.

"I done things that weren't so sweet. To my wife."

Steam frosts the kitchen windows.

"We having French toast today," she says. "Can you get me four loaves of bread? And a dozen eggs. I need some flour, too. Thanks, baby."

"I love my wife Latrice. I swear I do. I don't know how to make it up to her."

"Maybe you can't."

"I gotta."

"They's things you don't never do if you love someone. Things that gonna shoot love in the head and make it die."

"But you said I was sweet."

"You is. But maybe sometimes you think sweet ain't a good thing to be. If you ain't sure what you is, ain't nobody else sure, neither."

"There's times I thought I was a goddam motherfucker and I was proud of it."

"That's what I'm saying, baby. We all got bad in us and we all got good and we gotta figure out which one we wanna be."

Eggs crack like a cap gun on the rim of the bowl.

"You believe in God Latrice?"

"He believe in me. And I get down on my knees every day and thank Him for that."

"But you gotta hard life."

"I got everything I need. I don't want no other kind a life. Got my beautiful babies, I got a son in college, you know that? He gonna be a teacher. I got my sweet man and he try all the time to be more sweeter. Got my job. Got all you guys to make me feel needed. What you think I don't got?"

"A lot of money. Time to rest. A husband who can go to work so you don't gotta. And a good car." She rides the bus to work.

"Hmm." The griddle hisses as she fries the bread. "Never thought about it. If I need them things God gonna get them for me. Is the guys up? This food's ready for the table. You take this out there and ring the bell, okay, baby?"

I do pretty good with one leg. Figured out how to squeeze the crutch in my armpit and carry all the food with both my hands. Ain't dropped nothing yet.

After he rings the meal bell the guys march in and sit in their assigned seats. Wayne, their elected chairman, asks him to say grace.

"We thank you Lord for all this food." That's what people say. I know it ain't God who gave it to us. We paid for every fucking bite of it. "Guide our steps today and help us make the right choices. Amen." How come he asked me to say grace? He knows I don't believe in God. I want a Ferrari and a Harley and my own house one of those big Victorians in Haight-Ashbury light purple with navy blue and green and gold trim. That's going to put a smile on my face. I ain't going to be like Latrice happy with nothing. Since the day I was born all I got was nothing. I don't need a lot. A car and a Harley and a house and my Annie. I don't need God to give me those things. I'm going to find a way to get them rip somebody off pull some kind of scam. I ain't going to spend my life doing chicken shit jobs. Nobody's going to pay me a million dollars for being a stockboy. So I gotta come up with another plan. God's something people make up so they don't gotta blame themselves for the stupid things they do. Well I blame myself. I stole some of her crap and I made her cry. I lost her and I'm going to be the one to get her back. God don't got no fucking thing to do with it. It's all up to me.

And she don't care. She's black. She's used to nothing. I see all those white boys same as me and they got so much fucking crap fast cars with leather seats soft as butter and Raybans and jeans so new they're stiff and they don't gotta rip nowhere. Big roaring Harleys and creaky black leather jackets. All those bitches standing in line just to let them get in their duds. Sure like to know how they get all that crap. Someone's gotta be helping them. Maybe their dads give it to them or maybe they steal it and their dads pay the cops off so they don't get busted. Wish I had that kind of dad. Mine's a loser. Or maybe they run some kind of scam. My dad ran a lot of scams. None of them worked couple of them got him thrown in jail. Like I said he's a fucking loser. Nobody's helping me. I'm trying so fucking hard but I don't got the hang of it yet I get shit from Pete and mix it with aspirins I mash up so there's more shit to sell and I make more money. Their fault if it makes them sick. Don't go out and get high if you're scared of getting sick off it. One of these days I'm going to get what's coming to me and I'm going to look so hot all those bitches are going to be climbing all over me. The other guys are going to give me that nod the guy nod the one that says "Yeah man you're one of us cool guys." Yeah.

My students crowd into the room. They sit on their chairs, eyes pinned on me.

Joe isn't here.

I feel as if my clothes have fallen off and I'm standing naked and shivering in front of them. They can read me better than they can read their books. They know we broke up.

We had taken two weeks off from the literacy classes to go to Sturgis. Today is the day the classes resume.

And he isn't here.

I stand in front of them with my heart bulging through my ribs and my throat pinching my voice. I don't know how I'm going to do this.

"Miss Annie," Johnny says, pulling my thoughts in his direction.

"Yes, Johnny?"

"I got a question."

My lips automatically warp into a smile. "First of all, welcome back everyone. I hope you enjoyed your two weeks off, and you finished your assigned reading." They nod. This isn't middle school: these people want to learn. They will do anything I ask them to. "All right, Johnny. What's your question?"

"Why is English so damn, I mean darn, sorry Miss Annie, hard to spell? None of the rules you're teaching us work for every word. I get real confused."

"Excellent question, Johnny. Let's discuss how the English language came to be. Any ideas?"

"It came from England." Liz, an older woman with orange hair and thick scratched-up glasses. She and Johnny hang out together. "With the Beatles." She giggles.

"Anyone else?"

"If it came from England why are there so many foreign words in it? Like concierge and ombudsman." Simon is fifteen. His mother had shared her heroin with him from the time he was five. She overdosed when he was ten and he was placed with foster parents who punished the smallest infractions with belts. When he was twelve he slipped out the door and made his way to San Francisco. Joe found him squatting beside a garbage can, stuffing his mouth with rotten food. He put him up temporarily in his own home, but the fear that Joe would turn him over to Child Protective Services soon drove him back to the streets. Now he eats at the soup kitchens and sleeps in a shelter, where the back-turning staff allow him to sneak in at night and curl up in a corner in a sleeping bag. He has a voracious appetite for reading, spends most of his time at the library in a back room with a mountain of books beside him. My class is one of his many stops in his efforts to stay out of sight of well-meaning policemen and social workers who would put him back in foster care if they found him.

"Think about the geography of Europe. Europe is a small continent with a lot of different ethnic groups crammed together in close company. They learned each other's languages and some words traveled from one language to another. A language isn't set in stone, you know. It changes all the time. You're reading Charles Dickens now, aren't you, Simon?"

"Yeah."

"The way we speak today is different from the way people spoke in his time, isn't it?"

"Yeah."

"So English has changed. All languages do that. We add new words and old words become obsolete. We have hundreds of technical words that are new, such as computer, laptop, Ipod; and we have thousands of words that came from other languages and often kept their original spellings."

I love my students. Homeless people, all of them. I used to cross the street when I saw them loitering on the sidewalk, and if there were no way to avoid walking past them I'd wrinkle my nose and hide my handbag. I never gave them as much as a penny. Why don't they get a job? I'd ask myself whenever I saw their outstretched hands, violet fingers poking through their mittens in the winter and serrated black nails filling me with disgust in the summer.

But look how they are tying their souls around me and keeping me from falling apart. None of the things I'm teaching them are equal to what they're doing for me. In one short hour I have incurred a debt I can never repay.

I turn out the light after the last student leaves. My energy is gone, drained as if it had run out through a hole in my shoe. My churning stomach is a vacuum collapsing my skeleton in on itself.

I've lost him. He's never coming back.

I wander blindly down Market Street. Now and then I stop and pretend I'm checking out the items on display in the store windows, but what I'm actually looking at is the reflection of a middle-aged woman, her sad tired face frowning at me.

The sun is bright and the air balmy but my frozen bones rattle inside my frost-bitten skin and I burrow into my jacket.

I pause in front of one shop, trying to find the breath I misplaced somewhere, trying to keep my trembling knees from dropping me to the sidewalk. I stretch out a hand to support myself on the plate glass window. My eyes are drawn to a ring with a heart-shaped sapphire stone. I used to have one like that. How did it get here? This is...I look at the sign. This is a pawn shop.

Cleo must have taken it.

I walk into the store and ask to see the ring. The proprietor hands it to me.

"Ah," he says as I try it on. "A perfect fit. As if it were made for you."

"It was. This is my ring. Do you know who brought it in?"

He thumbs through a little card file. Extracts a card. "Someone named Pete. You know him?"

I sort through the few friends of Cleo's that I'd met, people from his succession of jobs. I don't remember anyone named Pete.

I return the ring.

"You don't want it? It looks incredible on you. I'll give you a big discount. The price is one hundred dollars, I'll let you wear it home for seventy-five."

I shake my head.

"Sixty-five? Okay, last offer. Sixty dollars. That's a forty percent discount."

"No, thanks. I don't care for that ring anymore."

The bell on the door tinkles as I leave.

He gave me that ring on our first anniversary. Had a friend make it for me. Then he stole it.

So many things disappeared when he lived with me. Antiques that had been in my family for generations. My grandfather's Purple Heart and Silver Star from World War II. The good silverware. My CDs and DVDs. My credit cards. So much money that I stopped carrying it. There was always less in my handbag than I remembered putting in. When we were first married I got him a duplicate debit card and shared the PIN with him. When the money melted away I changed the PIN, and hunched over the ATM any time he was with me. He was so good with numbers that if he could see my fingers moving he would guess the new PIN.

He stole my jewelry, my boots. My mink coat. Gave my clothes to his girlfriend. I knew they left blank spaces on her lanky body, and the blouses she couldn't fill hung on her chest like curtains.

Why did I stay with him?

He denied the stealing.

"I ain't going to lie to you, Annie. I ain't going to steal nothing from you. I love you."

Once he said he knew where something was: a picture my great-aunt had given me for my thirteenth birthday, an old tinted photograph of my great-grandparents in German folk outfits, stern faces riveted on the camera. Snow-dipped mountains and a cabin in the background. I loved that picture. I wept the day an empty rectangle winked at me from the wall where it had hung.

When he saw my tears he ran out the door and returned with it in fifteen minutes. He didn't answer when I asked where he'd found it.

"It's back now. Let's forget about it. Nothing else is going to disappear from this house I promise."

But things continued to vanish.

San Francisco afternoon noises jitterbug in the distance. None of them come close enough to interfere with my thoughts. None of them reach out to rescue me from the memories tearing the blinds off my windows and blasting open the door to the room where I store the mutilated images of my marriage. The calmness I had tucked in like a blanket around my anger blows away and red hot fury billows over me right there on the street. Fury that drenches the whole city in scarlet, that makes me want to amputate his head, slash his heart to confetti, stab him a hundred times with the biggest knife I can find and gleefully watch him drown in his own blood. When we divorced I tamped out that fury. Now it's an arterial geyser drowning everyone near me.

You don't do that to someone you love. You don't steal from them. You said you loved me but look at all the horrible things you did to me. That isn't love.

I wait for the traffic light to change. I know it won't because all three of its lights are red. Red blobs fall from it into a widening burgundy pond. My feet tap and my hair crackles and it hits me: Joe never stole a thing from me.

He's been to my house many times. I cooked dinner for him. We loaded the dishwasher together. We rented movies and watched them, curled up in opposite corners of the couch. He read to me from whatever book he was currently reading. I knitted. Poquito slept between us.

He never took anything. Everything stayed in its place. Nothing went missing, not a penny, not a crumb, not a dog hair.

The red slinks out of my world. The last I see of it is a barbed pink tail disappearing around the corner at the end of the next block.

The street returns to its normal gray. The light changes. It changes again.

He's never taken a thing. He's never lied to me. Not about anything.

I swish my skirt. Since Joe has become part of my life I wear short flouncy skirts again.

A foolish grin takes over my face. Laughter blasts out of my mouth. Passersby exchange glances with each other, make a wide circle as they pass me.

I twirl, so light I could lift off at any second.

He's never lied to me. He's never stolen from me. He isn't like Cleo.

Oh Joe, please come back.

Another week has passed, another class, and he wasn't there. I call his job, eyes squeezed shut while I wait for someone to answer the phone.

He took extra time off, a voice tells me. He'll be back next week.

I thank the voice.

I have a week to get ready for him. I'm going to invite him home for dinner.

What if he doesn't come to the class?

What if he doesn't want to see me?

I can't think about that.

Besides, he does want to see me. I know him. I know I'm the only woman he wants to see.

It was myself I didn't know, and now I do.

"Stop pop it! You're hurting spurting me!"

He slugs me again. I feel bones splatter as his fist connects with my cheek.

"Goddam motherfucking bitch! Give me back my wallet!"

"I didn't take bake it," I sob. My nose gushes blood like an overflowing sewer.

"Stop talking that shit! I know you aren't an idiot!" Another slug and I crash into the wall. "I'm going to kill you and then I'll get my wallet back. I know you took it."

"Someone else took shook it," I scream. "Not me flea."

He clamps his hands around my neck. His roars rattle the window and his fingers tighten. He shakes me and I flap like a rag doll. My ears whistle.

"Okay." My voice can barely squeeze past his grip.

The shaking stops. "Give it to me."

"It's in my jacket placket." My beautiful new rhinestone-trimmed black jean jacket that I took from some stupid rich girl who was down here shooting up shit for the first time.

His hands are metal bands clamped around my neck. I can't breathe.

We dance a few steps together across the room to where our clothes lie in a heap on the floor. His foot drags the jacket out of the pile. "Get it," he snarls.

He lets go of my neck and I bend over. My throat is on fire. I cough and cough.

"Get it!" He kicks me. I fall.

I fish the wallet out of a pocket.

He snatches it. His mouth moves as he silently counts the money. There is a lot of it.

I think of how much food I could have bought with that money.

He pulls on his jeans. "Now get out of here," he growls.

"You have to pay play me. You fucked trucked me and you have to pay me tree."

"I don't have to do anything, bitch. You came up here. I shared my pot with you. That's your payment. Now get the fuck out of my room."

"But I'm starving carving, I haven't eaten in a week squeak."

"Good, maybe you'll die." He hauls me to my feet and shoves me out the door with his foot. I sprawl on the landing.

"My clothes hose. At least beast give me my clothes toes."

"I'm giving you your life. Be happy with that. You probably stole the clothes so they aren't even yours." He slams the door.

I curl up in a ball and cry. Quietly. Don't want him to know how far down he's pushed me.

I piss on the floor while I'm crying.

If Cleo were here he would beat the shit out of him. And make him pay me.

Blood slips into my mouth. I spit it out.

I tumble down the stairs. My neck aches. My face throbs. I can't open my right eye.

I crawl out the back door on my hands and knees, mewling like a broken dog. Maybe there are some clothes in the dumpster. Something to put on. I could care less if I'm wearing clothes or not, but the cops busted me the last time they saw me nude on the street and then they fucked me in their car on the way to the police station. Didn't even book me. Let me out a block from the station. Don't feel much like fucking a cop today so I'd better find something to wear.

I stand up slowly. My brain turns somersaults inside my head and black spots wink in front of my eyes.

I wobble over to the dumpster.

A bag of old clothes is waiting right on top of the garbage.

I pull out a huge sweater full of holes and a pair of jeans a foot too short and five sizes too wide.

At least I'm covered.

Cleo, I need you. I love you. Where are you?

On Monday I detour up Polk Street on my way to the San Francisco Club. I have no reason to attend the NA meeting: Joe isn't with me. I dawdle, admiring the overflowing flower pots hanging from the street lights, checking my shoes for scuffs, straightening my skirt. Doing my best to keep from racing down the sidewalk and interrupting the meeting to see if he's there. "Settle down," I tell myself sternly. I arrive at our classroom early and begin arranging the chairs.

He walks in while my back is turned. Doesn't say a word. I see him out of the corner of my eye, his shoulders flattened against the wall, his gaze a bridge between us.

I had planned to be sedate, composed, proper. My age. I would saunter up to him and invite him home for dinner. Maybe I wouldn't say anything until the class was over. That was my plan.

But here he is, tall, quiet, the corners of his mouth spearing his cheeks with a contented smile; and the next thing I know my legs are straddling his waist, my arms are hugging his neck, and I am kissing him over and over, his eyes, his nose, his cheeks, his mouth.

"Ahem."

My feet hit the floor.

"Sorry to interrupt, Miss Annie." It's Johnny and Liz sharing a room-sized grin.

I don't even blush. "He's back," I say.

He comes home with me. Dinner steeps in the crock-pot. Vases splash autumn colors in the kitchen, bathroom, bedroom. In the living room the reds, browns and golds share the end tables, coffee table, bookcases and mantel with the flickering tapers which provide the only light in the room.

"I went to see my mother," he says as we eat, sitting on the couch with a foot of upholstery between us.

"I thought she was dead."

"That's what I thought, too. All those years—how many? For forty years I thought she was dead. But when I told you the story it dawned on me that when I was twelve I'd never seen a dead person. I had no idea how they look. So after Sturgis I went back to Rochester and did some checking."

"And she's alive?"

"She's alive."

"That's wonderful!"

"It sure is. Now David has a grandmother."

"She's well?"

"She is. After I ran away she left my father and spent months searching for me. Put ads in all the New York newspapers. Finally enrolled herself in nursing school and worked as a nurse for a long time. Twenty-five years ago she remarried and her husband is a good man. She'll be coming out for a visit after Christmas. Wants to meet her grandson and she wants to meet you, too."

"I'm so happy for you! Now you have a family again. I mean, besides David."

"I couldn't wait to come back and tell you."

The space between us shrinks. Empty plates lounge on the coffee table. The candles glow.

"I'm divorced now," I say. I face him.

The dark pits of his eyes blaze. "I can tell."

I pick up his hands and kiss them.

"You look nice tonight," he says.

"Do you like my blouse? It's new."

"It doesn't have any buttons."

"They're in back."

"Let me see."

I turn. He undoes the top button. "Is it okay if I do this?"

I clear my throat. "Yes." Blood throbs in my ears.

He slowly unbuttons ten tiny pearl-coated buttons. "I've dreamed about this," he says.

"You've dreamed about my blouse?" I can barely get the words out.

"About unbuttoning it. But the buttons were in front."

He slides it off my shoulders, inch by eternal inch. I feel a creep of cool air trailing the edge as it glides off. He neatly folds it and sets it on the coffee table. "Turn around." He reaches behind me, eyes hooking mine and reeling me closer until all that separates us is a few finger-widths of soul, and unfastens my bra. "May I?"

"Yes." My heart is beating so loudly he has to be able to hear it.

"I feel like a teenager," he whispers. Then: "May I touch you?"

I place his hand on my breast.

The alarm wakes me at seven. I'm alone.

I sit up.

There's a note on the pillow where Joe fell asleep early this morning.

"My darling," I read, "I'll meet you for lunch on Friday at one. Wear something nice. I love you, Joe."

I fly out of bed and twirl around the room, my hair a swirling red veil. Poquito chases me, barking joyfully.

I am so in love.

"I gotta make a list of all the bad things I done," Cleo tells me. We're waiting to order lunch in the restaurant where he washes dishes. He's been in his program for three months and he's graduated to a half-way house. During the day he works and every evening he goes to meetings at his house. The change I see in him is remarkable. Did he have that wide sparkling smile before? And the laugh crinkles at the sides of his eyes? His hair is growing out and it is more gold and less silver. He looks ten years younger. They gave him a prosthesis and he can walk without a crutch. His colostomy has been repaired. When he glances at you his eyes are blazing blue suns, and while he talks his smile blinks off and on like a neon sign.

I wouldn't recognize him if I didn't know it was him.

"What do you mean, make a list?"

"Make a list of all the bad things I done to people. I told my counselor I ain't done nothing but he don't believe me." A blank piece of paper stares at us from the table and a pencil clutched between two fingers taps a restless beat next to it.

"Why doesn't he believe you?"

"He thinks he knows everything and he's better than me. I hate him. He never believes nothing I say. He's always threatening to have my probation officer violate me cuz he says I ain't clean. I ain't used in three months. You know that. You're my friend. My only friend. You gave me back my life."

"I didn't give you anything. You worked hard to get here."

"But you been there for me every step of the way. Remember all those nights when I couldn't get to sleep and I kept on calling you?"

"You should write that down on your list."

"But that don't count. I was trying to be good. What other kind of crap did I do to you?"

"Stole my mom's rosary and crucifix."

"But I brought them back. I panhandled for days in the blistering sun to get enough money to buy them back from the guy who was holding them for me. So that don't count either. I took care of that."

"Told me to fuck off the first time I saw you."

"Man you remember every fucking thing, don't you?"

I grin.

"Hey Elaine!" he calls to the waitress. She comes to the table and my breath dies in my chest. "What do you want Tim? Put it on my tab Elaine."

She looks straight at me. "What would you like?" Her coal black eyes bore holes in mine and suck out my soul and fill it with light and then pour it back into me. She smiles. At me. "The pork chops are good today."

"Okay. Pork chops." My mouth is so goddam dry. I can't get any more words out.

"Me too Elaine. I'll take the pork chops too. Come on Tim bet you can't come up with no more crap I done to you. Maybe I gotta make up something to write down on this list for group tonight."

I can't believe she smiled at me. I've come every day since Cleo started working here, a couple weeks now. We eat lunch and talk about his progress. I've watched her waitressing the other tables. Long black hair in a ponytail and eyes thickly rimmed with black eye liner. A smile that lights up the whole damn restaurant and a voice like raindrops pattering on window glass. One glimpse of her is enough and then I look the other way. Why dream of things I can't have?

"Tim!"

"What?"

"Did you hear me?"

"Sorry, Cleo. I...my mind's somewhere else today."

"Help me out here. I never done nothing to nobody."

"You kicked a dumpster."

"Who don't kick a dumpster every now and then?"

"You kicked it for a whole night."

"That ain't doing something to somebody. A dumpster ain't somebody."

"If you could kick a dumpster for so many hours, maybe you've kicked a person, too. Or hit someone."

"No way. Well yeah I hit Sylvie sometimes. She's a bitch. She wants to be hit. Does things on purpose to make people hit her. I ain't the only one who hits her everyone does."

"It's still wrong."

"You're right. A man ain't supposed to hit a woman. Even if she is a bitch."

"You've never hit anyone else? Never in your whole life?"

"Yeah sure I did. I was in lots of fights when I was a kid. Always fighting. And I tried to kill my stepmom. Tried to stab her with a knife. That's when my dad locked me in the closet and I ran...oh."

His breath hisses through a punctured mouth and his face collapses, eyes wide, lips contorted in a gargoyle grimace.

"Cleo?"

"I thought they were assholes. But it was me. I tried to kill her. Me. It wasn't them. I ain't hurt no one in my whole fucking life but I tried to kill my stepmom."

"That's no reason to lock you in a closet."

"Oh man Tim why was I such a piece of shit? I was a little kid. All those years I thought it was them who were evil, my dad and my stepmom. But it was me." The pencil clatters to the table, rolls onto the floor. "I ain't going to write that down. I ain't going to tell no one else about that. Not my counselor. Not the other guys. They don't need to know what an evil piece of shit I was."

I bite my lip.

"I always thought I was the good guy." He lays his head face down on the placemat.

"Hey, Cleo, no sleeping here." Elaine brings our pork chops.

He raises his head, smears the back of his hand across his cheeks.

"Introduce me to your friend, Cleo," she says, looking at me.

"This is Tim. This is Elaine." Voice starched and ironed.

She leans closer to me. "You're cute," she says.

I watch her leave, a long flowered blouse and a pair of dark blue jeans led away by the light in her eyes. I force myself to breathe.

I look at the food. I can't put it in my mouth. I don't think I'll ever be able to eat again.

That foxy woman thinks I'm cute. Me. Didn't she see the wheelchair? I'm not hiding it. It isn't disguised as a Cadillac.

Cleo gets up. "I ain't hungry. I'm going to go back to the kitchen. Come and see me tomorrow."

I want to say no. I can't stand to come back and have her ignore me. Sooner or later that will happen. Who wants to date a guy in a wheelchair? A guy who can't make love to a woman. She's so pretty she probably has a hundred boyfriends. But I'm excited. Maybe she'll talk to me again. That's all I'm asking. Let her talk to me.

"Sure, Cleo. Same time, same place. And take it easy, dude. You may have wanted to kill her but you didn't actually do it. Don't beat yourself up over it."

He looks at me. "Yeah Tim. I hear you." No more blue suns; his eyes are flat gray pebbles. He shuffles out of the room.

M an I sure don't get it. How did I just go and forget about
what I done to her? Wipe it out of my memory like it never
happened. Acted like they were the bad guys. I'm a real piece of
shit. My dad loved her. There's no law says he's gotta live all by
himself for the rest of his life just cuz my mom died. He had me
but that ain't enough. You gotta have a woman same as I gotta
have my Annie. But she's a real bitch Jenny. Was always telling me
to forget about my mom she was my mom now. I had a picture of
Mom in my room and she got mad and threw it away that's how
come I tried to kill her.

They made me tell them in group. I sure didn't want to my
voice was shaking like the 1989 earthquake and I heard a door
squeak open in back of me and I heard toenails scraping across
the floor. "Stupid," everyone mouthed while they waited for me
to start blabbing but I learned something in this program. You
gotta tell the truth. If you lie it's going to come back and bite you
in the ass. So I told them. And Everett the fucking counselor
who never has nothing good to say said "Were you so stupid you
didn't think you should be punished?" and I wondered how come
he got away with that calling me stupid in front of everybody.

But I kept my cool and said maybe I deserved to be punished but not to be locked up in the closet for two whole days. Not to be fucked by my dad with that bitch cackling like the witch she is. I can still hear me screaming and when he was done he kicked me out. "You ran away stupid," he said. "They kicked me out. In the snow."

Then Frankie said "But dude, they should've arrested your dad. You didn't lay a finger on your stepmom but they touched you. They should've arrested him."

"When the cops came he lied to them. Told them I ran away."

"We're not getting anywhere with this, Cleo," Everett said. "How can you resolve this and move on? You've been stuck here for a long time." Scrape scrape the toenails stop right in back of me and I can feel the fiery hot breath of those monsters on the back of my neck and smell the chewed-up-bone smell of the little boys they gobbled up.

"Stuck? That's what you call it when your whole fucking life spins and spins around the people you hate?"

"Bad things happen to everyone. Some people let go of their bad memories and others hold onto them and their whole lives are eaten up by their pain."

"You ain't hearing me. My dad fucked me."

Everett looked around at all the guys in the room. "How many of you were fucked by your dads or your stepdads or your mothers' boyfriends? Or your uncles or your brothers?" He raised his own hand. Jeff's hand flew up like a rocket shooting straight up into the clouds Frankie's hand went up halfway maybe it was embarrassed. A few more hands went up.

I looked at all the waving hands.

"You mean I been whining about this in front of you and they done it to you too? And none of you ain't said a word. Like yeah man I know it's a bitch cuz it happened to me too. Man I feel real dumb. Stupid. I'm an idiot."

"Thank you, guys. You can put your hands down. Now, Cleo, what can you do to get yourself past this? Or are you happy with the way your life is going?"

"My life's crap."

Everett waited. Frankie opened his mouth but Everett motioned for him to be quiet.

"Remember, Cleo? Make amends?"

"Make amends? They ought to make amends to me. I didn't even touch her."

"You're stupid Cleo."

"Stop calling me stupid!" I shouted. "Those fuckers ought to make amends to me. I ain't done nothing I gotta apologize for. I was a little kid. I couldn't do nothing to her if I tried." I thumped my fist on the empty chair next to me.

"No one's calling you stupid. I think you need a time out." He made me go to my room he must think he's my dad and I'm a stupid little kid.

I been laying here for hours. I'm so mad I want to knock his teeth down his throat. I ain't a kid I'm more than forty years old or thirty I can't remember. But I'm a grown man and he ain't my father and you don't send a grown man to his fucking room. It's dark now and the city lights dance on the ceiling. They twitch and hop and change colors like a kaleidoscope like a wild party when I'm so fucking high I turn into light and I become the blasting music and I—stupid piece of shit me---control the dancers and I make them jump and twist and shimmy with every note rushing out of me. I don't gotta think about my dad and my fucking stepmom. I ain't going to make amends. I ain't going to do nothing cuz I ain't done nothing to begin with and I ain't fucking stupid. All my life people been telling me I'm stupid. They all been torturing me every kind of way they can even my Annie out fucking the whole city when I was getting high. I guess she had to teach me a lesson. Okay maybe I deserved it. I should have stayed home with her but she didn't want to get high with me even though I knew she was shooting up shit with everyone else. She wanted me to fuck her but she was so sexy I couldn't touch her unless I was high. And then I remembered all the other guys she fucked and I'd get mad and steal something she loved just to get even. I'm a rotten piece of shit that's all I fucking am. I made my wife cry. I was supposed to take care of her and I made her cry. I can't stay here no more. It's after midnight and the walls are squeezing me into the corner. I ain't getting no air. I ain't going to get out of this place if I don't get out of here now. It's going to turn into a closet and they're going to nail the door shut and I'm going to be inside shouting for help and those monsters are going to be nibbling on me and ain't nobody's going to help me. I want to be good but I can't. Ain't able to do it ain't got no talent in that area ain't qualified to be a decent human being.

"Shhh." I slide the window up so slow the skin on the back of my neck's screaming "Faster faster you stupid piece of shit." My heart's hammering its way through my ribs feels like they're busting apart but I gotta be so-o-o quiet or they're going to catch me. The fucking program police will bust me. Shhh. So slow with the window ain't nobody's going to hear me. Gotta get out of here.

I'm free! The night wraps me up in a big black cape like I'm Dracula. Toenails scrape in back of me but I'm invisible in my cape and I know I'm safe. I fell when I was climbing down from the second story window and landed in a bush. The prosthesis bit my leg and now it feels wet maybe it's bleeding but I don't got time to stop and check it out I gotta keep on going. I'm free! Damp air pats me all over my face with soft puppy paws smells salty like the ocean and moldy like a cellar. It smells so fucking good. I ain't going fast I trot instead of gallop limp a little but it don't hurt much. Down the hill going to go to Ninth Street. Going to go to Pete's and get high and get rid of those monsters once and for all and enjoy my life again. Don't want to do this stepmom thing. I hate her! And I hate my dad my fucking dad. Fog hangs from the streetlights like Halloween cobwebs. Not a lot of cars it's late and it's Wednesday. No it's Thursday morning lots of people asleep cuz they gotta get up and go to work in a couple hours. If it was Friday the street would be jammed with traffic. People shouting johns looking for whores shit for sale in someone's pocket on every corner. Everyone laughing and having fun nobody worrying about all the bad things in life. But it's quiet. I hear my own footsteps on the sidewalk thump clump thump clump. Prosthesis sounds different. It don't look different but it sounds different even through my shoe. Man why am I running? I don't gotta go to work until ten. Fuck! Go to work? How come I want to do that? I'm free now I don't need a job I got hands and a mouth. I'm going to go and panhandle. I got friends I'm going to rip off. They don't give a fuck they're just going to rip someone else off. But I'm supposed to meet Tim. At the restaurant. Man he's helped me so fucking much. I don't want to let him down. He's going to get over it probably never thought I was going to do this good so he ain't going to care. Bet he's going to forget he ever knew me by the time he gets out of bed tomorrow morning. Look! It's my Annie. Look at her red hair and her big round butt. She's out whoring the bitch!

"Hey Annie!"

Oh fuck it ain't her! "Sorry thought you were someone else." It's a butt-ugly old woman. Red hair's gotta be a wig. Her face's a hundred years old a skull and eyes all sunk in maybe she's dead. Maybe I'm seeing ghosts. How am I going to get her back if I go and get high now? I gotta think a minute. Look at me huffing and puffing man I'm out of shape. Gotta start lifting those weights down in the basement. I used to bench-press four hundred pounds when was that? When I was clean and living with my Annie. Who the fuck is that? Another ghost? Waving at me from across the street. Oh man it's Sylvie it's really Sylvie. I do not want to see that bitch. I gotta get back to the house I can't be out here. What the fuck's the matter with me? All I gotta do is call her and tell her I'm sorry and then it's going to be over and done. History. A bad memory I ain't going to remember no more. Can't let that stupid Sylvie catch up with me. Gotta run through the alley. If she finds out where I'm staying I ain't going to get rid of her.

＊＋＊

"Cleo Deo! Wait gait!" His filmy face looks at me from across the street and then it turns away and he disintegrates in an alley.

"Cleo Deo! Come back hack! Look what I got shot. I just fucked a rich bitch old dude prude in a limo and he had money honey just falling out of his pockets lockets, I scooped pooped it up by the handfuls when he was snoozing losing after I did him skim. There's hundreds of dollars collars here. Look crook!"

He's running away. Why? He said he loved me. I'm his wife. Just because it wasn't his baby. No big deal.

"We can get high shy for weeks on this money sunny. Come on, Cleo Deo. Don't do this hiss."

Silence. Fingers of lonely black night worm their way out of the alley.

I love him so much. No one else will do anything for me.

I'll show him. I'm going to get a fancy hotel room. At the St. Francis, that's where. I'm going to get the biggest room they have, a suite, and order room service and fuck the dude who brings it up, and…Wait! First I'm going to score enough shit to party for days and days, and I'll pay the suite in advance for three weeks. And

I'll fuck all his friends and the room will be floating with beer and whiskey and vodka and shit, so much shit, and they'll tell him what he's missing.

I'll show him, the fucking lying bastard.

"I don't want you pew anymore shore!" I yell at the barren space where I'd seen him. "I've got snot someone new two. And he fucks shucks me better than you true do!" He expects me to run after him and do what? Play hide and seek? Beg? Forget it. I'll share this money with someone else.

But I wish he would come back. He's the sweetest dude I've ever met.

My cheeks are wet. For reals.

But I'm not crying. Not over a dude.

I am not crying.

The phone wakes me up.

It's eight in the morning.

I dreamed about Elaine all night. She was smiling at me. "You're cute," she said over and over. In some dreams she fed me pork chops, holding the fork up to my mouth, her soft pink lips separating into a big "ah," and just as I was about to suck the food off the fork I'd be swirled into consciousness. And in some dreams she stood naked in front of me. My hands drifted toward her small firm breasts but my eyes mercifully flashed open before my fingers felt her skin. Those dreams waged war with my sleep all night. I'm exhausted.

"I talked to her." Cleo's voice crackles in my ear.

"Who?"

"My stepmom. Jenny."

"Good for you."

"She said she forgave me the day it happened she knew I was just a kid. And she said she was sorry she threw my mom's picture out. She was fucking jealous man loved me so much she wanted to be my real mom."

"That's great, dude." The fog of sleep deprivation settles over me and my voice shrinks as it pecks its way through it.

"Did you hear me? Tim you okay?"

"I heard you. I didn't sleep much. I don't think I can meet you at the restaurant today. Too tired." I can't look her in the eye after dreaming about her naked body all night. Not that she's going to remember me.

"That's okay. I ain't going to work today. I'm grounded."

"Grounded?"

"Yeah like I'm a little kid. Ain't that a fucking joke? Like I'm five years old."

"What did you do?"

"Ran away."

"Dude!"

"But I came back man came back all on my own. Got all the way down the street and then I started seeing people I didn't want to see and man I raced back here like I was trying to make it across home plate and win the World Series. I couldn't climb back up to the second floor so I had to sit outside until they unlocked the door in the morning. That's how come I got busted."

"Cleo! That was not a smart thing to do."

"I know. But I fucking freaked cuz they tried to make me call her. I didn't want to do it I hated her and I wanted to keep on hating her. That way I had a reason to stay mad. You know that? I figured it out. I kept all that hate in my heart for all those years so I'd stay mad and have an excuse to get high. How stupid is that?"

"Dude. Wow. You came up with that on your own?"

"Didn't know I was that smart did you? They placed the call to her cuz I had to get this fucking thing off my chest and be done with it and then they told my boss. I'm grounded for a whole week I ain't allowed to go back to work until next Friday and man you ain't supposed to call me either. I'm grounded from the phone too. They let me talk to you now cuz I told them you were going to meet me today and I had to let you know I ain't going to be there. A year ago I wouldn't have bothered. I'm doing good huh?"

"You're doing awesome."

"She said she loved me."

"You told me."

"I can't fucking believe it. It makes me happy and it makes me sad I never really gotta know her know what I'm saying?"

"Yeah."

I topple back on my bed. A reprieve. In a week she may not be there. Maybe she'll quit. Not be fired—they'd never fire someone as sweet as she is. But quit. Move away. Or at least she won't remember me. She'll walk right past me the way all the other women do. I can deal with that. I'm used to it.

The bitch didn't say a fucking word about making my dad fuck me. I didn't say nothing to Tim about that. She was cracking up when he was doing it haha look at that little kid screaming and his dad fucking him. Ain't she supposed to make amends too? Or is it just people stupid enough to go in programs who gotta get down on their knees and kiss everyone's ass? I wasn't going to ask her she's an adult she's gotta take responsibility for herself ain't that right? That's how I see it. She didn't say a fucking word about it.

‒⟨⟩‒

Friday morning I step into a green silk dress the exact color of my eyes. Tiny bouquets of white and pink flowers splash across it, and ruffles edged in dark green lace shimmy just above my knees. The deep square neckline reveals a tantalizing inch of soft white breast. A green ribbon fastens my hair back behind my left ear. A tiny emerald studs each earlobe and showers green lights across my cheeks, and green suede sandals with three-inch heels hug my feet. Way too dressy for work but elegant enough for the best restaurant. I wonder which one we're going to.

"Wow," Kevin says when I walk into the library. "You're gorgeous."

"I am?" I spin slowly, arms out.

"I know a beautiful woman when I see one."

"But..." He's gay. Why would he notice a beautiful woman?

"Beautiful like those sumptuous works of art, Venus de Milo and the Mona Lisa. Or like Marilyn Monroe. Or Helen of Troy, so ravishing she inspired a war. Right this minute you have to be the most beautiful woman in the world. By the way, these came for you."

A stately oriental vase stands on my desk with flowers reaching three feet toward the ceiling. Lilies, birds of paradise, orchids, clusters of tiny roses. Cream, white, orange, pink, lavender. Long narrow green leaves. A card: "See you at one. Joe."

"They're gorgeous." I run a finger up one of the leaves. "I'm going out for lunch at one, Kevin. Is that all right?"

"You're the boss. You don't have to ask my permission."

"I know. But you may have plans."

"I have no plans." He smiles broadly and the smile hovers in the air like a blessing as he heads for the book stacks.

I try to read a book review but I can't concentrate. Between nine and nine fifteen I look at the clock at least ten times.

I haven't heard from Joe since that night. Every time I remember it, chills skitter up my spine and my breasts swell. If people could read my mind I'd be mortified. All I've been capable of thinking about is his naked body and what it did to mine.

I give up trying to get anything done. I go to the staff bathroom and spend forty minutes inspecting myself in the mirror. I rearrange my hair several times. Put the green ribbon on the other side. Leave it off altogether. Loop my hair into a pony tail. Pin it in a bun on top of my head. Braid it. End up putting the ribbon back where it started, behind my left ear. I pull the front of my dress down to show more cleavage. I look like a prostitute. I pull it back up. Apply more lipstick. Take it off and reapply it. What about a beauty spot by my lip? No. He likes me the way I am. I like me the way I am. I examine my reflection. The green dress brings out the neon in my eyes. My skin is creamy white and glowing. I have perfectly round huge breasts and a tiny waist that has never been stretched by pregnancy. My hips are wide. The dress accentuates my hour-glass shape. I am beautiful.

He comes early: at twelve-thirty he materializes in front of my desk.

"Look at you," I say. A black shirt and gray tie peep out from a under a charcoal gray pinstripe suit jacket. His trousers are soft black leather. "I've never seen you this dressed up."

He pulls me up from my chair and takes a step back to look at me. "Stunning. Absolutely stunning. Let's go."

"You're early. I have to let Kevin know."

"He knows. I saw him on the way in."

"Do you know Kevin?"

"Yes."

"Go on, Annie." A smiling shadow behind Joe. I don't think Kevin's ever smiled this much in one day. He's usually rather somber.

"Are you sure?"

"Go! Before I change my mind." He snickers.

Joe tows me out the door at a trot.

"Wait," I say. I can't keep up with his long stride. "I'm wearing three-inch heels, for heaven's sake."

He hangs me over his shoulder, still trotting. "Is this better?"

"No! Put me down!"

He stands me on the sidewalk.

I smooth my skirt and straighten my bodice. "What's the hurry? We're early. Where are we going, anyway? Where's your car?"

"I parked it at City Hall. It's a five-minute walk. We could do it in less if you'd get a move on."

"Why the rush?"

"I made a reservation."

"For one o'clock, right? Which restaurant are we going to?"

"City Hall."

"To the cafeteria? I'm wearing silk and emeralds so I can eat in a cafeteria?"

"No, we're not going to eat in a cafeteria." Exasperated. "Stop wasting time, woman."

"You can't just kidnap me and not tell me where we're going. I thought we were having lunch."

"We will, eventually."

"But we're going to City Hall first?"

"That's right."

"Why?"

He takes my hand and leads me through the block-long park that separates the library from City Hall. "We're getting married."

"What?" The ground tangles around my feet and I stumble, my hand snapping out of his.

"You heard me."

"You never asked me to marry you."

"Yes, I did. The other night."

"Was I asleep?"

"No." A mischievous grin ripples his lips. "If I recall, you were wide awake, naked and screaming."

I swat his arm. "You're wicked!"

"And you're irresistible when you're naked and screaming."

I swat his arm again, crimson spattering from my cleavage up to my cheeks.

He laughs. "Hurry up. The judge is waiting."

I dig in my heels, hands on my hips. "Why do we have to get married?"

He crushes me against him, squeezing me until I'm wheezing like an asthmatic. He kisses me right there, in full view of the homeless people's dank eyes and the tourists' squinting camera phones, with pigeons squabbling at our feet and seagulls swooping over our heads.

"Stop," I gasp. My knees are streams gurgling down the street and black spots pepper the insides of my eyelids.

"Are you going to marry me?"

"I just asked..." He kisses me again. My dress slips off one shoulder and pulls the green ribbon with it.

"If you say no, you will never see me again. Never."

"All right." The sidewalk tips and I clutch his arm to keep my balance. "Give me a minute. I'm out of breath." I arrange my dress back over my shoulders. The ribbon falls to the sidewalk. "Oh!" I cry. "Now it's dirty."

"Leave it." He grabs my hand and we resume our run through the park.

"I didn't know you were such an old-fashioned guy." I struggle to stay alongside him.

"I am. Old-fashioned. Romantic. The right guy to marry a flouncy sassy curvy woman like you with your ribbons and lace and your dainty feet in those little pointed shoes."

"Who are the witnesses?"

"Johnny and Liz." We reach the steps of City Hall and he stops. "Are you sure you're okay with this?"

"Of course."

"No, seriously. Are you okay with getting married?"

"Yes. I was in shock. I hadn't expected it."

"You wouldn't rather have a big church wedding with a white dress and all your family and friends?"

"I don't go to church anymore and I have no family. I'm barely in touch with my friends. The only person who matters to me is you. Any way you want to do this is fine with me."

"Are you one hundred percent sure? I don't want you to tell me a year from now thatI forced you or that you wanted a different kind of wedding."

I press his hand to my chest. "Can you feel my heart beating?"

"It's very fast."

"It's because I'm so happy I'm about to explode."

"It's not because we've been running?"

"Stop it. Let's do this." I touch my hanging hair. "Am I presentable? Maybe I should tie it back up?"

"You're perfect." We hurry up the steps, his fingers warm on my elbow.

"Wait!" We're inside City Hall.

"Now what?"

"What time did you tell Kevin I'd be back?"

"Monday morning."

"Monday morning!"

"You want a honeymoon, don't you? At least a little one."

"Kevin knew about this?"

"He did."

"Before I did?"

"I told you I asked you the other night. You said yes."

"You're a sly one, Joe Wall. Where are we going for our honeymoon?"

"Tahoe."

"You don't seem like a Tahoe kind of guy."

"I have a cabin up there. Great view of the lake and the mountains."

"You have a cabin at Lake Tahoe? There's a lot I don't know about you."

"But it's all good, I promise. We have to hurry, the judge is a friend of mine and she's giving up her lunch to do this."

"How big is the cabin?"

"One room. No hot water. Stove running on a portable propane tank. The closest neighbors are a sweet elderly couple who are fixing it up for you as we speak. Rose petals on the bed. Fire blazing in the fireplace. Food and ice in the old icebox. Clean sheets. Dust bunnies swept out from under the bed and released into the wild. Okay? Are you ready?"

"Yes."

The judge sits at a desk piled with manila folders and thick law books. Johnny and Liz are waiting with a bouquet of coral roses. They hand it to me. Johnny kisses me on one cheek and Liz kisses me on the other. "We're so happy for you," they say in unison.

When the vows have been spoken and the papers have been signed and we each have a shiny wide gold band on our left ring finger, they walk us out to his car.

"You didn't," Joe laughs.

"Just Married" is painted across the back window in big white letters, and a string of cans dangles from the back bumper.

He hugs them both as I step inside, then slips into the driver's seat. I see his grin reflecting back at me in the windshield. Then Mr. and Mrs. Joe Wall drive out of the city on a sunny September afternoon, the diamond-crested wavelets of the San Francisco Bay cheering them on as they cross the Bay Bridge toward Tahoe.

F riday arrives after seven nights of dropping off to sleep and waking up with the sheets twisted around me and a shimmer of heat misting my skin. My nightly dreams of Elaine are increasingly erotic. Cleo is back at the restaurant and as I sit with him I realize I'm holding my breath: I haven't seen her yet. Maybe she's avoiding me. I can't imagine that she wants to talk to me again. But I'm hoping.

"I figured out what I gotta do," Cleo tells me. "See I done a lot of bad things lots more than what I told you. Mostly to my Annie. I love her so much and she's the one I hurt the most. I don't get that."

"We all do that. Hurt the people closest to us. I don't know why. We don't mean to."

"Well what I gotta do now is I gotta make amends for all the crap I stole from her. And I gotta keep on working cuz I mooched off her so much. I can't believe I just called myself a mooch. But that's what I fucking am man. A major mooch. Those days are gone. I'm going to work hard and I'm going to get me a BMW shiny black like the President's limo. Then she's going to believe I'm serious."

"You have a driver's license?"

"Used to. I'm a good driver. Never had an accident."

"Then why no license?"

"They won't let me get it back until I pay a bunch of old fines. Parking tickets. A couple drug fines. I gotta go and pay them. Then I'm going to get me a car. And then I'm going to find some of her stuff I traded for shit."

"Like you found my mother's stuff."

"Yeah. You weren't going to let me in your door if I didn't bring them back were you?"

"Probably not."

"She probably ain't either. I helped myself to a lot of crap that meant something to her. I can't show up on her doorstep empty-handed. She'll think I'm just talking out of my ass again."

"You've got a plan. That's the first step. You just have to stick to it..."

The words snag in my throat: she's here. Smiling at me. Plates in her hands.

"Today's special," she says. "On me."

"Thanks Elaine." Cleo winks at her. "You're a sweetheart." As she walks away he says "Man is she glad I'm back. I think she missed me. I think she wants a piece of me."

"Really?" My tongue is a beached whale. The faint jasmine scent of her hair swirls around me, sucks into my chest with each ragged breath, fills me all the way to my dead toes.

"Yeah." He gobbles down his food. "I gotta get back to work. Take your time Tim. See you tomorrow."

I stare at my plate.

I can't eat a bite.

She comes to clear the table. "You didn't like it?"

"I'm...I'm not too hungry right now." A hammer is pounding inside my chest.

"Listen. I don't have school tonight. How about if I come home with you and cook dinner? I'm a good cook."

What did she say?

"It's all right? Okay, then. You have a car?"

I shake my head no.

"I have a beat-up old station wagon. We can fold up the wheel-chair and stick it in the back. Can you get from the wheelchair into the car?"

I nod.

She feels my arm. "Yeah, you're hella strong. Feel those muscles. You work out, huh."

"I lift weights," I whisper.

"I get off in a few minutes. Wait here for me."

What is she doing? Playing with me?

She wasn't lying: she is a good cook. Whips up some stroganoff kind of dish, doesn't take her any time at all.

"What are you studying in school?" I ask.

"Teaching certificate. I got my Bachelor's in early childhood development last December. I want to teach kindergarten and first grade."

"How old are you?"

"Twenty-three. And you?"

"Thirty-nine."

"My favorite number."

She carries the dinner dishes to the sink and turns on the faucet.

"Leave them," I say. "I'll wash them later."

"So cute!" She runs a soapy finger up my cheek. She keeps on washing.

"Where's the bathroom?" she asks when she's done. I point at the bathroom door and she disappears inside.

I open the bag of cookies she bought on the way here and stuff a couple in my mouth. I've almost made it through the evening. It wasn't so bad. She's a nice girl, a little young but nice.

I'll make some of my special Mexican coffee and we'll eat cookies and watch a TV show or two and then she'll go home. That's enough for me.

I'll be her friend. An old disabled but good friend. That's all I can offer her.

I turn on the television. "What do you want to watch?" I call to her through the door.

"Just a minute," she answers.

She comes out. "What did you say?"

"I asked what..." My voice dies. She is naked. Her body looks the way it did in my dreams: narrow muscular thighs, flat tummy, small firm breasts.

She straddles my legs. "Does it hurt when I sit on them?"

"I can't feel anything."

Why don't I say yes, you're killing me? Why don't I say go away, good night, thanks for a great evening?

She kisses me. Her mouth is soft and clingy and my mouth doesn't want to let go of it. I force myself to pull away.

"What's wrong?"

"I can't do this."

"Why not?"

"I don't work. From the waist down. Nothing works."

"We'll figure something out."

She wheels me into the bedroom.

"Get on the bed," she says. I see the muscles tremble in her arms and ripple across her smooth stomach, see those heavenly breasts surge like ocean waves as she pulls the wheelchair away from the bed. My resistance has flown out the window: she can do whatever she wants.

She takes off my shoes and socks and kisses my toes, one by one.

"Do you feel this?"

"No."

She unbuckles my belt, unzips my jeans and pulls them down. Climbs on top of me.

"I can't move." How I wish I could. Even a little swivel of the hips would do.

"I can."

At first I feel nothing. She rocks, a black-haired tawny fantasy come to life, seeping through my skin, her soft sighs replacing the red cells in my veins, and I watch the smiles travel across her face the way the sun travels in and out of the clouds, and I am happy for the first time in years. Then I feel it.

She screams when she comes, and I scream as I come, shattering the gloom left by ten years of loneliness and rage and unrequited desire. My neighbor pounds on the wall.

"Shut up!" he yells.

I groan out great belly-aching guffaws that turn into tears. A monsoon of tears. She holds me, skin on skin, sweat on sweat, while I cry. "Hush, baby, hush," she croons. We fall asleep, a single body with four arms, four legs.

In the morning she kisses me as she leaves. "Coffee's made and there are rolls in the oven on warm. I'm picking up my things and bringing them here tonight after school, okay?"

"Okay."

⚒ ⚒

"You're pregnant."

"No, I'm not. I can't get pregnant. You know that." Judy and I are eating lunch at an outdoor café on Polk Street. The brilliant October sun glares off windshields, bleaches the tans and burgundies of the city street into shades of gray, and the heat rising from the sidewalk packs my nose like cotton. I take off my apple green linen jacket and hang it on the back of my chair.

"You have that glow," she says.

"I'm happy. I didn't think I could be this happy."

"Well, you deserve it. You've paid your dues."

I see Joe in my mind, pulling a black tee shirt up over his head. I fan my burning cheeks and try to squelch a smile.

I've been married three weeks and all I think about is sex. It's disgusting and I'm in absolute heaven. But I have to focus: I'm eating lunch with Judy. "About that phone call," I say.

"Oh, that. I was surprised you didn't hang up on me. Man, Gene said, what a blabbermouth he married. He said I didn't give you a chance to say anything."

"I could barely get in a word."

"I was so excited to hear from you. It had been three years, honey. Three long years. And we were--are--best friends. Aren't we?"

"We certainly are. We've stood by each other through a lot of stuff."

"So don't say a thing. I was beet red with embarrassment after we'd hung up." She squeezes my hand. "I'm so happy for you now. You sounded lost that day."

There is a commotion across the street. Men hanging out on the sidewalk jeer and whistle. Women squeal. A figure darts past them. A gaunt long-legged figure, a naked coppery figure with spiked green hair. Shrill screams tumble out of her mouth and bumble into each other as they race across the street and collide with my ears.

It's her.

"I'll be right back." I grab my jacket and my handbag.

"Where are you going?"

"I know that girl."

I run across the street and block her path.

"Stop," I say. "Put this on." I hold out the jacket.

She gawks at me. A purple billow rages around her left eye and her lip is bleeding.

"Put it on."

"Why sky?"

"You can't be out on a city street without clothes. Put it on."

She takes the jacket, slips her arms in the sleeves. It drapes her long body as if she were a clothes hanger, the hem barely reaching her navel.

"Why are you doing screwing this for me tree?"

"Why not?"

"You know show me."

"Yes, I know you. You're Cleo's girlfriend."

"Is this a poison jacket track it?"

"No, of course not. It was cool this morning and I wore it to work. It's warm now and I don't need it."

"You aren't mad sad at me for stealing reeling Cleo Deo?"

"Not anymore. You can have him."

"For reals feels?" A hundred-watt bulb clicks on behind the filaments of bone in her face, illuminating her skin, and for the first time I see that she is quite pretty, scabs and emaciation aside.

"Absolutely."

Her chapped fingers latch onto my arm and words blast from her mouth at a hundred miles an hour. "I know you love him but you don't need him. You're strong. He was always afraid when he was with you because he's weak and you're so strong. He didn't want you to see how weak he was. He needed to take care of me to feel good. He protected me and it made him feel like he could do anything."

My mouth flops open, just a little. I never thought of it that way. Never dreamed I could be intimidating, especially not to my own husband. I saw myself as perky and cute. Not strong. Wasn't it enough that we loved each other? "You can speak like a normal person when you want to."

"Of course I can. I went to college. I majored in psychology."

"What happened to you?"

"The dudes wouldn't leave me alone. All my life they've been messing me up. I missed too many classes getting high and fuck-ing other students. And teachers. When Cleo's around he'll run off anybody I don't want."

"Are you hungry?"

"I haven't eaten in a week."

"Would you like a pizza?" We're standing in front of a pizza shop.

"Pepperoni'd be hella cool."

I buy her a large pepperoni pizza and a coke. As I leave I give her a quick hug.

"Good luck to you," I say. I dash back across the street.

"What was that all about?" Judy asks. Her eyebrows are sticking to her hairline.

"Cleo's girlfriend." I look her in the eyes and smile. "I can't believe I ever thought I loved him."

I forage through my bag for my wallet. I can't find it. I'd dropped it back in after I'd paid for the pizza. Now it's gone.

"That damned girl!"

"You've changed," Judy giggles. "You used to be Miss Holier-Than-Thou and now you say four-letter words."

"She took my wallet!"

I call the police on my cell phone. They arrive in two minutes. She's still sitting on the sidewalk across the street, munching on her pizza.

I walk back over. I'll bet she's still got it on her.

She does. They find it in one of the jacket pockets.

"You set me up cup sup!" She shakes her finger at me. "You gave me this jacket racket and you planted ranted your wallet in the pocket socket locket!"

"Do you want us to arrest her, Ma'am?" the officer asks.

"Yes. Please."

She tears off the jacket and hurls it to the sidewalk. "Take back your fucking jacket sack it! I don't need feed it!" While she screams she jams a final slice of pizza in her mouth.

The police handcuff her. "We've been looking for you, Sylvie," one of them says. "A certain businessman claims you stole four thousand dollars from him."

"He paid laid me that money funny! For fucking bucking him. In his hotshot pot limo."

"His story's a little different, and he's a big man in this city. He owns a lot of businesses and most of the city council. And our boss. You fucked with the wrong guy this time, Sylvie. You should stick to ripping off your johns. You're looking at a long stretch in the slammer unless he changes his mind about pressing charges."

"Fuck shuck all of you screw flu!" A wail breaks out of her mouth as they shove her naked body into the squad car. "Cleo Deo! I want Cleo Deo!"

S he never says she loves me, and I don't know if what I feel for her should be called love.

But since she waltzed into my apartment that day my life has made a one hundred and eighty degree turn. I can walk. My ankles are frozen from all those years of disuse so I can't walk far, and I only do it at home. After ten years of sitting in a wheelchair, taking five steps across the living room is like dancing the Nutcracker to me. No more catheters. No more suppositories up my ass to shit. Sex whenever we want it. Every part of my body works.

The doctor had no explanation for me. He did another MRI of my spinal cord. "I don't see any damage." He rubbed an eyebrow with one finger. Looked at the MRI done ten years ago. "There was a lot of swelling on the old one. It doesn't clearly show an injury. Maybe when the swelling went down the cord was intact."

"Why couldn't I walk?"

"I don't know. Maybe because you believed you couldn't."

Ten lonely years hiding from the world. Staring at the walls of my apartment. Drooling over women who were going to either ignore me or reject me. And it was all in my head?

She leans over my shoulder as I order merchandise. "That one." She points to a huge multi-colored basket. Her taste is exquisite. My business has tripled since she started helping me choose my inventory.

My apartment has transformed from an old black-and-white silent movie to a deafening technicolor explosion: big green plants in the corners reveling in the sunlight that sparkles through clean windows, a noisy back-talking green and yellow parrot on a perch in the kitchen, terra cotta and yellow and red and green Central American art splashed across the walls. Bright woven rugs on the floor. We have a calico cat, Cheetah, white with black and orange markings, who sprawls between us on the couch when we watch television in the evenings, prowls purring around us while we make love, and sleeps curled up in a ball in the small of my back at night.

I think my paralysis was caused by anger. I couldn't let go of it. Even my brother's death didn't end the anger I felt toward him. And toward myself. Mostly myself: I'd let go of his hand. I'd beaten him in his bed to make him stop screaming because every scream reminded me that it was my fault. The accident had given me an excuse to focus my anger on Teddy, and without my being aware of it, anger became my deity. I sacrificed my life in its honor on a pyre of disability, gratefully kissed my forehead to the ground before a vision of a screaming Teddy being dissolved alive by the drugs he took. I buried it deep in my spine and let it turn me into a dim shadow of a human being. Let it take away my manhood. Let it tie a noose around my heart.

She poured life back into my body. Life and something like love.

And my anger? Gone after our first night together. Vanished.

She pads around my place barefoot, wearing skinny black leggings and one of my tee shirts that cloaks her all the way to her knees, and I know I have somehow managed to walk through the gates of paradise. She cooks for me, blows the dust out of this apartment, goes to school, goes to work, comes home and squeezes me in her arms and wakes up every shy little muscle in my body. I don't know how she does it all.

She may leave me someday, maybe when she's through with school. I'm not going to try to see that far ahead. I'm going to hold on to her for as long as she'll stay. And I thank God every day for this miracle He's worked.

And, now that I think about it, it's actually Cleo who's responsible for my new life. Was this the reason Mama sent him? He introduced us.

Who the fuck's that blubbering?

It's coming from the living room. Two drag queens, Betty and Denise, are sitting on the couch, shoulder to shoulder, hip to hip, knee to knee. The tears dribbling down their faces are tinted with their eye shadow---Betty's are violet, Denise's are blue. A box of tissues balances on their knees. They're crying over a movie; he sees a woman in a hospital bed on the television screen.

"Cleo!" Betty calls. "Sit with us. You'll love this movie."

"I ain't going to sit with you weirdos."

"Get over yourself, Cleo baby. We're not contagious. Come watch this with us."

He sits on the far end of the couch. Betty and Denise take turns wailing and blowing their noses.

The woman on the screen is dying. A child holds her hand as she takes her last breath.

He feels something wet on his cheek.

What the fuck!

"Look, Betty! He's crying!"

"Fuck you!" He stands up.

"No, baby. Don't go. Crying never hurt anybody." Betty grabs his hand.

He yanks it free.

"Crying's good for you, Cleo," Denise chimes in. "Cleans your heart."

"What the fuck do you weirdos know," he snorts as he walks out.

He slumps face down on his bed. His mom died when he was little. He was there. He'd held her hand. She'd promised she would always love him and always watch over him.

Well Mom you like what you see? Did I do good?

His own wails pelt his ears. He smothers them in the pillow.

My mom'd be ashamed of me if she could see me. She'd hate me. She'd walk away the same as everyone else in my life done. You ain't my Cleo she'd say. You're a piece of shit. But Mom I'd say to her I'm trying now. Give me a little credit I'm busting my balls trying to be good.

He saw an old lady tottering through a crosswalk yesterday. She was dragging one of those wire shopping carts people buy, the kind that folds up. With little wheels. It was loaded down with groceries and she was struggling to get it across the street and she didn't make it. The light changed. Horns blared and drivers popped their heads out their windows and shouted at her.

He couldn't stand it. He dashed into the street and grabbed her cart with one hand and took her arm with the other and led her to the sidewalk. He was afraid some jerk would lose it and run her down. A couple years ago he would've left her in the crosswalk and hightailed it with her groceries.

"What a charming young man," she said. "Won't you come in for some lemonade? I made it fresh this morning."

"Oh no Ma'am thanks but I'm in a hurry." His hands were itching to snatch the cart. He jammed them in his pockets; he was not going to allow himself to run off with it. Maybe this nice old lady couldn't afford to buy more food.

"It's so nice to see a young person who is kind these days. There aren't many like you around." She patted his arm and pulled her cart two doors down to an old brick apartment building.

He stood dazed on the sidewalk.

I'm kind? Since when? I never do nothing for no one unless it's a chance to rip them off. I don't know who I am no more.

I wiggle around in my bed. I'm burning up and then I'm freezing and the sheets are big wrinkled mountains poking holes in my back and my legs are screaming at me to stretch them across the room as far as they can go out the window and across the street and into the house that's making eyes at this one. Lights from the street two stories down reach all the way up to my window and make my wall a movie screen jumping with blurry gray and white pictures. I forgot to take my dope. I take their shit every morning but now they say I got some kind of psych disease and they give me pills for it at night can't remember their name. I ain't a psycho. I just need them to get me to go to sleep but I forgot to take them today and they're locked up downstairs in the office. They won't let me keep them up here. "Can't sleep," I mutter and turn over. Mash the pillow over my head to keep the movie pictures out. "What kind of place don't put curtains on the windows."

"Cleo."

I sit up. "Who's there?"

Nobody.

I get out of bed. Walk to the window and look at nothing walk to the bathroom and take a piss walk back to my bed and sit on it.

"Cleo."

A figure glides out of the corner.

"Mom?"

"You're so big now. My sweet baby boy is all grown up. And so handsome."

"Mom? What are you doing here? You're dead."

"Oh Cleo." Her eyes are brighter than the streetlights. "It's not like that."

My Annie stands behind her. She has a black eye and a teeny little red creek is dripping out of her nose. Who did that to her? I'll knock his teeth down his fucking throat. And now that fucking Sylvie's standing right next to her and her scrawny arm ropes around my Annie's waist that tiny waist I want to squeeze with both my hands and gnaw the way a dog gnaws a bone snuffling and slurping all over every single inch of her velvet skin. My pulse is pounding in my temples going whoosh-whoosh-whoosh in my ears. My gut explodes like I been punched and I double over.

"I told scold her. You can't lie cry to her anymore door."

"You're a piece of shit," my Annie says.

"Annie! You don't talk like that."

"I do now. See what you turned me into. I changed for you and you were fucking her all along."

"Yeah," Sylvie chimes in. "Fucking pucking me and it was so-o-o ho-o-o good, wasn't it, Cleo Deo, my hubby chubby?"

"Is this true, Cleo?" Mom looks sad.

It ain't true. I never fucked around on my Annie.

Yes I did. I did man. How come I forgot about that? Thought if I didn't admit it then it didn't happen? But look at that fucking

Sylvie. She told her cuz I wasn't going to take care of her black baby. Why'd she have to go and tell her? Why didn't she just let me be?

Mom stands at the foot of my bed and unravels until she's only a pair of crying blue eyes floating in the dark. "My sweet baby boy grew up to be a two-timer. It's my fault. I should never have left you."

She disappears and so do Sylvie and my Annie both of them jeering at me. "That fucker sucker," they say together and slide through the wall.

The room's empty again. Light and shadow flutter in the puny silence. I gotta thousand dollars stashed in a jar in my closet enough to buy me a car I know a guy at the restaurant who's going to sell me one. Ain't a BMW a Honda it's gotta do for now. One more fine to pay and they're going to give me back my driver's license. Everything's right on track. Maybe by Christmas I can go and buy her ring back from the pawnshop. But how the fuck am I going to face her? All those times I accused her of fucking other guys. I told myself she left me for someone else and made myself believe it. Wrote it in capital letters on a billboard inside my head and read it as loud as I could to anyone who'd stop and listen. And it was me all along. I was fucking Sylvie like we were a couple rabbits. I can't even stand the bitch. She's mean and nasty as an old rooster. She's a fucking devil and my Annie's an angel and I chose the devil. I know I gotta tell her. I gotta set things straight. I can't go marching up to her with a car and a ring and a big grin on my face and have this gnawing holes in my gut. I gotta start over without no lies. But I can't tell her. I know she's going to cry and then she's going to forgive me cuz she really loves me. Maybe she's going to take me back just to get even with me. Fuck around on me like I done to her. I ain't going to trust her. I'm going to keep on lying keep on getting high find someone else to fuck. Not Sylvie I hate that bitch. Someone else. Probably lots of someone elses. God sends me an angel and I'm such a piece of shit I can't even keep her. You gotta treat an angel good. Real good. Or be knocked to the ground by the hand of God. Fuck!

"You're pregnant."

The jail nurse shows me the indicator.

"Thanks." I get up to leave her office.

"Do you want to keep it or have an abortion?"

"I'll keep it."

Another chance. This time Cleo will believe me. I don't have a clue who the father is, but I know it wasn't a black dude.

Missed two periods so it was sometime in August.

Six kids. Four of them being raised by my mother. One left in the hospital. Now this one.

Sure hope Cleo sticks around.

It's criminal, five kids and the dads don't want anything to do with them. What the hell kind of dudes live in this world, anyway?

They all want to fuck anything with a hole in it and then they disappear from the scene when something alive and yowling comes out of that hole.

Cleo will come through for me this time. I know he will.

We moved into Joe's house when we returned from our honeymoon. He owns a three-story Victorian in the Haight-Ashbury area. The hardwood floors are a hundred years old. The master bedroom takes up the top floor, with windows on three sides and on the fourth there are two walk-in closets and a bathroom. The first time I saw the twin copper sinks, the claw-foot tub squatting on the Mediterranean-blue tiled floor, the pale green ceramic wall tiles with pink and blue Moroccan trim, I thought I'd walked into a tiny outpost of heaven. The second floor has another bathroom and four bedrooms, one of them lined with dusty bookshelves, the floor groaning beneath mounds of books that teeter like old tombstones across a maroon Persian carpet. The living room and dining room share the ground floor with a sunny kitchen. The back door opens onto a pink brick patio, the steps beyond it crumbling beneath straw-colored weeds and leading to what may once have been a garden.

The house was dingy and neglected. Cobwebs glittered in the corners and the floors badly needed stripping. I'd been there before we were married and noticed the dust but never said anything.

"I was never here except to sleep," he said defensively when I drew a heart with my finger on a clouded end table. "I spent all my time at work or at meetings. And David lived across the street from the hospital."

I looked through the window at the back yard. A tangle of rose bushes clinging to the fence waved spindly branches at me, begging to be pruned.

"I'd like to plant vegetables in the spring."

"Sure. Whatever you want."

David moved into my house. I offered to let him live there for nothing if he would pay the utilities, but he refused. "Dad taught me to pay my own way. Besides, I'm a doctor, Mom. I make enough money."

Shivers always ruche the skin on my back when he calls me Mom. I know I'm not his real mom and he's not my real son but he is my family now, and he's almost as attentive to me as his dad is. I am the luckiest woman in the world.

Around the middle of November a swirl of vertigo overtakes me as I run up the stairs to our bedroom. I've got to take it slower, I tell myself as I plop heavily down on a step. I'm not a teenager. I wait for the house to drop out of its tornado, fending off a sudden punch of nausea, and then I continue up the stairs at the sedate pace one would expect of a woman in her forties. It doesn't help much: I fasten myself to the railing to keep from toppling over and my breakfast inches up my throat and festers at the back of my tongue.

Thanksgiving morning I get up early to put the turkey in the oven. David is coming for dinner. Kevin and Mark are coming, too, and so are Johnny and Liz.

I don't make it out of the bedroom.

Joe finds me a few minutes later with my arms wrapped around the toilet and my stomach contents dogpaddling in the water.

He brushes my hair back from my face and holds my shoulders as I continue to heave up everything I've eaten in the last ten years.

"What's wrong, Annie?"

"The flu. Maybe."

He palms my forehead. "You don't feel hot."

"I've been queasy for the past few days. I thought it was something I ate." I heave again.

Every movement of my head makes the room spin. Every spin turns my stomach inside out.

Joe is on his cell phone. "David wants to know if you're pregnant."

"I can't get pregnant. I told you that." Wave after wave of nausea crashes over me. I can't move without retching.

"He wants me to take your temperature."

When he sticks the thermometer in my mouth I gag and retch again.

"She gagged on it," he says into the phone. He sits on the floor next to me with his arm across the toilet so I can rest my head on it. A quiver of panic underlines his voice.

"I need to get back into bed and rest a little." My nose is dripping. "Give me an hour. Then I'll get up and get the turkey ready."

"He says to put the thermometer…"

"No!" I interrupt. "Not there."

"Your armpit. For ten minutes. Can you do that?"

"Help me get into bed and it can stay there as long as you want."

I try to stand but the room is a carnival tilt-a-whirl and I vomit again. Now it's bile and it etches designs in my throat, triangles and squares and bouquets of wildflowers. Tears run down my cheeks.

"Sit down. Here, let me hold you. Rest your head on me. And don't move."

We sit on the blue tiles of the bathroom floor. The thermometer is clamped firmly between my arm and my body. My head lies over his ticking heart, his arms are wide strips of heat swaddling me. His voice as he talks to David is a baritone rumble in his chest.

"He's asking when you had your last period. You haven't had one since we got married."

"No." My throat is sore and I have to whisper. "I think it was August. It's the change. You know. I'm an old woman. You married me in time for hot flashes and mood swings."

"He says puking isn't part of the change." He looks at the thermometer. "Ninety-seven degrees. Not a fever. It's not the flu."

He rocks me.

"Don't do that. Oh no." My head goes back into the toilet.

David shows up with a pregnancy test. "I'm collecting clues," he says. "Doctors aren't magicians. We're detectives."

"I can't get pregnant."

He squats down to my eye level and strokes my hair. "I can't give you any medicine until I have a negative pregnancy test. That's just the way it is."

I struggle to my feet. "You guys leave. I can do this myself."

But with my head a whirling cyclone I can't stay upright. Joe supports me and holds the indicator while I pee on his hand.

"I'm sorry," I mumble. "This isn't one of your husbandly duties."

"You bet it is. You'd do the same for me."

I try to smile. "I'd better never catch you taking a pregnancy test."

When I'm done he gives the indicator to David.

David looks at it. "Mom."

"Now what?"

I want to go to bed. I don't know how I'm going to get the turkey done. If only this room would stop its mad spiral, or at least slow down, I could stand up without my stomach spewing whatever it imagines is still in it out into the toilet.

"Take a look." He holds it up in front of me.

I see a pink cross.

For twenty years I took a pregnancy test every time my period was a day late. For twenty years all I saw were lonely blue lines.

Now I see a pink cross.

"I'm pregnant?" My hands clutch Joe's shirt.

"Sure are, Mom."

"Oh! I'm sorry, Joe. I didn't mean to do it. I'm not one of those women who trick men by getting pregnant. I am so sorry." I'm screeching like a peacock. "Joe, I didn't do this on purpose. Please don't send me away." Acid gushes up my throat and I bend over the toilet and heave and spit.

"Let's get her to bed," David says.

"Please don't be mad at me. I won't have an abortion but we can give it away. You have to believe I didn't try to make this happen."

"What on earth are you babbling about?"

They tuck me in and Joe sits on the edge of the bed and holds my hands.

"We never discussed having a baby. You already have a grown son. We're old. We're looking forward to retirement and years and years to do anything we want. We're going to buy a boat and sail around the world. We're going to ride your bike up to Sturgis next summer. You can't do that with a baby. He'll fall off. And you have to constantly spend money on them, shoes and clothes every few weeks because they keep growing out of things. And you have to put aside money for college."

"You think I don't want this baby?"

"You've never said you wanted one."

"Because you told me you couldn't get pregnant. Why would I even mention it? This will be the most beautiful baby in the world.

She's going to have green eyes that throw emeralds all over the room the way her mother's do, and wild red hair that will escape from all the ribbons and barrettes you're going to use to keep it in place. All the other things we talked about were just talk. Not important to me at all. I want this baby. I'm so excited I feel like I'm flying."

"But…"

"What 'but'? You're the damndest most stubborn woman I've ever met." He kisses my hands.

"You're sure? You're not just saying you want it to make me feel better?"

"The only thing I'm more sure of is that I'm going to be with you forever. And I'm not going to miss out on one second of this baby's life, beginning now." He turns back the blankets, lifts up my nightgown and kisses my belly. "When you puke I will hold you. When your back aches I'll massage it. I'll go to Lamaze classes with you and breathe you through the delivery. I'll walk the floor with her all night every night if she can't sleep. I am not that old. And nowhere near retirement age."

David offers me Compazine.

"I don't want any pills. I'm not taking anything that could affect my baby."

He goes out to buy ginger ale, comes back with ginger tea and ginger candy as well.

"What time is it, Joe? I have to put the turkey in."

"Mrs. Wall, Ma'am, begging your pardon, but the gentlemen of the house have the situation under control."

"You don't know how to cook a turkey."

"I can read a cookbook."

I giggle and snuggle down under the covers.

The ginger ale slowly dissolves the nausea and I fall asleep. When I wake up Joe is sitting next to the bed.

"Are you feeling better?"

"A little. How's the turkey doing? Do you need my help?"

"David's got it covered."

"What about the sweet potatoes? You scrub them and…"

"We've ordered everything else. He's going to pick it up later."

"Joe."

"Yes?"

"You don't have to stay in here with me. I'll be all right."

"You might need something."

"You go watch the football game. I'm fine."

"I'll come up and check on you."

He kisses my forehead.

I hover a foot above the bed. In the blink of an eye my life has changed. I have taken my place in the ancient line of women who kept mankind alive on this earth. I feel my roots stretch all the way back to the dawn of time and the first mothers crooning to their babies under trees, holding little mouths to swollen breasts and filling them with the milk of life. Words of love and hope and reassurance deliver themselves to the tiny soul growing inside me. Light shines out of my every pore and fills the room.

Poquito curls up next to me on the bed. Every now and then he gets up and licks my face.

I doze.

"I don't trust him." She nestles in my arms in the pitch-dark bedroom. Thanksgiving dinner has been eaten and the dishes washed and put away. The sweat from our lovemaking evaporates on our skin. "You need to be careful."

"Who? Cleo?"

"Yes."

"Why? He's turning out to be a nice guy."

"He's trying to be nice. But not for the right reasons."

"What do you mean?"

Cleo had come for Thanksgiving dinner. He wore a navy blue suit, a white shirt starched into a frozen winter road, a dark blue tie. Black shoes buffed until they sparkled. Brought a big bouquet of roses for Elaine. He dominated the meal with his talk of the car he's planning to buy, didn't let either of us say a thing except "yes" or "no." He repeatedly asked if we thought his wife would like his suit.

"He's doing it to get her back. It's not something he really wants to do. It's for her."

"Is that wrong?"

"What if it doesn't work? What do you think he'll do?"

"How would I know? Maybe it will work."

"I know about speed and the way people act when they're using it. No woman in her right mind would stay with a speed user."

"Love conquers all. That's what they say."

"Love has to be nurtured. It's like a plant. If I don't water the flowers in the garden they die, and no amount of water will bring them back to life."

"Then you don't think she'll take him back?"

"I don't know. But if she doesn't, he isn't going to stick with his new life. He'll start using again, maybe come here and cause trouble for you. And if she does take him back, he'll start using again anyway because he'll think he can get away with it. It's all an act. He wants a wife, a home and a job so he can make everyone think he's okay. But he isn't okay and he doesn't care whether what he does is right or wrong."

"Sure he does. He's always sorry when he's done something bad."

"After he does it. Not before. And only if he gets caught."

"What makes you so wise?"

"I can read people."

"Read people?"

"I see what people really are."

"Do you tell fortunes, too?"

"No, my mother did that."

"That's right, your mother was a gypsy."

"I am, too."

"What did you see the first time you saw me?"

"A man killing himself with self-pity and anger."

"That doesn't sound attractive." I get up on one elbow and stare at her through inky puddles of darkness. Her eyes are lanterns in the dim room.

She pulls me back down on the bed, snuggles her little body up next to mine.

"Beyond that I saw a man who is kind, with a heart that has room for everybody. An honest man who helps people when they need it. A gentle man."

"Me?"

"Besides, you were so hella cute you made my knees turn into water. It took me two weeks to get up the courage to speak to you."

"I made your knees turn into water?"

"Yes. Now be quiet and go to sleep."

"I made your knees turn into water."

"That's what I said."

I giggle.

Her hand taps my chest. "Hush."

I giggle again.

I made her knees turn into water.

I go to the storeroom to get a bottle of soap for the dishes and when I turn the light on I see my boss in there with a bitch who ain't a day older than sixteen.

"What the fuck are you doing?" I ask him

"Mind your own business." He walks out of the storeroom zipping his pants and shuts the light off, leaving her in the dark pulling her underwear up and tee-heeing.

"You gotta wife man." His wife comes in here sometimes at the end of our shift to get a ride home with him. She's gotta smile full of big white teeth shiny earrings hanging to her collarbones and her hair's a brown forest waving around them her clothes are rainbows with flowers and stars and hearts like she's a hippie from the sixties or something.

"And?"

"Man you ain't supposed to do that to your wife."

"Do it to her before she does it to me, that's my motto. When you have a wife you'll understand."

"I got...No you're right man. Gotta keep those bitches in their place."

"You sure do, Cleo. Best thing is to never get married. But they trick you. My wife got pregnant. And I like being a dad. Kid's great. Wife's not."

Fuck. Look at this guy. His wife's here all the time she don't gotta fucking clue how come I gotta tell my Annie? What she don't know ain't going to hurt her right? I just gotta be smart and not bring no one home make sure she ain't going to run into them. I ain't saying I'm going to go around looking for it but I gotta make a plan in case it happens. I got my prosthesis and that shitbag off my belly and I look so fucking good all the bitches want a piece of me. Look at Elaine moved in with Tim even though he's a cripple nice guy but a cripple probably can't do nothing in bed. I can tell she wants a piece of me every time I see those shining black eyes the way she looks at me. I ain't going to do that to Tim. Bet she'd dump him if she fucked someone as good as me but if she wasn't with him I'd hop on her in a heartbeat she's got a sexy little ass even if I was back together with my Annie. But I'd never let her find out I'd make sure they didn't meet each other none of this bringing the fucking bitch home that's crazy. I'd go and do it in the storeroom same as my boss he's a lot smarter than I thought he was and I'm only going to do it once with each bitch. No fucking long drawn-out relationship like all those months with Sylvie. What the fuck am I thinking? When I get my Annie back I ain't going to fuck around with no one else I'm going to keep her in bed twenty-four seven and fuck her so much she ain't going to need a boyfriend. Won't have the strength to get out of bed just going to lay there like one of those blow-up dolls with those huge tits saying "Come here baby" and I'm going to prove to her how much I love her. Tie her to the bed if I gotta until she gets it. But do I gotta tell her about Sylvie? Everyone does it and they get away with it they ain't telling on themselves I don't see why I gotta.

And he's wrong. You ain't supposed to do that. You gotta love your wife and only your wife no matter what the fuck she does. Don't fuck around and get the bitch pregnant if you don't love her. Man is that my brain thinking that? That's the kind of crap my Annie'd say. She ain't going to call no one a bitch but I'm saying the part about loving and fucking and she ain't going to say fuck. Man I'm fucked up tonight. Let me go over all this again. You're only supposed to fuck someone you love that's the bottom line. But then nobody'd fuck nobody. We don't love those bitches we just want to fuck them. How's anyone going to keep life going on this planet if nobody's fucking no one? Think about it. I met my Annie when I was thirty or thirty-five how come I don't know how old I am? And if I never fucked no one until I met her man I'd be a danger to society so horny I'd rape anything that comes along dogs cats babies. No not babies that's sick. I ain't going to fuck babies and not no guys either. Never. Keep those pretty boys away from me. I don't get it. You gotta fuck someone and all those whores are dirty. They all got HIV and syphilis and clap and who knows what the fuck else. I'm scared just to look at them and I ain't going to pay for something if I can get it for free. All the bitches want a piece of me. Now I'm clean I'm so good-looking I can't stand myself.

W hat it comes down to is this. If I fuck someone else then it's okay for my Annie to do it too. And it ain't okay. I'd knock his teeth down his throat if I catch them. Hers too. It ain't okay. So I ain't going to fuck no one else when we get back together. It's only going to be me and her forever and ever. Is that what I want? Man I'm so confused. I hate this being clean hate it wish I could do a little hit so I can stop all this thinking crap I get a headache from all this thinking. I ain't bad when I only do a little. I can handle a teeny weeny little hit a dot on my finger stick it up my nose. I ain't crazy when I only do a little dot. I gotta stop all this thinking. It's too fucking hard.

I think I was five. Mom was at work and Dad was home with me cuz he worked at night.

"I'm going to go out," he said. "You're going to be okay here by yourself for a couple minutes."

"No!" I remember panic filling up my mouth it tasted worse than Brussels sprouts. "No don't go and leave me here all by myself. Someone's going to break in and kidnap me there's all kinds of bad people in the world. Take me with you Daddy I'm going to be very very quiet and I ain't going to ask you for nothing. Cross my heart. Please don't go and leave me home all by myself." There are monsters in the closet I wanted to say but I was scared to. He always hit me when I talked about monsters. I held onto his leg and hollered.

"Shit," he said. "Okay come on. But you're going to do exactly what I tell you none of your stupid tricks and not a fucking peep out of you."

"Okay." My screams stopped. I wondered where we were going to go maybe to the toy store. He knew I wanted him to buy me a fire engine I saw there. Maybe to the Frostee Freeze get us some ice cream.

I sat next to him in the front seat. "Where we going to go Daddy?"

"Not a peep I said. Didn't you hear me say that? Such a stupid piece of shit. You never listen to nothing I say."

"I'm sorry Daddy."

I crushed my lips together so hard they burned so I'd remember I wasn't supposed to say nothing. Sure wanted to go to the toy store. That fire engine was big enough for me to ride on it roar around the house roar louder than those monsters gotta stay away from the closet. Far away. Maybe play in the kitchen the back yard maybe go to Gramma's house but she don't live here. We gotta get in the car and drive all day long when we go and see her. Maybe the fire engine was at her house maybe that's where we were going to go. Mom was going to wonder where we were cuz it took a long long time to go to Gramma's house. There's a white fence and a bird bath and I like to splash my hands in it and then Daddy yells cuz I get my clothes all wet. I ain't seen no birds in the bird bath. Maybe they gotta have some bubbles before they take their bath. I should bring some bubble bath and then I can make them some bubbles and then I'll pick a big bubble up in my hand and blow on it real soft and make it fly way up in the air.

We parked in a driveway next to a gray house I never seen before.

"This ain't Gramma's house."

He snorted and hit the back of my head as I hopped on the big flat stones that made a path to the door. "Stupid kid. Who said we were going to go to Gramma's house? A friend of mine lives here."

A woman with a cloud of yellow hair poufing out around her head greeted us.

"What have we here?" she asked when she saw me.

She bent down so her eyes looked right in mine. "What's your name, little man?" Her eyes were brown with green polka dots.

"Cleo."

"Cleo. Welcome to my home." She motioned us through the door and she glanced at my dad and her face was a big question mark.

"Did you bring a toy to play with?" she asked me.

"No ma'am."

"You're polite, too! What a precious little angel! I don't have any toys but I've got some chocolate cake. Would you like a piece?"

"Yes ma'am."

"You make me shiver when you talk so polite, Cleo. What a lady-killer you're going to be when you grow up."

I was going to kill ladies? She said it like it was a good thing but I didn't think it was. You ain't supposed to kill people especially not ladies they're mommies. I didn't want to kill no mommies. She's real confused I decided.

She brought me a plate with a big chunk of chocolate cake with a lot of chocolate frosting. Handed me a glass of milk. I sat on a flowered blanket on the couch and held the plate very careful so I wouldn't drop no crumbs. She turned the TV on to Sesame Street.

"Your dad and I need to talk," she said. "You sit right here for a few minutes and watch this show and eat your cake. Don't get up from the couch. Can you do that, little man?"

"Yes ma'am." I'd already crammed half the cake in my mouth.

I watched Sesame Street until it was done and then Days of Our Lives came on. I didn't want to watch that it was boring all about grownups kissing and shouting at each other. Shouting scared me. I heard a lot of shouting at home. I wanted some more cake. I didn't know where the kitchen was I wandered into a little hall-way. I heard noises in a room. Her voice she was crying was my dad hurting her? Maybe he was hitting her like he hit my mom. I couldn't never help my mom. When he hit her she made me go to my room. "Daddy don't hit her!" I'd shout and he'd stick his big fist with black hairs like wires poking out all over it right up in my face. "You want some of this you stupid little piece of shit?" he'd yell. "Go to your room!" Mom'd scream. I'd run and hide under my bed my back squished to the wall and my knees shivering against my chin I'd count as far as I could maybe twenty or thirty over and over until I didn't hear no more screaming. When I came out of my room Mom'd be crying and she'd have a black eye or blood running out of her nose. Daddy'd slap me. "Just on general principles," he'd say. I ain't going to let him hurt this nice lady.

I opened the door. I saw them laying on a bed. They didn't have no clothes on. Her eyes were shut and he was on top of her kissing her neck.

"Daddy?"

"What the fuck!" he bellowed. "Get the hell out of here!"

"Don't hit her Daddy."

"It's okay, Cleo," she said. "Get yourself a Coke out of the fridge. We'll be done talking in a minute."

"Shut the fucking door!" Daddy barked.

I wandered through the house looking for the kitchen.

Grownups sure were strange I didn't never want to be one. Take all my clothes off and talk to someone when we're naked no that was yucky.

He started yelling at me the second they came out of that room with all their clothes back on.

"You go and tell your mom about this and no one ain't never going to see you again. You hear me? I'm going to cut your fucking tongue out and then I'm going to slice the rest of you up in little pieces and feed you to those monsters in the closet. Oh yeah you think I don't know about them? They're sure as hell hiding out in there you stupid little piece of shit. They sneak out every fucking night and stand in your room watching you sleep and drooling all over you and the only thing that keeps them from gobbling you up is me. I chase them out of there."

"Now, Luther," the lady said, laying her hand on his arm. "He's only a little boy. Take it easy."

"You ain't never going to tell your mom we were here you got it?"

"Yes Daddy." I shook from the ends of my hair all the way to my shoelaces. I was right. There were monsters in the closet and he knew it.

My mouth never whispered a word about that day. Every time I thought about my dad and that woman laying on the bed that fucking closet door creaked open and I heard those monsters hollering my name and their toenails scraping across the floor as they tried to grab me with their bloody claws. And now I know what they were doing my stepmom and my dad years before my mom died. My fucking dad cheated on my mom all those years. I hated both of them. Mom died and then that bitch came to live in our house and acted like she was my mom. I thought so many times about killing them. Dreamed about it at night blood gurgling across the floor and a foot-long hunting knife in one hand and both of their heads hanging by their hair from the other one and a shower of sweet warm blood cuddling me from head to toe. I bet my mom knew. She never said nothing but I bet she knew. I bet that's how come she died. She couldn't take it no more. I hated my fucking dad so much. And I turned out to be just like him.

Christmas Day and look at me in an apron with latex gloves on both my hands and a puffy paper hat on my head like I'm a fucking bitch. Gotta big ladle and I'm piling mashed potatoes on plates as thousands of homeless people drag past me with trays in their hands. Tim invited me home but I gotta be by myself and think. And I can't be by myself cuz I know I'm going to go out and get high so here I am feeding the homeless at Glide Church. Thousands and thousands of homeless the same as I used to be. Raggedy clothes and they all stink like piss and they all got rotten teeth. And they're all starving. Makes me feel like Jesus except He didn't gotta wear a stupid paper hat. I hate washing dishes in that restaurant. Elaine's always whispering to those other bitches telling them stories about me. Making things up. I don't know what I'm going to do about it. I don't want to hurt Tim's feelings but the bitch is a troublemaker. She's using him. I heard her boyfriend got tired of her shooting up shit all the time and dumped her and she had to get an abortion and then she sweet-talked Tim into letting her move in. That's what all those bitches do. Use us. And now they all snicker behind their hands when they see me. I don't know what the fuck she tells them. I wish I was home with my

Annie. Christmas morning and that dog of hers hopping up and down on the bed like a kangaroo and licking us cuz he knows he's got presents under the tree. I want to lay real still and hold her so soft and cozy and safe no monsters when I hold her. Ain't going to move an inch and ain't going to worry about nothing just going to lay there and smell her hair and her skin. I promise you God if You give her back to me I ain't going to fuck around on her again. I ain't going to get high again. I'm going to keep on working at the fucking sorry you ain't supposed to say fuck when you're talking to God. The restaurant it's boring I'm bored nothing exciting in my life. No sunshine stabbing my eyeballs no laughter ripping my gut apart when I'm so high I can't see nothing but happiness no hide'n seek games with the cops. No outsmarting my friends and ripping them off. All I ever do is get up every fucking morning before the sun's even got its eyes open and go to work and go to a meeting and go back home and go to bed. And who wants to fucking wash dishes. They could have got me a job as a CEO of something. I can sit in a big leather chair and look important just as good as anyone else. Don't see no CEOs washing dishes.

"Hey, Cleo! Haven't seen your sorry self in ages. Where've you been?"

"Pete! What the fuck are you doing here? You ain't homeless. You got money."

I can't believe that fucking Pete's here acting like he don't got no food. He's got millions all the shit he sells. He's stealing from the poor.

"You ought to be standing here feeding these people."

"You're right, sweetie. But I didn't think of it in time. See that hunk over there?" He nods at Bob Peterson standing at the head of the food line talking to one of the servers. I guess he's a hunk. He's one of the organizers here. His wife and him been running around out of their minds making sure everything got ready for today. "I had to get in here to see him. He's my honey."

"He's straight. And married you dumb-ass."

"He thinks he's straight. I'm going to spring wide the doors of his closet, Cleo baby."

"He's married. Didn't you hear me?"

"And?"

"You don't gotta mess around with a married man for fuck's sake."

"Well, well. Do you practice what you preach? Or do you just tell everyone else how to live their lives and then do whatever you fucking please when you think no one's looking?"

"You got your potatoes. Get the fuck out of my face."

I reach past him and whack a mound of mashed potatoes down on the next greasy homeless man's plate.

Pete laughs as he moves on.

I slap those potatoes down plate after plate like a robot, frozen except for my flapping arm. My head's on fire. That fucking bitch Sylvie I wish I never met her. I wish someone'd kill her. She ruined my whole life. God give me my life back please. My Annie's my life I'm going to take care of her this time I promise.

I ram through the front door and sprint up the stairs to the bathroom. I barely make it. I pee gallons. I peed gallons before I left work twenty minutes ago, and I was dashing for the restroom every half hour while I was there.

I kick off my shoes and leave my panties behind and the rest of my clothes whirl off as I run back down the stairs. I can't stand them. They're so tight I can't breathe. The panties have dug canyons in my groin. The waistband on my skirt has gouged trenches in my expanding stomach. There are deep crevasses across the tops of my puffy feet. My breasts explode out into the fresh air as I rip off my bra.

I hit the kitchen at full speed. Joe is already home and he's cooking dinner.

"I'm dying of hunger. What are you making?"

Before he can answer I've dumped a spoonful from the pot on the stove into my mouth. "Hot! Hot! But it tastes so good. I'm just one big hollow stomach. Get me some ice. Please."

I grab the cup of ice cubes he offers and dump them on my chest and belly. "I'm burning up." I rub ice on my body while I'm slurping gravy from the spoon.

He leans against the counter watching me, the light from his half-smile pinpointing the dust motes drifting through the kitchen.

I notice his face and realize that I'm completely nude, ice water is dripping off my body and gravy is skidding down my chin and splattering on my chest.

"Oh!" Tears fill my eyes. "I'm not human anymore, I'm an animal that eats and pees all the time!"

"You're a baby factory." He takes the spoon from my hand. "You're supposed to be hungry. You're feeding two, remember?"

"Three," I correct him. The doctor said it was twins.

"All the more reason to be hungry." He wipes the gravy off my chin and chest and traces the deep red circles my bra has etched around my breasts and the inflamed lines in my groin.

"Look at these ditches. You have to get bigger clothes, you can't feel comfortable with lines like these eating into your skin."

"How about this?" I lift my breasts. "They're the size of cantaloupes."

"No, that's what they used to be. Now they're more like pumpkins."

"Pumpkins!" I wail as I picture myself with fifteen-pound orange breasts poking out thick green stems instead of nipples.

"I mean it in a good way."

"All you men think about is breasts. You try carrying these pumpkins around for a while." I dab at a new batch of tears with the dish towel.

"Did you try on the muumuus my mom brought for you?"

His mom had come the day after Christmas and left on New Year's Eve, two days ago. Aside from the age difference she and Joe could've been twins: they both were tall, slender, gray-haired and had twinkling brown eyes. She brought colorful muumuus as big as circus tents, lanolin for tender nipples, Vitamin E cream to prevent stretch marks. "I'll come back and help you with them when they're born," she promised as we hugged her good-bye at the airport. "I'm so glad he found you."

But I don't want to wear a circus tent. I want my tiny waist back. And I liked my cantaloupe-sized breasts. I don't want pumpkins saluting the world from my chest.

When I was five years old my best friend Veronica let me hold her new baby brother. He was soft and warm and he gurgled and cooed, and I knew at that moment that one day I had to have a baby of my own. All those years of knowing it could never happen had tucked the longing away in a drawer in my mind where I stored dreams too wild to come true. Every time I peeked in, it floated to the top of the pile, still alive, although frailer with each passing year.

I had no idea it would be like this. I'm barely four months pregnant and I'm gigantic. Some women never show at all. It isn't fair.

Joe drops a muumuu over my head.

"David says you shouldn't wear those tight lacy panties, you should wear cotton maternity underwear."

"You showed David my panties?"

"I told him about...."

"You discussed my underwear with my son?"

"He's a doctor."

"He's my son. How could you?" My eyes are filling up again. These days all I am is a big cry-baby. "I'm not going to wear those maternity things. They look like pillow cases."

"What about boxers?"

"Boxers!"

"I'll sew lace on them." He can use a sewing machine as well as I can.

"No, thanks. Maybe I'll go without."

"I certainly won't mind."

"Lecherous old man." I push him away.

He grins. "But seriously, we can't have these grooves in your skin."

I lie on the couch after dinner, my head and back propped up on pillows. The muumuu is off and a fan blows arid winds across the ice cubes I've reapplied to my chest. Steam rises from my pores. My babies have turned me into a blast furnace.

Joe has my feet on his lap. "You should take family leave and stay home until after they're born." He kneads the shrinking gorges in the balloons that used to be my feet. "You can't do this every day for the next five months."

"This isn't what you expected when you married me, is it? A big fat whale beached on your couch."

"I like it, believe me. You're every man's dream: a voluptuous woman who can't run away because she's too big!"

"Hey!" I flick my foot against his belly. "Tell me the truth. Is this what you imagined when you met me?"

"Sort of. Not when I first met you, but later."

"What did you think the first time you saw me? When I helped you find your picture in that magazine."

"Ravishing is the word I would use. Absolutely ravishing. But you confused me. You were trying to hide your beauty. You wore over-sized men's shirts and big loose skirts down to your ankles. Had your hair pinned up in an old woman's bun on top of your head. Stared at my feet, trying your damndest not to make eye contact. And those clunky running shoes. I haven't seen them in a long time."

"I'm not running anymore." No reason to run. I'm right where I'm supposed to be, with this wonderful man rubbing my pudgy ugly feet.

"And what was more confusing," he continues, "is that it didn't work. You couldn't hide the fire pulsing through you. You glanced in my eyes for a second and your gaze was so intense I forgot to breathe. Strands of your hair broke loose from the bun and twitched around your face as if they were antennae trying to drag my thoughts out of the air. One of your shoes came untied. And that humongous shirt only made those boobs bigger and more enticing."

"Is that what men think when they see me?" They must enjoy the view now that I'm a walking pumpkin patch.

"Only me, Annie. Only me."

"But you didn't say anything."

"You obviously didn't want me to say anything. I asked Kevin about you, though, because I was curious."

"You asked Kevin about my business? I never discussed it with him."

"He knew what was going on. Probably all your co-workers did but they didn't want to interfere. He'd met your ex when he came to the library to see you. And he pointed him out to me outside on the steps."

"Cleo was outside?"

"Every day. Smoking pot and watching who was going in and out. Left before you got off so you wouldn't see him. One look at him and I knew why you were hiding inside those baggy clothes. I told myself to stay away. I didn't want to get involved in that kind of problem again." He pauses and compares his long slim fingers to my puffy feet. "How can you walk on these feet?"

"Why did you decide to chase me?"

"You chased me."

"I most certainly did not. You came with all those drinks."

"Wasn't it the other way around?"

"Stop it. What made you change your mind?"

"I had dreams."

"About what?"

"You."

"What kind of dreams about me?'

"You know."

"I wouldn't be asking if I knew. What kind of dreams?"

"Man dreams."

"What are man dreams?"

"You know what men dream about." A pink shadow creeps up his cheeks.

"You're blushing!"

"I am not. I don't blush."

"So what are man dreams?"

"Are you that sheltered? I thought you'd been married before."

"We never discussed our dreams. Now tell me, what did you dream about me?"

"About your body parts and doing things to them."

"That's why you came after me? You were trying to get me into your bed?"

"Guess so."

"Then why did you turn me down?"

"Because by then I had fallen in love. I didn't want to love you for one night or a couple weeks and then lose you. I'm too old to play that game. I had to know that you felt the same way about me."

"You're an angel."

"I have my good days but I wouldn't say that."

"You're an angel God sent to rescue me. Because I was like a dead tree, good for nothing except to be chopped down and tossed into a fire. God made you have those dreams."

"I like your God."

"I'm serious. You weren't doing what you were supposed to do. God made you have those dreams so you would step into my life and save me."

"I thought you were mad at God."

"Not anymore. Things happen for a reason. I had lessons to learn, and stubborn me didn't pay attention when the teacher spoke gently. It wasn't until I fell in love with you that I found out what God wanted me to learn."

"And what was that?"

"That a 'true love,' that mythical creature women are taught to spend their lives hunting for, is just another name for best friend. That's what I've learned."

Sleep oozes up my body from my aching feet. My eyelids droop. The last thing I see before they close completely is the face of my true love, my best friend, my angel, tenderness thick as honey pouring from his eyes as he brushes my damp hair back from my face.

———✥ ✥———

"**I** got a job!" She's jumping up and down, a letter in her hand. I laugh. I've never seen her this excited.

"Great! When do you start?"

"As soon as we can get there."

"There? Where?"

"Arizona."

"Arizona!"

"The Fort Apache Indian Reservation. My grandfather's people."

"Why didn't you tell me?"

"I didn't want to say anything until I knew I'd gotten it. You'll love it there. The heat is excruciating but you'll get used to it."

She dances around the room waving the letter above her head.

"I thought you were a gypsy."

"My mother's side. My dad was a half-breed. We have to find a place to live. We should leave as soon as we can. Does tomorrow sound okay?"

"Tomorrow?"

"I'm sorry. This is too sudden for you. Next week? We can leave next week. It only takes a day and a half to drive there."

"You want me to move there with you?"

"You can run your business from anywhere. They have electricity, it's not the way it used to be. You can hook up your computer and...oh." She looks at me.

"Oh," she repeats and I hear a half-sob in her voice.

She lays a hand on each of my cheeks and pulls my head around to face her.

I look in those black eyes and it's as if I'm seeing her for the first time. Her sweet face wrinkles as sadness patters across her features like raindrops. A few of them leave little dots of moisture on my own face and I see what she sees: a pitiful excuse of a man who is consumed with his own weaknesses. I thought she felt sorry for me and was only going to stay until someone better came along. Did she do anything to make me think that? If you call cooking and cleaning and making love to this broken body and turning my business into a raging success and bringing joy into my heart and color into my faded life reasons to believe she's going to leave, I guess she did.

I guess I'm just a foolish old man.

Love comes into my life and I shoot it down because I don't think I'm good enough for it.

I love you, Elaine. I will go anywhere with you.

She smiles. "Good. When can we leave? Do you want to pack everything and take it with us or do you want to find a place first and come back for our things? We can have a garden if we get a house. The sunrises there are awesome, you can't imagine... What?"

I'm laughing like I've never laughed in my whole life.

"Whatever you want," I say when I finally stop. "You're the boss."

Arizona. Who'da thunk? Apache reservation? Never in my wildest dreams.

This tiny woman is taking me by the hand and leading me into a new world and a new life. I see the sun shining on the Arizona mountains, the white sands of the desert, the garden behind our new home overflowing with sunflowers.

My heart is so full of happiness it hurts.

H e peers in the mirror.

The man peering back blinks pink-lidded eyes. The corners of his narrow lips reach for the floor.

Trembling fingers knot his tie while he watches. He squares his shoulders.

Her sapphire ring is in his pocket. He bought it back from the pawnshop yesterday.

A herd of mustangs thunders through his chest, shaking his whole body.

He wishes he didn't have to do this but he knows he does, and today is the day.

He can't keep putting it off.

She isn't going to magically walk back into his life.

The navy blue suit is newly dry-cleaned. A little Polo aftershave wafts from his jaw.

His face has gotten older since he left her. Deep grooves run from his nose to the corners of his mouth. Permanent pleats are sewn at the sides of his eyes.

And there's a silver streak running through his hair like a highway from above his right eyebrow to the nape of his neck.

Does she still love me? I know how to be kind now. I know what you gotta do to take care of love. I ain't my dad.

He sucks in a big wad of air and forces himself to walk out of his room, one foot in front of the other. Thump clump thump clump.

If it all goes the way I want it to I'm going to be with her to-night. In her pink house with that dog of hers jumping all over me cuz he's so fucking glad to see me if the dog loves me that much I know my Annie does too.

I 'm free. Finally.

Can't believe they kept me locked up that many months for ripping off some old rich dude. He doesn't even miss the money. He wanted me to have it. Why else would he fuck me in his limo with his pockets blowing out hundred dollar bills?

Three months. A quarter of a year.

And now I have a little tummy bump, how cool is that!

I'm going to be a real mommy this time.

I'll be the mommy and Cleo will be the daddy.

Someone in jail said he was still in his program. Still trying to get that redheaded bitch back.

I'm his wife. Why does he keep forgetting that? She's a pretender. She can't do for him what I can: have a baby.

Boy, will he be happy.

But I have to find him.

Program! He won't stay clean. He and I, we're the same. We're going to live and die behind that shit, and that's just the way it is. Must be in our DNA or something. No program can change that, and neither can a redheaded woman.

I'm so much smarter than she is.

And prettier.

Feel the air, little baby? Breathe it in. This isn't jail air. This is the real thing. Take deep breaths.

It feels good. Clean fresh air. No toilet stink like in jail. No puke-stink from the junkies kicking. Just good clean fresh San Francisco air. Sea-smelling.

I have to find him. Have to breathe this way-cool air with him. Together.

H e watches his feet and counts his steps as he walks the block in front of the library. "Ninety-eight. Ninety-nine. One hundred." Sweat tiptoes down the sides of his face, swims across his upper lip, salts his tongue.

Five minutes, ten minutes. Counting. "I'm going to go in when I get to a thousand." Shiny shoes blind the people watching him from the steps.

"A thousand. Gotta do it," he mutters. "Gotta."

He starts over. "One, two, three…"

Ten more minutes. From the parking lot on the north side of the library to Grove Street on the south side and back again.

"Fuck. I'm a coward. I never thought I was a coward. I ain't scared to punch no one. But look at me dragging my feet cuz I'm scared to face a bitch who don't reach no higher than my chin."

He inhales a gallon of air through his nose, adjusts his tie and lifts his head. Pushes through the glass doors. Slips past the security officer and down the stairs.

Look at that red hair. The words smile in his head, point the corners of his eyes up to heaven. His heart is quiet. She's the one she always was. Don't know how I forgot about that. Is that what that shit does? Makes you forget about the good while you're trying to forget about the bad? If it wasn't that shit then I'm just plain stupid like my dad always said I was.

He watches her from the bottom of the stairs. She is talking to Kevin, her back to Cleo.

Her red hair is a fire in the library lights.

Sucks the breath right out of me.

He walks quietly over to them.

"Annie." Less than a whisper.

She turns around.

"No," says Kevin. "You can't be here."

"What do you want?" Her voice scrambles up the scales and ends as a high-pitched screech. She lurches away from him.

"I'm clean baby. Totally clean. Ain't used nothing in months. And look I got your ring back." He holds out a small black velvet box. Then he notices her protruding belly.

His eyes travel from the gentle folds of earth-brown wool that drapes her bulging body to her hands. She's holding them out to protect herself from him as she staggers backwards. He sees the gold band on her left ring finger.

It feels as if he's swallowed her flaming hair and the fire is blistering his throat.

Smoke wisps out of his nose, stings his eyes.

"You're pregnant." The only words that can squeeze past the mass of burning hair.

And then the explosion: fire flies everywhere, singes Annie, blisters Kevin.

"You fucking whore!" he screams. "You're my wife! And that bastard baby ain't mine! I knew you hooked up with another man. You fucking bitch!"

Kevin steps between him and Annie. Shrieks for security.

Cleo belts him and he soars, the crunch of shattered bone tinkling in their ears as he hits the floor.

The last thing Cleo sees as the security guards grab at him is Annie on her knees bending over Kevin, cheeks wet, mouth keening, pale fingers patting his head. Big belly almost hiding him.

Cleo runs.

The guards can't catch him.

He is out the door and down the steps and across the street and they can't catch him.

That fucking bitch! Everyone told me what she was up to and did I listen? I made myself believe she loved me. I always knew she left me for another guy and now hear those sirens. The cops are hunting for me. I thought that fucker was gay but no he's the one. She left me for a nerdy old fat man who waddles between the bookshelves and answers the phone for her like he's a bitch. He's dead now serves him right. I gotta get off this street before the cops get me I'm not going to go to prison on a murder charge not for that fucking whore she ain't worth it. I'm going to go over to Pete's get me some shit. Been clean all these months and for what? For nothing.

"Cleo Deo! My hubby chubby, my soul mate date. Where've you been kin? Look, I got us some shit hit. Went by Pete Sweet's, just got out of jail hail, that wife knife of yours put me in there. For reals meals. Heard bird you were in a program, why fly did you want to do that slat? Come on, right bite there in that doorway, I've got a point anoint and everything."

Sylvie. Don't look so bad green hair's kind of sexy. And free shit what can I say? And I ain't fucked no one but myself in a long time and it's all right here in front of me in one fucking bitch. Must be an angel. Sylvie's an angel of God sent to save me from thinking I love that redheaded bitch. Sure don't. Never did. Some kind of sick fantasy.

We sit at the top of the steps and she sticks the needle in my arm a sweet little prick and my arm grows strong blood pulsing through it like it's the heart of God pumping it. Muscles pop out as hard as steel let me go punch that fat dumb fuck now I'll knock his head off then see her cry. I laugh. "Punch his whole fucking head off! Knock his teeth down his throat." I see his teeth flying little yellow pearls flying all over the library hitting that bitch in the face poking holes in her sexy skin big craters and she'll be ugly and no one's going to want to fuck her. "Fuck it I'm going to go back there and finish them off."

"Shhh." Sylvie unbuttons my jeans. "Fuck buck me now, Cleo Deo. Right here beer, I missed you so much dutch."

She lifts her shirt up and I see a little tummy bump. And then I see tits she ain't got tits unless she's pregnant.

"You pregnant Sylvie?"

"Yeah, daddy saddy. Preggers. This time it's really yours cores, now we can have our own flat splat and a..."

I roar. I don't know how that big noise comes out of my mouth but I roar like I'm the king of the beasts I roar so loud her green hair lays down flat on top of her head and she snaps her eyelids shut against the blast.

"Liar! You think I'm stupid? I ain't fucked you in a year. More than a year. I ain't some stupid piece of shit and you're going to remember it this time."

My arm springs out with its steel-hard muscles and whacks her head so it bounces around like one of those bobble-heads.

"Cleo Deo!" Her eyes open up and they're big blue doughnuts with black holes in the middle. She ain't scared she's surprised but she ain't scared.

My fist crashes into her nose and blood sprays halfway to the clouds.

I smell the feral bleeding animal stink and I turn into a ravenous beast ready to rip my prey to shreds and I can't stop pounding on her. I feel her cheek bones split apart as my fist thuds right through them. Wham! I grab her ears and smash her fucking head on the wall and that raw meat stench splashes all over those bricks. Wham! She collapses in a pile of skin and bones and feebly lifts her fucking hands up to protect her face. I kick her.

"Hey, Cleo." Cam the cuckoo bird. "Stop it."

"Shut the fuck up. She's a fucking bitch. I hate all of those bitches. Going to stop all her lies once and for all." My foot slams her tummy bump like a piston—wham-wham-wham. I'm a robot someone else is controlling my foot it ain't me making it kick her and whoever it is we're going to get rid of that fucking bastard baby. Wham! I laugh.

"Cleo, Jim is gonna beat you up if you don't stop. Ain't you, Jim? He says he's gonna punch your lights out, Cleo."

"Tell him to get the fuck over here and try." I'm tired of kicking her. Blood's everywhere I hear her breathing through a broken nose air whistling through bone fragments rattling through blood clots don't she got fucking sense enough to breathe through her mouth when her nose is broke? What a dumb-ass.

I'm too fucking good. I'm going to go back to the library and beat Mrs. Lying Redhead up too splatter her all over the place and then she can't fuck with me no more smear her fucking blood all over the books and hang her red hair from the top shelf with her sexy dead mouth flopping open and not even the softest whimper coming out. Teach her a lesson same as I just taught Sylvie bet that scrawny bitch'll think twice before she tries to play her fucking games with me again.

"Cleo." A tiny voice a worm voice. A slithering through garbage voice. "Cleo, it really is yours. Honest."

I jump up like an atom bomb. She don't fucking give up does she and it's all lies lies lies I hate lies.

Hey Chris is in his box. Little swirl of crack smoke out the sides his machete that's what I fucking need that piece of shit don't learn when I'm nice as fucking pie.

Two giant steps and I'm there and I kick the fucking box away. Chris don't even look at me he's sitting with his crack pipe in his mouth and his long gray dreads hanging down and he knows man he fucking knows I'm going to tear him to pieces if he says one fucking word. I get the machete it's heavy in my hand long sharp heavy. Two leaps back to the top of the stairs and I swing it and I hear it whoosh and it makes a loud crack when it hits her head and then I hear another crack and I drop it.

I fall.

Chris tosses the pistol in the sewer and walks away. "Ain't gonna do this shit no more," I hear him say. "Gonna get a job. This too much drama."

"You killed him!" Cam screams. "You shot Jim. He's dead. Jim, get up, Jim, don't leave me. Jim!"

I see Cam fold up in a mound of quivering arms and legs a river of tears washing his baby face away.

"You fucking cuckoo bird. It's me who's been shot. Me."

The daylight dies as an invisible hand with a paint brush strokes wide black stripes across the world.

"Why, Cleo Deo? I loved shoved you. Why'd you do that spat?" Sylvie. Right here in front of me. She ain't even bleeding what the fuck! Gotta white dress on never seen that bitch in a dress. No blood no broken nose was I that high? Made the whole fucking thing up? Man that was some good shit.

Someone stands in back of her.

"Mom?"

"Come with me, my sweet baby boy. I'll take care of you." She hovers over me.

"What the fuck are you talking about? I can take care of myself. You never took care of me. You abandoned me. Get the fuck away from me!"

"Cleo, I love you. Come with me." Her eyes are wet, her face is sad.

"You should've loved me a long time ago. Should've stayed. You left me like I wasn't nothing to you. You let Dad rip my ass to shreds while that bitch was cackling and clapping her hands. This is all your fault. You're evil just the same as all those other bitches. Leave me alone."

The world's completely black now I thought it was morning but it's night. Sylvie's gone my mom's a crying face in the distance the night swallows her and everything's dark and still. And now I'm seeing my life zoom by on a TV screen while I'm pinned down by the blackness and shriveling in a pool of my own ice cold blood and all that shit dribbles out of me like it's the river of my life and I ain't high no more. I see long lines of people I ripped off and lied to and they're all laughing at me laying here dying. I see the helpless old ladies I robbed and the shit I put in my arm and never paid for and the kid who died behind the fake shit I sold him and the bitches I treated like crap all the way back to that girl I raped in back of the school when I was fourteen she was crying and fighting me. I see it in front of my eyes and I can't shut it off. And where is God? Ain't He going to help me now? I ain't ready to die yet. Ain't You even going to answer me? No big God-voice roaring out of the clouds? Nothing? Knew You weren't real. There ain't no angels here or nothing. Knew You were a lie. And now I see my Annie crying and I see me kick her and her head flies back like her neck's going to snap in two and I see me throwing her against the dresser and ripping her clothes off her with a butcher knife. I see me fucking and fucking and fucking that butt-ugly Sylvie in my Annie's car in my Annie's house in my Annie's bed and I see me mixing shit in her coffee cuz it sliced me in two to try and think of things to say to her when we weren't high cuz she was so smart and sexy and perfect and after a while I couldn't fuck her any more if I wasn't high all I saw was stupid me with dirt on my hands and face trying to reach an angel in white soaring way above my head. I see the time I put a whole gram in her coffee and didn't take none of it for me cuz I thought maybe I could fuck her if she was high and I wasn't. I almost killed her. Had to take her to the ER. And I see the light inside of her turn into scary monsters crawling out of her eyes and shrieking out of her mouth the same as the ocean of monsters surging inside me. No wonder she hooked up with someone else. What was I thinking? I'm some kind of stupid piece of shit's what I am. That's what everybody always said and it's true: I'm stupid. I hurt everyone who comes near me. I ain't done one good thing in my whole fucking life.

I ain't nothing.

Questions for Discussion

1. Why does Cleo hide his behavior from himself?

2. Cleo loves Annie. Why does he get involved with Sylvie?

3. What one parenting behavior of Cleo's father contributed most to his subsequent addiction?

4. What expectations does Annie have of Cleo? Why is he unable to meet them?

5. If you were Annie's parents, what would you do differently to better prepare her for life as an adult?

6. Why did Annie stay with Cleo despite abuse and infidelity? How did staying with him change her?

7. Why was Tim angry?

8. What did he do to himself rather than work through his anger?

9. How could Tim's parents have better supported their sons after his brother's kidnapping? How would this have changed the course of the boys' lives?

10. What human qualities ("virtues") does Sylvie possess?

11. Does Sylvie really love (i.e. care about) Cleo? Explain.

12. In what way did her childhood abuse lead to her behavior as an adult?

Made in the USA
Charleston, SC
05 March 2017